INFUSION

STAN C. SMITH

ISBN-13: 978-1517247096

ISBN-10: 1517247098

To those who would do good with the powers they possess.

INFUSION

Definition:

the introduction of a new modifying element or quality into something

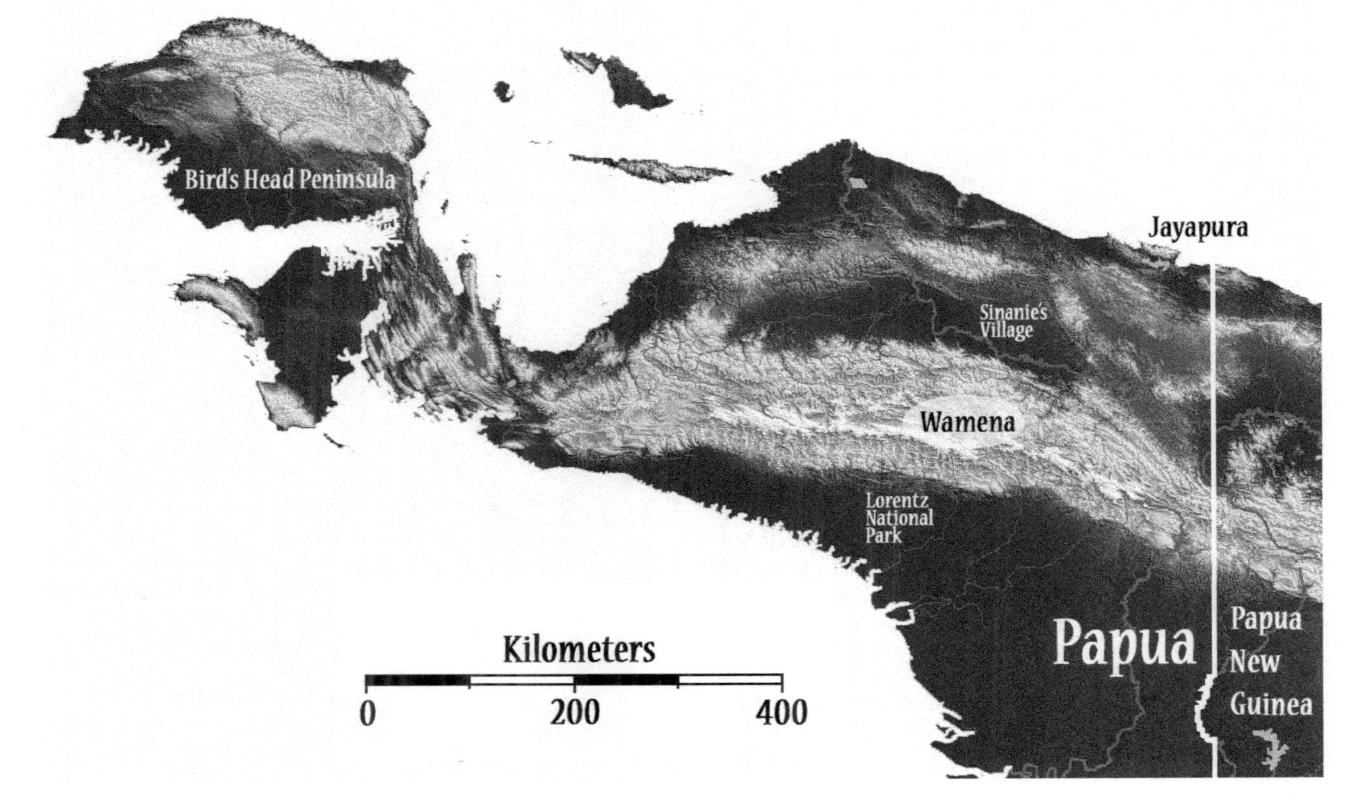

Bird's Head Peninsula
Jayapura
Sinanie's Village
Wamena
Lorentz National Park
Papua
Papua New Guinea
Kilometers
0
200
400

CHAPTER ONE

1977 - IRIAN JAYA, INDONESIA

PETER WOOLEY MADE his way up the rope ladder, feeling strong but awkward as his feet searched for each woven rung. He paused and looked down. The forest floor was at least forty meters below. The rope, made of intertwined strands of spider silk, was remarkably thin, but Peter knew it wouldn't break. What did concern him, though, was that this was likely his last opportunity to climb it.

The rope ladder, or *yebun*, was suspended from the ceiling of a hanging hut, and Peter entered an opening in the hut's floor as he climbed the last few meters. He stepped from the ladder to the floor. The hut bounced from the added weight, but he had become accustomed to this during the three days since his arrival at the hanging village.

Two tribesmen stood to the side waiting for him. Both were a good ten centimeters shorter than Peter and were easily recognized by the pincushion arrangements of feathers protruding from their hair—green lorikeet feathers for Sinanie and white cockatoo feathers for Matiinuo. Both men appeared to be no older than thirty, but Matiinuo was actually the village elder. Besides the feathers, the men wore few adornments and no clothes other than short, functional penis gourds, or *mbayap*. Behind the tribesmen stood Samuel, a peculiar Englishman who for some reason had been living among these villagers. Samuel gazed at Peter for a moment, allowing him to catch his breath, and then raised his brows as if asking if he were ready for what was to come. Peter felt unsure but nodded anyway. Without a word spoken, the men turned and walked out of the hut into a long hanging corridor. Peter followed.

Once again Peter marveled at the sensation of walking through a tunnel suspended in the canopy of the tallest rainforest trees he had encountered in all his travels. But this time it felt rather like a death march.

He fiddled with a talisman hanging from a cord around his neck. It was a sculpture of a tree kangaroo, meticulously carved from stone. Matiinuo had given it to him the previous day. Peter had assumed it was a token of friendship, but then Samuel had explained that it was more an offering of assistance. Matiinuo believed the tree kangaroo might help Peter succeed in the task demanded of him, but Samuel had also made it clear that if Peter failed, he would be killed.

They made their way through perhaps a hundred meters of hanging tunnel before it opened up into a larger hut. Doorways to five other tunnels were evenly spaced around the walls of the hut. The hut was like the hub of a wheel with six spokes. It was the most important hut in the village, but there were no sleeping mats, fire bowls, or other amenities. At the center of the hut was a section of tree, growing up through the floor and branching into two thigh-sized limbs at chest height. Molded around the Y in the tree was a brownish mass that resembled a ball of clay. From a distance it could have been mistaken for an arboreal termite nest. But Peter knew it was much more than that. It was like nothing he had encountered in his life. It was the reason he had been allowed to live for the last three days, and it was the reason he probably would not live to see another.

After entering the hut, Sinanie and Matiinuo stood to one side of the brown mass and Samuel stood to the other. They waited for him to approach.

"Samuel," Peter pleaded, "I need more time with it. Maybe if I had a few more days."

Samuel's face, which was typically hard to read, now showed what might have been pity. "I will endeavor to convince them of that. You have indeed shown considerable propensity for your task. But I fear they do not believe you are the man they have waited for, and I am inclined to agree."

Peter sighed. Samuel probably couldn't help him even if he wanted to. He stepped forward and held his left hand just over the brown substance. He closed his eyes, thinking of the reasons he now had for living. The substance beneath his hand had extraordinary power—he felt obligated to let the rest of the world know. He had to live so he could do that. And he had to live so he could return to Rose, never to leave her again. She deserved that from him. Peter braced himself for the challenge before him. There was too much at stake to fail.

Without opening his eyes, he placed his hand on the substance. As before, it was cool and pliable. His palm tingled slightly. Suddenly a jumble of symbols appeared before his eyes, hanging there in the darkness. He opened his eyes, and the symbols were still there, superimposed over his view of the inside of the hut. Some of them looked vaguely like letters or numbers, but most of them were spirals, angles, or shapes that prior to the last few days would have been meaningless to him. He took a deep breath and reached for one of the floating symbols with his free hand. The symbols had no physical substance, but they responded to his gestures. He shoved them into piles based on characteristics such as the presence or absence of right angles. Once they were sorted into clumps, they disappeared, and another jumble of symbols filled his vision. He sorted them again, and then again, working faster with each group.

To his side, Matiinuo and Sinanie exchanged unintelligible words. Matiinuo was getting impatient. Peter had done these exercises before. He had to go beyond what he had already done or it was all over. With a violent swipe he cleared the virtual slate so that it would populate with all of the 128 symbols. Whatever this substance was, it had been trying to get him to complete an exhaustive sequence of tasks that gradually resulted in him assigning numeric meaning to each symbol, and then conceptual meaning to combinations of the symbols. Apparently the end result was that he would be able to input commands the substance would understand. Back home, Peter had recently purchased a new computer, a Tandy Radio Shack TRS-80, and he had quickly learned to input instructions using the BASIC computer language. He was now convinced the substance in this hanging hut had to be some kind of computer. But it was unlike any he had ever imagined. And he was confident that outside of Matiinuo's tribe and Samuel, no one else had seen such a computer—at least no one on Earth. Because Peter had seen where the object had come from. It had been shown to him in a dream, a dream so astounding that his life would never be the same even if he did survive this day.

He took a deep breath and moved five of the symbols into a cluster. The rest of them faded away. He had already discovered that this combination resulted in a response. As expected, his cluster disappeared and was replaced by three clusters. This was the computer's response to his command, but he wasn't even sure what the initial command meant, let alone the response. He needed more time to master the language. Feeling defeated, Peter sighed.

Matiinuo grunted and then spoke. "*Nu ne khelép-té. Wolakholol be-lembu-té-n-da.*" Sinanie grasped Peter's arm, ready to lead him out of the hut.

Samuel stepped forward and spoke to the tribesmen. "*Mbakha-lekhé-nggolo? Nokhu be-Khelép-telo-n-din-da!*" After a moment of silence, he turned to Peter. "My friend, for reasons unknown to me, you have shown great capacity for understanding the *Lamotelokhai*. But my indigene hosts appear unsatisfied. Perhaps if you would agree to stay here and assist me with my studies, they might see that you can be useful to them."

But Peter sensed that his opportunity had passed. He would likely be killed before the evening rains set in. He simply shook his head at Samuel and turned his gaze one more time to the Lamotelokhai, the mass of clay that was somehow also a computer. He quickly repopulated the symbols and moved some of them into two piles. He had no way of knowing how accurate it was, but based on the meanings of symbol groupings he had established, he hoped that it said, "Help me."

Sinanie firmly guided him away from the object and placed the rope ladder into his hands.

SAMUEL AND SINANIE took Peter to the hanging hut where he had been forced to live for the last three days. After speaking earnestly to each other in Sinanie's language, they left Peter alone. As he descended through the opening in the hut's floor, Samuel assured Peter he would do what he could to convince Matiinuo to allow Peter more time.

Soon the rope ladder went limp. Peter was alone. He waited a few minutes and then climbed to the ground and began running. He knew this was probably suicide, but if he could get far enough before his absence was detected, maybe he could get away. Considering the stakes, he had no choice. For the first time in his life he had something consequential to contribute to the world. And he was willing to risk his life to return to Rose—to give her the life she deserved.

But the forest was extraordinarily dense and progress was challenging. Before long he was bleeding from multiple cuts and had lost the tree kangaroo talisman when it had been ripped from his neck. And disturbingly, one of the real tree kangaroos was trying to follow him. The creature could lead the tribesmen to him.

Skirting a dense stand of plum pines, he nearly collided with Samuel.

"Peter!"

Peter stopped abruptly. He felt a flame of hope. Perhaps Samuel had convinced the villagers to let him go.

"Samuel, I had to leave! I wanted to say goodbye, but I couldn't risk it. The others—do they know I've left?"

Samuel stepped closer, his face etched with concern. "They are aware. You must know you cannot leave this place. It is not yet time."

Peter scanned the forest but saw no sign of the tribe's hunters. "I can't stay here. Please, Samuel! You can stop them."

Samuel shook his head. "If I am to endeavor to save your life, you must agree to remain. Stay here with me, Peter. There is much for us to do."

Peter backed away. "All I ask is that you give me a chance. Try to hold them off."

Samuel's expression turned to alarm. "Do not, Peter. I beg you."

Peter turned to run. Suddenly he glimpsed a familiar array of green lorikeet feathers in front of him. But it was too late to stop. Sinanie's spear pierced his gut. Sinanie rushed forward, driving the spear deeper and knocking Peter off his feet.

Pinning him down with the spear, Sinanie stood above him, gazing into his eyes. Slowly, the tribesman smiled. Peter couldn't move, and it became difficult to breathe.

Sinanie wasn't alone now. There were two others. They

intended to kill him. He would not leave this forest, and Rose would never know what had happened.

One of the tribesmen picked up a tree limb. He hefted it a few times, assessing its balance, and then swung it at Peter. The blow glanced off Peter's forehead. Oddly, it numbed the pain of the spear piercing his gut. Peter stared up into the canopy above. For a brief moment, he tried to imagine he was relieved it was finally over.

WITH INTENSE INTEREST, the tree kangaroo, or *mbolop*, watched the violence from a low branch of a coral bean tree. Clubs pounded flesh until the flesh was no longer recognizable as a man. And still the clubbing went on. The villagers would make sure the body couldn't heal and would never leave this place. Suddenly the mbolop gripped the branch and shook it forcefully, its mottled brown and gold body jerking up and down. The creature was agitated at this new development. Although biological in structure, the mbolop was different from the naturally-evolved tree kangaroos it had been created to resemble. It understood its own purpose. And as it watched the disintegration of the man called Peter Wooley, it began to doubt its purpose for the first time. Peter had been important, nearly equipped for what was needed, but he hadn't been given enough time.

The mbolop jerked its body up and down one more time, then it turned away from the bloody scene. It paused for a moment, listening. It ignored the ambient sounds of the forest and the grunts of the men as they continued to pulverize the remaining flesh into the soil. It was listening for something else. Puzzled, it scurried to the main trunk of the coral bean tree and began climbing, its hind claws digging into the soft bark for leverage. When it reached the highest limb, it stopped and listened again. Nothing—no incoming instructions.

A concept began forming in the tree kangaroo's consciousness, a plan to do something consequential. The man, Peter, was gone, but perhaps he could still be important. The mbolop began descending the tree, but then it hesitated. Perhaps its plan had formed as a result of incoming commands it hadn't knowingly detected. It listened again, but still there were only the sounds of the forest and the men below.

The mbolop descended to the ground and approached the brutal scene until it was beside one of the laboring villagers. The tribesman paused only briefly when he noticed the creature then continued pounding the ground. The mbolop sniffed at a small mass of bloody tissue that had not yet been pulverized. It snatched up the mass with its mouth and scuttled back up the tree. It then bounded from tree to tree until it arrived at the churning brown river the villagers called *Méanmaél*. It descended to the water's edge, dropped the mass of tissue on the bank, and began gathering and preparing materials: leaves it had chewed, water it carried in its mouth, decaying vegetation, and soil. The creature worked meticulously and without urgency. Narrow shafts of sunlight moved slowly across the forest floor and then vanished as the sun dropped toward the horizon and clouds began to fill the sky. Rain began falling, trickling through the canopy. The forest shifted from green to gray to nearly black. Still the tree kangaroo worked, shoving one pile of raw materials onto another and stamping them together, expelling mouthfuls of river water onto the pile, traveling far down the edge of the river to return with several live beetles and a grasshopper to be chewed and added to the accumulated materials.

Late into the night, the mbolop finally sat back on its haunches and eyed the mound. It was as high as the creature's shoulders and as long as the height of a man. The tree kangaroo scratched its belly with one of its forepaws. Suddenly it plunged the entire paw through its skin and into its abdomen. After digging around for a moment, the paw emerged holding a glistening lump of flesh. The creature released the lump onto the pile of materials, then plopped onto its side on the ground, exhausted.

The mbolop listened to the soothing sounds of the roiling river water and night insects as it gazed at the product of its labor. It was almost asleep when the pile of materials began shifting, blending together, changing its shape.

PETER OPENED HIS EYES. He could see nothing but mud and leaves, faintly illuminated by dawn's first light. He realized he was on his side in a fetal position. He rolled onto his back. Above him was a dense forest canopy, sparsely punctuated with glimpses of gray sky. A cloud of flies hovered over him, but they did not descend upon him to bite. He sat up. He was naked. He rubbed his legs above the knees, then held his hands up, staring at them as he clinched and unclenched his fists. He ran one hand over his abdomen and frowned. His appendectomy scar was gone. And so was the birthmark below his navel. His frown intensified as his eyes moved downward. His penis was no longer circumcised. He pulled the skin on it back and then released it, watching with fascination as it moved back into place.

He stood up, testing his legs. They felt strong. He looked around and saw that he was next to a river. After gazing at the brown water for some time, he turned and began walking in the direction the water was flowing.

TRAVELING WAS SLOW, but Peter had made steady progress. Occasionally he was forced to wade or swim across smaller streams that flowed into the river he was following. When he was thirsty, he had to wait for rain or drink the river's muddy water. He found a few fruits to eat, but for the first few days he wasn't particularly hungry and it didn't seem important. On the fourth day he decided he needed protein. Finding it was not difficult; while walking next to the river's edge during rainstorms, he had seen large earthworms with their bodies partially extended out of the saturated soil. When the evening rains came he found one of these and pulled it from its burrow. The worm was nearly a meter long. He could only eat it raw, but he was beyond being finicky and it provided all the animal protein he needed.

On the first night, Peter had not slept. Instead he had continued travelling, picking his way in the dark through the tangled understory next to the river. But by the second night he had needed rest. The flies still were not biting, so he had found a soft spot at the base of a tree and slept sitting up with his back to the trunk. This is how he spent each of the nights after that as he methodically made his way downstream.

On the morning of Peter's eighth day of walking, still naked but feeling vigorous, he emerged from the forest into the blindingly bright clearing of a bustling village.

PETER DROVE his Ford Cortina to the top of his driveway, stopped next to Rose's car, and turned off the engine. He gripped the steering wheel for a moment, then turned his hands over and looked at the palms. They were clean and smooth, without cuts or calluses. He closed his eyes and sighed, trying to gather his thoughts. Peter clearly remembered being attacked by the villagers, at least until the blow that had rendered him unconscious. He was glad to be alive, although he had no idea why the tribesmen had spared him. He had come out of the bush with no possessions or money, and it had taken two days of phone calls and deliberations to arrange a flight back to Cairns. Before being allowed back into

Australia, he'd been examined by doctors. They found no health issues. Regardless, he should have been truly knackered by this point, but he felt fine, physically. It was the psychological exhaustion that was taking its toll.

He popped open the Cortina's door and emerged into the full heat of a December day. He glanced at the front of his house and saw the curtains move. Rose was watching him through the window but hadn't come out. Not good. He had called her from Jayapura, but she hadn't even asked why his trip had been longer than planned. She was definitely mad. Peter had developed an obsession with embarking on the most physically demanding excursions he could dream up. Rose believed he had a death wish. The truth was, she was right. His solo walkabout to Irian Jaya's interior had been ill-advised, in spite of months of preparation. It had been nothing more than his latest attempt at a glorified suicide. Well, today he would set things right. He would not leave her again.

When he entered the house, she was sitting at the table, fingers folded together in front of her. Three suitcases sat neatly arranged next to the door.

"Rose, what's going on?"

She turned to him. Her eyes were red. "Peter..."

"What's going on?" he repeated.

"I just—I can't do this. Sitting here—waiting for you to die!" She had paused before *waiting* and then spit it out like venom.

Peter was stunned. "No, Rose—please! Something happened to me this time. I'm not the same man I was before."

"You're always the same man!" She hesitated. "What do you mean?"

He sat down in the chair across from her. "I haven't told anyone yet. But I found something—in the bush. It's something that will change the world, Rose!"

She stared at him. "Well, what is it?"

He looked at the table for a moment. He sighed. "I don't know exactly what it is. It's still out there."

"I see. And you have to go back there to get it."

He shook his head. "I wasn't going to say that." He reached across the table and was slightly surprised when she allowed him to grasp her hands. "I know it's been hard living with me. You deserve more. I'm trying to tell you that something has happened to me. It's something so big I'm afraid if I try to explain it, you'll think I've gone *troppo*. I need your help figuring out what to do. Stay with me, Rose. I'll never leave you again. I want us to grow old together."

She gazed at his face. Her eyes probed his like she was searching for truth. Seconds passed, with no sounds but the hum of the fridge's condenser fan. Her brows creased as if she were puzzled by something she saw deep within his eyes. For a moment, Peter thought she might get up and walk out on him for the last time. But gradually her expression relaxed. She sighed.

"Promise me, Peter. Promise we'll grow old together."

"I swear, Rose. Bloody oath."

Peter got up and walked around the table. He leaned over and kissed her. She stood up and embraced him, her face buried in his shoulder. Finally, she pulled away.

"Okay, how can I help you?"

Peter kissed her again. Then he considered her question. Where to begin? He wasn't going back to Irian Jaya. He could never find the hanging village again. But eventually, someone else would.

He took her hand and led her to the bedroom. On a desk in the corner sat his TRS-80, with its keyboard in front and cassette storage drive to the side. It was gathering dust.

"I think we need to start here," he said.

He sat in the chair and switched on the computer. Rose sat on the edge of the bed. As Peter watched white text appear on the video display, he thought of symbols materializing before him, visible whether his eyes were open or closed. He hadn't been capable of learning to use the symbols fast enough. But someday someone else would need to. Perhaps everyone would.

Rose grabbed a cloth and wiped away the dust.

CHAPTER TWO

42 Years Later
Papua (formerly Irian Jaya)

QUENTIN DARNELL GAZED down at his bare feet as he trudged along the bank of the Méanmaél River. He no longer missed his hiking shoes. He had discarded them because they made it difficult to climb the rope ladders in the hanging village. He had offered them to his wife, Lindsey, and then to his students, but his shoes were too big for any of them. Their shoes and most of their clothes had been lost three days ago, dissolved into soil along with the wreckage of the Twin Otter that had carried them out of the Central Highlands. Quentin's feet were grubby, but they were mostly free of cuts and blisters, thanks to his body's new healing ability.

They had been walking nonstop for hours and Quentin was lost in his own thoughts and engrossed in the strenuous, repetitive effort to make progress. Which is why it took him by surprise when an arm encircled his neck and threw him roughly to the ground. The impact took his breath away, but the arm immediately released him and a hand clapped over his mouth, signaling him to silence. He turned to his side and his eyes met Samuel's. Beyond Samuel he saw the rest of his group, already on their bellies, cautiously watching something downriver.

Quentin nodded that he understood to be quiet, and Samuel withdrew his hand. With minimal movement, Samuel pointed downstream and across the river. There were several Papuan tribesmen there, standing in the water or sitting on exposed rocks. The men were talking, possibly taking a break from a long hike or hunt. Quentin counted five tribesmen.

He whispered to Samuel, "They can take us to their village. There may be an airstrip there."

Samuel shook his head slightly. "I know of this tribe. They are murderous and pugnacious."

Quentin looked at the men again. Oddly, they all seemed to be bald. Several of them were laughing at one of their companions, who was half-heartedly attempting to spear something in the water.

"They look friendly enough to me."

Samuel shook his head again. "You do not know them as I do. Those men are preparing to carry out a raid on another village."

"How do you know?"

Samuel tapped his head above one ear. "Based upon their headdresses."

Quentin looked closer. The tribesmen were not actually bald. They were wearing caps made of hairless animal skin. Suddenly a chill ran its fingers down the back of Quentin's neck. "They're human skin, aren't they?"

Samuel's expression was grim. "It is their custom to wear them for days before a raid."

Quentin suddenly felt vulnerable, and he hunkered down closer to the ground. "Why do they raid other villages?"

"In spite of the plentiful food sources you have seen available to the indigenes with which I have been a guest, this region can support few people. Sustenance is scarce. The chief source of animal meat for the few other tribes in the region is human flesh."

Quentin eyed Samuel. He looked dead serious.

"Such is their savagery," Samuel said. "The tribes regularly raid each other for the meat needed to sustain life. They know that Sinanie's village is in the area, but they have never successfully completed a raid there. Inevitably they retreat after some of them are killed. They always manage to carry away their fallen companions, so I suppose they do not return to their village without meat."

Quentin wasn't even sure how to respond to that. He turned again to stare at the tribesmen. There was something odd about their skin. Parallel rows of bumps covered most of their chests and backs, arranged in patterns that looked vaguely familiar to Quentin.

As if reading his thoughts, Samuel said, "You see the scars on their bodies, no doubt. They are prideful of them, and administer them to each other, inflicting great pain, I'm told. They are arranged so as to resemble the scales of crocodiles, a creature which they revere."

"Nice," Quentin said. "If there are crocodiles in the river, why don't they just eat those? I'd think that would be easier."

"Perhaps you have not attempted to subdue a crocodile, Quentin."

"Psst!" Lindsey hissed from her position several meters behind them. She then gave them a questioning look. She hadn't heard the details of their conversation.

Samuel whispered to Quentin. "We should remain cautious and withdraw from the river's edge. We can return to the river when we are far beyond these cannibals."

Quentin simply nodded. He glanced one more time at the men

with their skin caps and reptile scarification and then signaled Lindsey and the others to move silently away from the water.

A FEW HOURS LATER, after negotiating a two-meter-deep creek bed, Quentin stopped to help the others. One at a time he gave them a hand up the steep ravine, first Lindsey, and then Samuel, followed by the students, Ashley, Carlos, and Bobby. They all walked on ahead. The last to come up the slope was his son, Addison.

Quentin hesitated before holding his hand out to Addison, because the innocent-looking figure below him was not really his son at all. It simply looked like Addison, down to the last tiny, heart-wrenching detail. It had Addison's freckled face and wild curly brown hair. It had Addison's voice, and his frail frame and long fingers. It even smelled like Addison. But it wasn't him. It was an unfathomable mass of substance that could change its shape and chemical composition. And that was only the beginning of what it could do. The Papuan villagers who had been hiding it for centuries called it the *Lamotelokhai*. The real Addison was gone. His memory had been wiped clean, and he was either already dead or wandering aimlessly through the forest miles away. Finding him would have been impossible, so Quentin and Lindsey had been forced to leave him behind to die.

The Addison replica looked up at Quentin and extended its hand as it had seen the others do. Still, Quentin hesitated. The thing's eyes were the same pale blue as Addison's, but for a moment their color seemed to shift to an unnatural fiery golden hue. It only lasted for a second, and then the eyes were blue again. Perhaps it had just been a reflection.

The figure stood there with its hand held up, waiting. "You are afraid," it said. "Why?"

Quentin realized he was holding his breath and released it. He reached down and grabbed the thing's hand. With his help it scrambled up the slope. It stood there next to him, waiting for an answer.

Quentin released its hand. "We have no idea what you really are. Or what your intentions are. Why shouldn't I be afraid?"

It hesitated. "I cannot know why shouldn't you be afraid."

Quentin sighed. Although the Lamotelokhai was a fast learner, its speech still needed some work. As he turned to begin walking, movement caught his eye. Three tree kangaroos scurried up the ravine and then stopped at the Lamotelokhai's feet. The creatures had been following them since they'd left the hanging village. Quentin turned and started walking, and the Addison replica and tree kangaroos followed him.

"As I said, we don't know what you are."

It replied immediately. "It would take much talking to tell you. When you sleep again, I will show you."

Quentin turned around and raised his brows. "Another dream?"

It didn't respond.

"Do you mind telling me what you'll be putting into my head?"

"I will show you my creators."

"That'll definitely be interesting." Quentin kept walking. "Well, you should expect us to be afraid until we know more about you. That's the way people are."

They walked in silence for some time. Quentin realized he didn't like having the Addison replica behind him. He stepped to the side and gestured for it to pass by. It hesitated only briefly and then walked ahead.

When they caught up with the rest of the group, the tree kangaroos had disappeared. The Lamotelokhai joined Bobby, who then began asking it an endless stream of questions. The thing seemed naturally drawn to Bobby, probably because Bobby was the one who had learned to communicate with it first. That was before it had transformed itself into the shape of Addison. Bobby was predisposed to mastering the symbolic language the Lamotelokhai used. The language was based on the same set of symbols used in Kembalimo, a popular game he played. Quentin was baffled as to how there could be a connection between a computer game and this thing that had been hidden in the world's most inaccessible wilderness for so long. The only explanation he'd come with was that it was a coincidence, but his gut told him it must be much more.

Quentin skirted around the teens and joined Samuel and Lindsey, who were now leading the way. For some time they had to walk in single file, fighting their way through thick brush. But eventually the forest understory thinned out enough to allow Quentin to walk next to Samuel.

"I know you think we're making a mistake," Quentin said.

Samuel walked in silence for a moment before replying. "It seems that the fate of the Lamotelokhai is now beyond my ineffectual reckoning." He gave Quentin a brief glance. "However, I have been entertaining the notion of proposing to you that we halt our journey and establish our own tribal village here, where we might continue hiding it."

Quentin and Lindsey burst out laughing. But then Quentin saw that Samuel wasn't smiling. It had not been a joke.

Lindsey said, "I think we've already proven that we have no survival skills here, Samuel. You've had a century and a half of experience. We wouldn't be much help."

Samuel seemed to consider this, then he just nodded.

Quentin had been through a lot with Samuel in the four days since Samuel had found him, injured and delirious. But he still felt like he barely knew the man. Samuel rarely spoke of his past, other than to doggedly insist that he had been living with the tree-dwelling Papuan villagers for over 150 years, sustained by the restorative powers of the Lamotelokhai.

The funny thing was that Quentin now believed him. He had seen too much to doubt it was possible. So Quentin found it disturbing that Samuel was so reluctant to reveal his discovery to the rest of the world. Did Samuel know something about the Lamotelokhai he had not yet shared?

The understory became a dense tangle again so Quentin dropped back into single file and gave up trying to have a conversation. Soon after that it began raining.

AFTER TWO DAYS WITHOUT SLEEP, Bobby was starting to hear ringing in his ears and see movement at the edges of his vision. But his mind wouldn't rest. He had been forced to make decisions that had hurt people. To prevent the monster Addison had become from killing them all, Bobby had decided to have the Lamotelokhai erase Addison's memory. He realized now it would have been easier on Mr. and Mrs. Darnell if he'd simply killed Addison. And then, thinking it might improve that problem, he'd decided to have the Lamotelokhai change itself to look and act like Addison. But this was apparently a bad decision, too, because it freaked them out. So far, the Lamotelokhai would do everything Bobby asked it to, and it seemed more willing to talk to Bobby than to the others. In the coming days Bobby would probably have to make more decisions. He was eager to learn more about the Lamotelokhai, but he didn't want to be responsible for hurting more people.

It had been raining for an hour. The ground had become so muddy that Bobby had fallen three times. When Samuel slipped and tumbled down a minor ravine, they decided to stop for the night.

As the adults discussed how they might build a shelter from the rain, Bobby had to force himself to avoid staring at Ashley. She was muddy and soaked, and she frequently adjusted what little clothing she still had, trying to keep it in place. Bobby's legs were tired, so he sat on the ground. His own clothes were little more than a few strips of his pants and half of his shirt. The remains of his pants were wrapped around his waist, so to keep his privates hidden he pulled his feet up to his crotch and put his arms around his knees. Carlos sat down next to him and assumed the same position, probably for the same reason.

Bobby said, "Maybe in a few days we'll be home and sleeping in our beds."

Carlos didn't respond to this. Instead, he drew lines in the mud with his finger. Bobby wasn't sure what to say to him anymore. Carlos had lost his brother, Roberto, in the plane crash just days ago. One minute he would be talking and seem happy, the next he would turn quiet and gloomy. Several times he had said he didn't even want to go home.

Bobby looked at the forest canopy above them, trying to spot Mbaiso and the two other tree kangaroos. The creatures had followed them, but they would often disappear for an hour or more and then randomly show up again. He couldn't find them, so he returned his gaze to Ashley. She was walking away from the group alone, toward the river. He got up and followed her. Surprisingly, Carlos came with him.

The river was maybe fifty meters from where they were setting up camp. When Bobby and Carlos stopped at the jumbled boulders near the water, Ashley was nowhere to be seen.

"Jesus flipping Christ, you guys! I'm taking a pee!" Ashley was squatted in the trees a short distance away, glaring at them. "Turn around!"

Bobby felt his face flush as he and Carlos turned the other way. Before he could stop himself, he slugged Carlos on the arm, to show that it was his friend's fault that they had followed Ashley.

"Sorry for hitting you, man," he said in a whisper.

Carlos just stared ahead.

A moment later, Ashley was beside them. "All done." She looked at Bobby for a few uncomfortable seconds, and then she actually smiled. "I didn't like coming down here by myself anyway. It kind of creeps me out." She held up her hands and frowned as she inspected them. Then, apparently determined to wash them, she moved to the boulders at the river's edge. The jumbled rocks on the bank made it difficult to step directly into the water.

Bobby pointed downstream. "Maybe down there," he said. He and Carlos followed as she looked for a suitable spot.

"Did you guys want something? Or did you follow me to see me pee?"

Bobby said, "No, we just didn't think you should come down here alone."

"My heroes," she said. Finally she found a place where she could step on several rocks to get to the water. She hopped from rock to rock. The rocks were wet from the rain.

"Be careful," Bobby said.

"Seriously, Bobby?"

She ended up on a large boulder that sloped toward the water, and she inched her way down the slope on her butt until her toes were at the edge. She leaned forward and started scrubbing her hands.

Bobby decided to join her. He stepped on the same rocks she had used until he was looking down at her from atop the sloping boulder. Carlos had followed him, and they both sat down at the top of the slope and watched her. As she leaned forward, Bobby tried keeping his eyes from drifting below her bare shoulders.

Carlos surprised Bobby by breaking the silence. "There's something in there," he said. He pointed to the brown water in front of Ashley.

A large shape was rising to the surface. Bobby's muscles tensed up as if electricity were shooting through his body.

"Ashley," he cried. "Get back!"

She had already seen it. Just as she was pushing herself to her feet the shape exploded out of the water and lunged at her. Her arms flew up to protect her face and the thing actually rammed into her elbows, knocking her onto her back. It then crashed down onto the rock.

Bobby stared in horror, hardly able to comprehend what he was seeing. The head of a massive crocodile was on the rock between Ashley's knees. It swung its jaws to the side and barely missed Ashley's foot as she kicked and scrambled to get away, her feet slipping on the wet rock. The monster snapped again and almost caught her other leg.

At the edge of his vision, Bobby saw Carlos heave something. It was a football-sized rock, and it flew over Ashley and hit the crocodile squarely on the back behind its head. Apparently startled, the creature retreated into the water and sank out of sight.

Ashley rolled over onto all fours and fought to stand up. Finally her feet gripped the rock and she was upright. Her eyes met Bobby's. He had never seen her look so stricken.

Bobby leaned forward, his hand outstretched. "Come on!"

Her face became determined and she held out her hand. But she was short by a meter. He inched his way down the boulder, and she took a step up. Their hands met. Bobby gripped her hand as tight as he could. Carlos grabbed Bobby's other hand to keep him from sliding down.

"Hurry, Ashley!" Bobby said.

She took another step up the rock. "Did you freaking see that? Did you see it, Bobby?" She took another step.

With a wet swishing sound, both of her feet slipped. Her hand was yanked from Bobby's grip. Her head hit the rock with a sick thud. She stopped moving and her body slid down the boulder and into the water.

For several drawn-out seconds, Bobby stared in disbelief. Ashley's body bobbed to the surface, face down, and was carried downstream. Behind him, Carlos said, "Oh, shit."

"Get the others!" Bobby cried, and then he skittered down the rock and plunged into the river.

———

THE PILE of sago palm leaves in Quentin's outstretched arms was growing larger as Lindsey continued to add more. Samuel and the Addison replica were doing the same thing somewhere nearby. The plan was to use the meter-long fronds for the roof of a simple rain shelter.

Quentin was more than glad to be out of sight of the Addison replica. It was easier to take his mind off his son's fate when he didn't have to see a copy of him every time he turned around. Lindsey hadn't spoken since they'd started collecting the palm fronds, and Quentin made no attempt at conversation. They were descending into a pattern of episodic periods of somber silence. They hadn't actually articulated it, but there seemed to be mutual agreement that speaking during these episodes would only make things worse. Poorly chosen words could crumble the unsteady walls they were each trying to construct to hold back a tidal wave of grief.

"Help! You guys, where are you? We need help!"

It was Carlos, from back near the camp. Quentin made eye contact with Lindsey for a second that seemed longer than it was, and then he dropped the fronds and sprinted toward camp, crashing through the underbrush.

Carlos was babbling. "Hurry—real bad! It's Ashley—drowning! And Bobby!" He turned and headed for the river with Quentin and Lindsey on his heels.

Quentin had no idea what had happened, but the thought of

losing anyone else in his group prompted an upwelling of anger and determination. He wouldn't let that happen.

"She fell in here," Carlos panted, pointing to an area of jumbled boulders. "But the water carried her away. Bobby went in after her!"

Without waiting for further details, Quentin and Lindsey moved downstream, trying to stay close enough to the river to see the water. But the unencumbered sunlight at the water's edge had resulted in plant growth so thick that this was nearly impossible. After moving perhaps fifty meters downriver, Quentin turned and plunged through the growth until he was standing waist-deep in the water. He had to grasp an overhanging tree to keep from being swept off his feet. Bobby and Ashley were nowhere to be seen. But then, about 75 meters down the river, Bobby's head appeared. He was struggling, trying to get his footing while pulling something toward the shore. It was Ashley, her body mostly submerged and lifeless.

"Quentin, do you see them?" Lindsey called from shore.

Quentin pulled himself back up the riverbank. He tried not to show the terror that he felt. "This way!"

Moving downstream close to the water's edge was a nightmare—vines and roots encircling their legs and torsos, causing them to progress in slow motion. But Quentin didn't dare move farther from the river where he would be unable to see Bobby and Ashley. Finally he spotted Bobby through a gap in the foliage.

"There he is!" he shouted, not even certain the others were still with him. He bounded into the river and pushed aside the branches extending out over the water. The river was not as deep here, but slippery rocks and strong current made it hard to wade.

Bobby was perhaps ten meters out into the river, hanging on to a rock with one hand. His other hand was clamped onto Ashley's wrist. He was trying to pull her toward him, to get her flipped onto her back. Ashley still wasn't moving, and Quentin tried not to think about how long she had been face down.

Quentin slipped and then caught himself. He slipped again, this time floating several meters downstream before regaining his footing. He was making progress, but now he had to move upstream as well as across the river. Amidst his struggles, Bobby looked up and saw Quentin approaching, but he was obviously too exhausted to speak.

After slipping several more times, Quentin was at Bobby's side. He grabbed Ashley by the armpits and turned her over. She was unconscious and her face was unnaturally white.

"I've got her," Quentin said. "Can you get on your feet?"

Bobby still didn't speak, but without the burden of Ashley's body he was able to stand up.

Quentin looked at the far shore. It was at least fifteen meters away. They would have to haul Ashley back the way he had come.

Bobby didn't wait to be told. He linked his fingers together under one of Ashley's arms, and Quentin did the same with her other arm. They pushed toward shore with her between them. As they approached the shore, Lindsey and Samuel waded out to help. They all dragged Ashley up through the vegetation to a small clearing.

Quentin said, "Bobby, help me lift her! Samuel, we're going to lay her over your shoulder so her head is hanging down."

Carlos and Bobby helped lift her. When Ashley was hanging over Samuel's shoulder, a disturbing amount of water trickled out of her mouth and nose. Quentin pressed on her back and chest and even more came out.

As they put her on the ground, Bobby spoke for the first time. "She was under water way too long." He dropped to his knees and put his fingers on her neck, feeling for a pulse.

Lindsey didn't wait. She kneeled on Ashley's other side and

began forceful chest compressions. Quentin heard a rattling waft of air go in and out of Ashley's mouth with each compression.

"I don't feel any heartbeat," Bobby said. His voice was flat, as if he were too numb to emotionalize what was really happening.

Quentin gently pulled Bobby's hand away and felt her neck himself. He moved his fingers farther under her chin, and then closer to the collarbone. There were no signs of life.

Ashley had drowned.

Lindsey was now sobbing, but she continued the compressions. Quentin didn't bother to stop her. He released Ashley's neck, got to his feet, and paced back and forth, clasping his head with both hands. He didn't know whether to scream or to cry. For a few insane seconds he stared at a nearby tree and considered running full-speed into its trunk. Maybe it would crush his skull and put an end to everything. But he flushed the thought. He didn't deserve such self-indulgence.

Finally, Lindsey stopped pressing on Ashley's chest. She sat there on her knees, her tears creating lines of pale skin on her muddy face. She looked up at Quentin, and he saw more in her eyes than just tears. She was on the verge of panic. Like Quentin, she had reached a breaking point but knew that breaking would be disastrous for the entire group. She seemed to take comfort from this silent exchange with Quentin, and finally she nodded slightly.

Quentin turned to Bobby. "How did this happen?"

Bobby ignored him. Instead he spoke to the Lamotelokhai, his voice still unusually flat. "Bring her back. You can, right? I know you can."

The Addison replica kneeled down but didn't touch Ashley's body. "Ashley is dead. I helped you when you were hurt. When I helped you, you were not dead. This is different."

"I know you can do it." Bobby's voice now carried a slight edge. "Bring her back. I'm telling you to bring her back!"

Quentin was aware he should say something—he should intervene. But he remained silent.

The Lamotelokhai gazed at Bobby without expression. Its blue eyes again seemed to shift briefly to a peculiar golden yellow. It then pressed its finger against its own abdomen. With a faint pop, the finger pushed through the skin and disappeared all the way to the first knuckle. The finger came out covered in blood and curled around a walnut-sized mass of tissue. The Addison copy then moved its hand to Ashley's face. It shoved the mass into her mouth and then wiped the finger across her cheek, leaving a red streak on her deathly white skin. As Quentin stared at the streak, it gradually faded. Seconds later there was nothing left but dry, rust-colored residue.

Everyone seemed unwilling to break the silence. Quentin's eyes were glued to the stain on Ashley's skin, but his mind was elsewhere, engaged in a raging conflict. What would happen to Ashley now? Why had he not stopped this? Why hadn't Lindsey stopped it? Was their despair so consuming that they actually hoped this abhorrent copy of their son could bring Ashley back from the dead?

Quentin realized this was exactly what he wanted. As heinous as the idea was, at that moment he wanted it. After losing Roberto and Russ, and Miranda, and then Addison, he wanted it more than anything. He needed it in order to go on living. He looked across Ashley's body at Lindsey, and he saw the same need in her eyes.

Minutes passed. Still, no words were spoken. As they watched, Ashley's skin gradually turned from white to its original flesh color, as if the capillaries near the surface were filling with blood. The entire situation seemed surreal to Quentin. They were all gathered around Ashley, anticipating something that couldn't possibly happen, at least not in the reality in which Quentin had previously lived. He understood that when an animal died, there could be no turning back. When the heart stopped beating, the cells throughout the body were deprived of oxygen and they died. This was why Ashley's skin had turned white. And brain cells died even before skin cells did. Ashley's dead brain cells had likely already released the enzymes that helped microorganisms break them down. Her memories, her personality, all elements of her consciousness, were gone in the first few minutes after her heart had stopped beating. At least ten minutes—maybe twenty—must have passed between Ashley drowning and the Lamotelokhai's intervention. Decomposition began immediately after cell death, and there was simply no turning back.

Yet here they were, hoping and waiting for the impossible.

Ashley's face seemed to shift, changing its shape. Quentin blinked, uncertain he was actually seeing it happen. As he stared, her forehead receded, and the skin on her cheeks sagged as if it were no longer attached to the underlying tissue. But soon her familiar facial features returned and solidified.

Quentin was looking directly at Ashley's temple when it began to throb with a new pulse. At that moment he had witnessed the creation of life from nonliving matter. Minutes later, her chest began to rise and fall.

When Ashley opened her eyes, nobody had yet spoken since Bobby had ordered the Lamotelokhai to bring her back, perhaps a half-hour before. She blinked a few times, and then her eyes seemed to focus on the trees above her. She turned her head and saw that they were all gathered around her. Her brows furrowed and she frowned. She tried to speak, but all that came out was a strangled cough.

Lindsey leaned forward and placed her hand on Ashley's cheek.

Ashley turned to the side and spat out a mass of pale phlegm. Then she rolled over and vomited up a shockingly large mass of unidentifiable grey, viscous material. After spitting the remains from her mouth, she rolled on to her back again. She looked directly at Bobby.

"Nobody's saying anything," she said. "You're scaring the shit out of me."

Lindsey turned and looked at Quentin. Her tears were flowing again.

"This can't be good," Ashley said. "What happened?"

Bobby spoke to her. "You fell on the rocks, remember? A crocodile came at you, and then you fell in the river. I tried to get you out, but it was hard. It took a long time." Bobby shook his head and looked toward the river, like he didn't want to say any more. Then he turned back to her. "You drowned, Ashley."

Ashley seemed to think about this. "I don't know what you're talking about. I never went to the river, and I didn't see any crocodile. I think I'd remember that." She tried sitting up, and Bobby reached out to help her. When she was upright she brought her knees up and wrapped her arms around them. "I remember things just fine. We were all walking. It had started raining—raining for maybe fifteen minutes. It was getting slick. There was like, a gulley, and I stopped to give people a hand as they crossed it. Carlos and Bobby were behind me, so I helped them. Then there was—that thing." She nodded toward the Addison replica. "I gave him a hand, too. That's it. Then I woke up here, with everyone staring at me. What the hell, guys?"

The Lamotelokhai spoke. "Ashley, you died. Bobby asked me to reconstruct you. I did. You have the memories of the other Ashley that were available to me. The memories of the other Ashley that happened after the last time I touched her were not available to me. So I could not give you those memories."

The thing stopped talking. The only sounds were the pattering of lightly falling rain and the constant hum from the cloud of flies buzzing at a respectful distance above them.

Ashley looked at her hands, then she ran them over her legs, inspecting them as if it were the first time she had ever seen them. She turned her gaze back to the copy of Addison.

"What the hell do you mean, 'the other Ashley?'"

CHAPTER THREE

Bobby sat on the ground with his back to a tree, silently watching the others. They seemed upset, confused about what had happened, and uncertain that they had done the right thing. And again it was all because of a decision Bobby had made.

When he had ordered Addison to bring Ashley back, it seemed like the right thing to do. How could he have made any other choice?

"I feel perfectly fine!" Ashley exclaimed. She was on her feet now, pacing back and forth, apparently annoyed at being told she should be sitting down. "What's not fine is that I can't remember what I did during a big part of the day. And the reason why is because the person who did those things wasn't even me!"

"At least you're alive," Carlos said. "You almost got eaten."

Ashley shot a hard look at him. "That was someone else, remember?" She then hesitated, and her frown softened. She sighed. "Okay. Yes, I'm happy to be alive. But the original me died. How am I supposed to deal with that?"

Bobby stared at the mound of mud he'd been pushing around with his hand. "I couldn't save your life," he said quietly.

"Well, you tried," Ashley said, "and I'm grateful for that. You're batshit crazy for jumping in a river with a crocodile."

He stared at the mud.

"Bobby?" she said.

Reluctantly, he looked up at her.

"Thank you."

There was an awkward silence as Bobby held Ashley's gaze for as long as he could.

It startled Bobby when the Lamotelokhai was the one to break the silence. "Ashley died. Bobby asked me to reconstruct her. I did. Now I listen to all of you talk. You are afraid. You are angry. Why?"

Everyone was silent.

Mr. Darnell said, "Because we don't know how you did what you did. We don't know what it means."

"It does not mean," the thing replied. "It is what Bobby asked."

Mr. Darnell stepped closer and actually looked at the Lamotelokhai as if it were one of his students. "Remember what I told you earlier? If people don't understand something—fear. That's how people are. It's not possible to bring someone back from being dead. That's something I know." He held his arms out to include the others. "We all know that. But then Ashley woke up. How can that happen?"

The Lamotelokhai glanced over at Ashley before responding. "I did not bring someone back from being dead. I cannot do that. I made a new Ashley, using what I know of the other Ashley. It was easy, because most of the parts I needed were there, in the dead body of the other Ashley. I did not have to go elsewhere to get them."

Mr. Darnell looked at the copy of Addison for a few seconds. Then he just shook his head and turned away.

It spoke to him again. "You are afraid. You are angry. Would you like me to take the parts I used to make this Ashley and put them back where I got them?"

Mr. Darnel and everyone else seemed too shocked to answer this.

"No!" Bobby said.

A SHORT DISTANCE from the group of humans was a small-leaved fig tree that had fallen years ago but was still alive, supported by woody vines that had broken its fall. Three tree kangaroos sat on the angled trunk. Mbaiso, in the top position, watched the humans while wrestling with thoughts like none he'd ever had. Below him on the sloped trunk, the tree kangaroos Bobby had named Tupela and Tripela seemed more interested in sleeping than in contemplating the current situation. Mbaiso was not surprised or concerned at their indifference. They had been created long after Mbaiso, and for different purposes. They had never shown any inclinations toward decision-making or autonomy. Mbaiso was different. He had always carried out his instructions from the Creator, but he understood that things were changing and soon the instructions would stop coming.

Mbaiso turned to the other tree kangaroos and made a purring sound with his throat. When Tupela and Tripela opened their eyes, he lifted the front of his body and moved his forearms in a controlled gesture. His companions understood. They hopped to the ground and followed Mbaiso to the river.

Once at the river's edge, they moved downstream until they were at the bank of jumbled boulders where Mbaiso had seen Ashley fall in. In single file, the tree kangaroos leapt from rock to rock until they were perched atop the large sloping boulder. Mbaiso then faced Tripela, sat back on his haunches, and began a long series of intricate gestures. As Mbaiso had predicted, Tripela signed back, ears flattened against his head showing agitation.

Mbaiso patiently provided further information. Tripela's role was important to his plan. Finally, the gesturing stopped.

Tripela crept down the sloped boulder. He stopped briefly to sniff a dark stain where Ashley's head had struck the rock. When he was at the water's edge he paced back and forth, pausing every few turns to thump his hind feet on the rock, creating as much movement and noise as possible. He then stopped pacing and abruptly leapt off the rock in a high arc and landed in the water. He swam back, climbed out, and went back to pacing and thumping.

Mbaiso observed from atop the boulder. Tupela had stretched out beside him and appeared uninterested. Abruptly, Mbaiso sat up straight, his muscles tense. A dark form rose to the surface in front of the rock. Without meaning to, Mbaiso let out a nasally, alarmed grunt. Tripela stopped and watched the water before him. He then thumped the rock. He thumped it again.

The crocodile cranked its tail to the side, propelling it forward and onto the rock amidst a storm of flying water. Its jaws swept to the side and caught Tripela's head and left forelimb. Mbaiso heard bones crack as the jaw clamped shut. The crocodile slid back into the water and disappeared, dragging Tripela with it.

The flowing water carried away all signs of the disturbance, and the river was silent again. Mbaiso gazed at the water, the muscles in his haunches twitching, ready to flee if necessary. Tupela had retreated when the attack occurred, but now she returned to Mbaiso's side, and together they watched the brown water slowly churning past.

Something large moved just under the surface. The crocodile's head and back appeared, and then the creature went into a death roll, as if trying to tear apart a prey animal. Its legs and tail thrashed wildly, throwing water into the air and showering the tree kangaroos. Then the thrashing stopped as abruptly as it had started. The crocodile rolled over and floated with its white belly and diminutive legs sticking out of the water, motionless.

Tupela let out a throat-purr, indicating she was eager to return to the safety of the trees, but Mbaiso stayed put, watching and waiting.

The crocodile's legs twitched, and then they began to move in a more coordinated way, as if the creature didn't realize it was upside down and was trying to walk. Its tail then swept to the side, rolling its entire body over. For some time it floated there with its eyes and snout just above the water's surface.

Mbaiso cautiously crept down the rock slope and stopped at the water where Ashley had washed her hands. The crocodile saw the movement and swam toward the rock. Its massive head inched closer and closer. Mbaiso's haunch muscles began twitching again. His instinct was to flee, but he fought this urge and held his ground.

The crocodile's snout bumped the rock, almost touching Mbaiso's feet. Black pupil slits extending from the top to the bottom of its golden eyes revealed nothing of the crocodile's intentions. Still, Mbaiso held his ground. He ignored Tupela's throaty distress calls.

Abruptly the crocodile turned away. It began swimming, steadily and with purpose. Mbaiso watched it clamber over some exposed rocks until it disappeared on the other side, making its way upstream.

Tupela's calls diminished in intensity and then stopped. Mbaiso climbed to the top of the slope. He turned to gaze up the river, but could see only rocks and water. The crocodile had a long distance to travel and much to do once it reached its destination.

WHILE THE OTHERS worked on setting up a shelter, Bobby's job was to get the tree kangaroos to help him gather fresh fruits to go with the *khosül*—the sago and bug paste—Samuel had brought from the hanging village. Bobby had asked the copy of Addison to join him. The thing had been just standing there watching the others, so Bobby figured it might help to take it out of sight of Mr. and Mrs. Darnell for a while. And out of Ashley's sight, too, for that matter. Understandably, she was still freaking out, trying to figure out what the Lamotelokhai had done to her. Bobby was still trying to wrap his head around what had happened too, but he was glad Ashley was alive.

Rain fell in spurts as it funneled though open holes in the canopy while Bobby and the Lamotelokhai watched the branches above for the tree kangaroos.

"I'm hungry," Bobby said.

The Lamotelokhai didn't reply.

"Do you need to eat food?"

The thing kept watching the trees. "No."

"Then how do you stay alive?"

"I am not alive like you."

"But you're a computer. How do you get your energy?"

"I get my energy from things around me. Sometimes I need little. Now, in this form, I need more."

"Because we walked all day?"

"Yes."

"So what are the things around you that you get your energy from?"

"The air. Light of the sun. Things I touch." It pointed to the ground.

"You get what you need from touching the ground?"

"Yes. And from touching living things." It put its hand on a green leaf that hung near its head. Then it moved its hand to Bobby's neck.

Bobby took a step away. "Well, I can't do that. I have to eat."

Something thumped the ground a short distance away. Soon there was another thump, and another.

"Sounds like they found food," Bobby said. Watching to avoid getting hit, he rushed over and grabbed up two of the fruits, which were shaped like small footballs and covered with spiny green skin. He held them up to the Lamotelokhai. "What are these?"

"*Yawol* is the villagers' name for them. Breadnut is the name Samuel would use."

Bobby sniffed one of the fruits. "Is it good to eat?"

"I cannot know if it is good. There are seeds in it you can eat."

When the breadnuts stopped falling, Bobby gathered about ten into a pile. Mbaiso came to the ground, followed by Tupela. They sniffed at the pile as if making sure Bobby had stacked them correctly. Then they both plopped onto the ground to rest, their hind legs sticking out to the side and their front legs tucked under their chests.

Bobby searched the trees for Tripela, but saw no sign of him. "What's going to happen to them? After we leave here, I mean."

"The villagers asked me to create the mbolop to help them talk to me. Now I am leaving the villagers."

Bobby had been thinking about this. Mbaiso had become his friend. He would love to take the tree kangaroos home with him, but that was impossible. Questions would come up, and people would want to study them. "So what will happen to them?" he asked again.

"I can take them apart. Put the parts into the soil."

Bobby's stomach tightened. "You mean *kill* them? Like you did to Miranda?"

"Miranda was a living thing. The mbolop are not living things. But yes, like Miranda."

"I don't want them to die."

"Why?"

"Because they're my friends. Mbaiso is my friend. Do you know what friends are?"

After a short pause it said, "Yes."

"Can't they just keep doing what they've been doing?"

The thing didn't answer.

"I want you to let them stay with Sinanie and the others in the hanging village," Bobby said. "You're gone from the village now, so I want the mbolop to help them learn to live without you. Will you do that?"

"Yes."

"And maybe they can look for Addison. Then if they find him they can help him, too. Can they do that?"

"Yes."

Bobby squatted in front of the lounging tree kangaroos. He reached out to pat Mbaiso on the head, but then both of them got up and hopped away. Instead of climbing a nearby tree, they kept going, headed in the direction of the river.

Bobby frowned. "Wait, they're leaving now?"

"You asked me to do that," the Lamotelokhai said.

"I haven't said goodbye or anything." Bobby watched the tree kangaroos disappear into the brush. "Can you let Mbaiso stay with us for now? Maybe just send the other two back to help the villagers?"

"Yes. I can send the mbolop you call Tupela. I cannot send the mbolop you call Tripela. I am not receiving information from Tripela."

Bobby was considering asking what this meant, but then Mbaiso appeared, running straight back toward them. He stopped and plopped down in the same spot he had just left.

"How did you make him do that?" Bobby asked.

"I send information to the mbolop. The mbolop receives the information. That is how I made him do that."

"So you talk to him, like wirelessly?"

The Addison copy looked at him. "Definition is needed."

"You talk to him through the air, without touching him?"

"Yes."

Bobby considered this. "You told Ashley you only had her

memories from before the last time you touched her. If you can talk to Mbaiso wirelessly, why do you have to touch Ashley to get information?"

"Ashley is not the mbolop. I can talk to the mbolop wirelessly."

Bobby sighed. "My mom would say, 'you're making my head hurt'."

The Lamotelokhai stared at him.

"Never mind." Bobby squatted in front of Mbaiso again. "I'm glad you're staying with us a while longer, boy."

Mbaiso twitched an ear to flick off the rainwater.

QUENTIN ARRANGED the last sago palm frond on the lean-to and stood back to inspect their handiwork. The shelter was crude, and everyone was already soaked, but it would allow them to sleep without being pelted with rain. The others were arranged beneath it, busily extracting seeds from the breadnuts. There was enough khosül to last a few days, but the prospect of supplementing this mundane staple with something new was incentive enough to engage them all in the process. With some effort, the breadnuts could be split open by hand. Inside they were lined with rows of large seeds the size of walnuts, which they ate raw. Samuel said they were better when boiled, but there was little hope of starting a fire in such wet conditions.

Quentin inserted himself under the lean-to next to Lindsey. Samuel sat at one end of the row of bodies, pulling off chunks of the sago paste and handing them out. There was room for all seven, but the Lamotelokhai sat cross-legged just outside the shelter, facing them.

"You can come in here with us if you want," Quentin said.

The figure did not respond.

Quentin held out the khosül Samuel had given him. "Do you want something to eat?"

"He doesn't eat that way," Bobby said, his mouth full of food.

Quentin withdrew his hand. "You don't need to eat?"

"There are things that I need. But my units are efficient."

This statement puzzled Quentin. "Your *units*? What are those?"

"They are my parts."

Samuel asked, "What exactly are these parts?"

"My parts were made by my creators. This was their greatest achievement. My parts can do different things, but they can also work together to do one thing. Now they work together so that I may talk to you."

Samuel frowned. "Your parts are separate things?"

"Yes. Working together they make me what I am. This gives me awareness and I can talk to you. And it allows me to tell my parts to work apart from me sometimes."

Lindsey spoke up. "So is that what you do when someone removes part of you? Like when Bobby took part of you to make Addison forget? You tell those parts what their job is?"

"Yes."

Lindsey seemed interested in this. "So if you keep giving portions of yourself away, how can there be anything left?"

"My existing parts make more parts when necessary. I must always have enough parts for my awareness to exist."

Bobby said, "Can you show us how you tell some of your parts to do something on their own? Something besides making the medicine?"

Without taking its eyes off Bobby, the thing swung one arm over and grasped its other arm, pushing fingers into flesh. Suddenly the arm detached just below the elbow. The Lamotelokhai held the forearm out for them to see and then released it. It plopped onto the muddy ground.

Impulsively, Quentin dropped the lump of sago paste he was holding and reached for the severed arm, thinking in a brief moment of confusion that his son Addison was hurt. But then he stopped and—like everyone else—simply stared at the arm.

The hand began grasping at the mud.

Ashley said, "Oh great, it's moving."

It began changing. The fingers shortened, pulling into themselves. The arm arched, pushing its middle section off the ground like a huge inchworm and then fell onto its side. They stared in silence as the arm warped around itself, becoming a shapeless mass.

Then the mass grew hair—dense, short hair, mostly white but with gold splotches like islands on a map. The thing unrolled itself. At one end was a pink prehensile tail, still tightly coiled. At the other end was an absurd face. Two large round eyes sat on top of the head, turned peculiarly upward, with vertical pupils cut into ginger-colored irises. There were no visible ears, which made the head seem as round as a tennis ball.

The little creature rolled over onto its feet. Its pink nose twitched, sniffing the air. Marble eyes rolled one way and then the other, and then froze when they spotted Quentin's lump of sago paste lying on the ground. With singleness of purpose, it waddled over and picked it up. Gripping the food in one forepaw, it climbed onto Quentin's knee and held the khosül out to him. Quentin could think of no other response, so he accepted it.

Samuel cleared his throat. "That is a cuscus, of the genus *Spilocuscus*."

After another moment of silence, Ashley said, "That thing would be the cutest animal ever if it hadn't just come from a severed arm."

"Very curious," Samuel said. "This is a cuscus species I have not encountered in all the years I have collected here. It is no doubt related to *Spilocuscus maculatus*, but there are distinct differences." He spoke to the Lamotelokhai. "What sort is this, if I may ask?"

The cuscus climbed from Quentin's knee and ambled back to the Addison replica.

"This sort no longer lives," said the Lamotelokhai, as it reached for the creature with its remaining hand. The cuscus stood on its back legs and raised its forelimbs, allowing the hand to grasp its chest. The Addison replica lifted it and pressed it against the stump of its arm. The cuscus began to transform again, and within a minute it was gone, replaced by a perfectly shaped and attached forearm.

Lindsey spoke to the Lamotelokhai. "These parts of yours— they are what, little machines? Like nano-robots?"

The Addison figure hesitated. "Definition is needed."

"Nano-robots. Tiny machines—microscopic in size—that work together to accomplish things."

"Yes," the thing answered at once.

Shaking her head, Lindsey turned to Quentin and muttered, "Nano-robotics is all theoretical. We don't even know if it's possible."

The Lamotelokhai must have heard her. "As I have said, my parts were my creators' greatest achievement."

DAWN WAS BREAKING. Quentin stared at the sun, an impossibly large, deep red orb. Wispy spires of nuclear inferno were visible on its surface. A network of thin lines, like a symmetrical spider web suspended high in the sky, moved across the crimson sun as it rose.

Quentin looked around him. Water was everywhere, reflecting the red glow. Tiny islands of rock emerged as far as he could see. On the islands were clumps of growth in dark patterns like lichens, with stands of thin stalks emerging from the center of each clump. Bulges at the tips of the stalks danced as they swayed in the breeze.

Quentin floated above the water and rocks, and he knew he was in a dream. The Lamotelokhai was communicating with him, showing him something.

The water below reflected cotton-candy-pink clouds as they drifted by. A ripple broke the water's surface, and then another. Soon the ripples were everywhere—aquatic creatures becoming active in the growing light.

Quentin began to fly, propelled through the atmosphere of this foreign place by some invisible force. Soon the rocky islands zipped by below him. He saw something far ahead—a thin vertical line, extending skyward from the horizon until it disappeared. There were others like it to the right and left, almost obscured by the haze of distance.

Quentin flew faster, until the passing landscape was a blur. But the vertical line still seemed far away. It was unfathomably tall, and Quentin sensed that it was part of the distant spider web he had seen silhouetted against the rising sun. The line gradually drew closer until its width was much greater than the others to the left and right. And still it grew, until it filled his field of vision. Its smooth surface reflected pink sunlight. Quentin slowed, and the ground below came into focus again. Large clumps of growing stalks dotted the landscape, mostly orange at their bases, but with dazzling blues and greens at the bulging tips. Winding among the clumps were thin paths, and small, distant figures walked the paths.

As the tower drew even nearer, the walking figures became more numerous, some of them in large groups. The tower wall rose directly out of the rocks and there were openings at its base. Countless figures streamed in and out. Quentin was swept into one of the openings and down a wide passageway with walls that emitted pinkish light. The moving figures were abundant here, but his speed prevented him from discerning their specifics.

Finally the passageway ended and Quentin emerged into a vast open space, the hollow center of the tower. While the outer surface was featureless, the interior was riddled with doors, balconies, and walkways. The doors glowed with specific colors, and the wall, gently curving inward for miles, resembled an array of shimmering pixels fading into the distance.

Before Quentin could adapt his sense of scale, he accelerated upward. Spherical pods flew about in the atmosphere of the tower, each of them emanating a color. There were no visible means of lift or propulsion, but the pods moved at great speed. He climbed higher, and they became more abundant, until the swarm of flying pods obscured the tower's floor below. Then without warning he plunged horizontally into another passageway. When he again reached the outer wall of the tower, a door opened and he shot out into the open air. At this height above the ground, the sky was darker, and stars sparkled through the thin air above. Still the tower rose higher. Again he accelerated upward, flying parallel to the tower's exterior surface.

Finally he spotted the summit. The tower was topped with a large disk-shaped node. Massive tubes joined the node, extending out in six directions. It was the spider web Quentin had seen from the ground. The tower connected the planet's surface to an unthinkably vast network, which appeared to envelop the entire planet in a perfectly stable geostationary orbit. Quentin was struck by the node's resemblance to the central hut of the Papuan village, which had housed the Lamotelokhai and was joined to six hanging tunnels.

He passed the lower edge of the node and rose toward its top. As he rounded the upper edge, the vast roof of the node lay before him. It was a disk the size of a city, joining six tunnels that were each at least a mile in diameter. There in the center of the disk something was happening. A cloud of particles was dispersing upward. He drew nearer and realized that the particles, which were not so small, were coming from openings in the disk's surface. He approached one of the openings. An object emerged from the portal and then shot into space to join the others. Another object appeared at the portal, held in place by clear, glass-like rods to a platform that had lifted it. It was about a meter across and roughly spherical. The clear rods pulled free of the object and retracted into the platform. The object shifted itself and sealed up the holes where the rods had been, and then Quentin knew what it was—the Lamotelokhai.

The platform snapped upward, shoving the thing off. Quentin watched it drift away, joining the cloud of thousands—perhaps millions—of others, all hurtling into space.

QUENTIN STIRRED, the dream lingering in his mind. It was still dark. The rain had stopped, but the silence was punctuated by pattering drops falling from the wet forest canopy. He rose to one elbow. The Addison replica still sat in the same spot watching him.

"I guess you don't sleep, huh?" Quentin spoke softly so as not to wake the others.

The figure did not respond.

Quentin whispered, "The dream I just had—you put that into my head, didn't you?"

"Yes," the figure whispered back. Either it was mimicking Quentin's tone, or it actually understood the purpose.

"That was the home of your creators, where you came from?"

"Yes, as it was long ago when I was created."

Quentin studied the Lamotelokhai. He was still struggling to grasp the enormity of what he had witnessed. The massive web that encircled the planet likely provided more living space than the planet's entire surface. It was beyond comprehension. Nevertheless, the Lamotelokhai had said it was the tiny particles in its own body that were the *greatest* achievement of its creators. And this achievement was here, sitting in the mud directly in front of Quentin.

"Why did you come here?" Quentin whispered.

In spite of the darkness, he saw the figure smile.

"Perhaps soon you will see why."

———

Bobby was the last to wake. He was aware the others were up—he heard them talking about the dream they'd all had—but he was still exhausted. He rolled over and covered his ear with his elbow, but it was no use. The morning birds and insects were making a ruckus, and it just wasn't comfortable lying in the mud. Besides, there was the dream. As he listened to the others talk, the details came back to him: The red sun; fish swirling the water; flying into a tower that went all the way up to space; and finally the Lamotelokhai. There wasn't just one Lamotelokhai. There were too many to count.

"Welcome to the living, Bobby," Ashley said.

Bobby wondered if she'd intended that to carry deeper meaning than just a morning greeting. He mumbled something that wasn't clear even to him. He squinted at Ashley. She was filthy, and her hair was a tangle of twigs and mud balls. And she was beautiful. "You look like a mudpuppy," he said.

Ashley snorted. "If I had a mirror, I'd make you look at yourself."

They were all grubby and damp. Carlos had managed—maybe on purpose—to spread mud over every inch of his body including his face. Even Samuel was a sight. He must have tried to wash himself in the river, because he was dripping brown water. The only one who looked normal was the Lamotelokhai. The thing still sat on the ground, perfectly clean, in the same spot where it had pulled off an arm the night before.

Bobby eyed the Lamotelokhai. It was easy to forget that the thing used to look like a mass of clay. It seemed so much like a person now. Not really Addison—because it said things Addison wouldn't say—but still like a person. He spoke to it. "That was the place you came from, wasn't it? In my dream?"

"Yes."

"What were those things swimming in the water? Were they fish?"

The Lamotelokhai nodded toward the adults. "Your questions do not fit the pattern of questions from the others."

Bobby frowned. The thing had always just answered his questions before. "They're grown-ups, I'm a kid," he said. "Were they fish?"

"No, not fish. But in some ways like fish. Would you like to see?"

Bobby wasn't sure what that meant, so he shrugged. "Sure, let me see."

The thing then repeated the same act it had performed the previous day. It pulled its own arm loose and dropped it onto the ground. Ashley and Carlos moved to Bobby's side. They stared at the arm, waiting. Like before, it curled up and then shaped itself into something else. Soon it was a perfectly formed creature, flopping in the mud. It was definitely not a fish, even though it had the shape of one. The tail looked like a fish's, spread wide and trying to swim by flipping at the air. But the creature's skin looked nothing like a fish's. It was more like hard leather with softer joints that let it move. The leather was the color of dried blood on the top of the body and pink lemonade on the belly. But Bobby's eyes were drawn to the strangest part, the head. Actually, there were two of them—or maybe two parts of one head. The hard skin did not cover the heads. This made the body look like a cone, and out of the open end of the cone came two thrashing eel heads about the size of Bobby's thumb. Each head had two eyes and whiskers that seemed to be feeling for something. There was one mouth just below where the two eel heads joined the body. The mouth opened and closed as if gasping for air. As they watched, the creature's flopping began to slow down.

Ashley was the first to say something. "Whatever that is, it's dying."

"It's not even real," Carlos said. Then he looked at the Lamotelokhai. "Is it real?"

"It is a copy, like I am a copy of Addison."

The adults came over and watched the thing die.

"That is a creature unlike any I have seen," Samuel said. "What exactly is it?"

"It's from the Lamotelokhai's planet." Bobby said.

The Addison copy picked up the creature, which was now hardly moving, and reattached it to his arm. Soon the creature was gone, and the hand was good as new.

"Why did it have two heads?" Bobby asked.

The Lamotelokhai flexed its hand. "Many of the living things on the planet of my creators had heads similar to this."

Samuel cleared his throat. He was frowning. "How much time has passed since you left the world upon which this creature swam?"

"A unit of time is needed," the Lamotelokhai said.

Bobby said, "It wants to know how long is—"

"Yes, I do see that," Samuel said. "Generally we measure the passing of time in years. A year is the time it takes for the Earth to complete its path about the sun." Samuel pointed up, even though the sun couldn't be seen. "Approximately 365 days and nights pass in a year."

The Lamotelokhai didn't even pause to think about this. "Six zero two three four two eight nine two years. That is the time that has passed since I was sent from the world upon which the creature swam."

Everyone was quiet. Bobby tried to picture the number on paper, but it didn't work. He noticed that Mr. Darnell was counting on his fingers as he repeated the number in his head.

He finished counting and said, "Nine digits."

"That's 602 million years ago," Mrs. Darnell said.

Mr. Darnell was still holding his fingers up. "The number you just gave us was six hundred and two million, three hundred and forty-two thousand, eight hundred and ninety-two years. It's easier for us to understand if you say it that way. Do you understand?"

"Yes."

"Is that number really correct?"

"Yes."

"So when did you arrive here on this Earth?" Mr. Darnell asked.

"I arrived 221,880 years after I was sent from the world of my creators." It stated the number correctly this time. "So I arrived here 602,121,012 years ago."

Again, everyone was quiet.

"Extraordinary," Samuel said. He paused for a moment as if thinking. "Last evening you showed something to us. It was a cuscus of the genus *Spilocuscus*. You claimed that the species no longer lived. Yet you seem to have memory of it, memory sharp enough to create an accurate imitation of a living individual. Do you have memory of other living things from the past?"

"Yes. I have memory of living things I have encountered since I arrived here."

Mrs. Darnell said, "You have that kind of information about living things on Earth for the last 602 million years?"

"Yes. There were no living things on the land when I arrived here. But many were in the water. Later, living things were on the land. I have information on all that I have encountered."

"My God," Mrs. Darnell said. "Quentin, it's a databank of the evolution of life."

An idea hit Bobby like a punch to his head. "You were here when dinosaurs were here, weren't you?"

The Lamotelokhai looked at him. "Definition is needed."

"You know, dinosaurs! They were big and kind of like lizards. They were reptiles—really big ones. Some of them ate plants, but some of them were the biggest predators ever."

"Yes, I was here when dinosaurs were here."

Bobby turned to the others, his face hot with excitement.

"Way *beyond* extraordinary!" he said.

<hr>

THEY CONTINUED DOWNSTREAM, along a trail that was often no trail at all. The ground was slippery, with treacherous slopes where minor streams merged with the river. It was slow going, and Quentin had little choice but to face his own beleaguered thoughts.

The Lamotelokhai had revealed medical and physical phenomena Quentin had believed impossible. Now the thing claimed to have occupied the Earth for over half a billion years, recording information on evolving life forms. So much information that it could create an exact copy of any living thing it had encountered. It must also have data on such things as water and air chemistry. And this was just for the Earth. What about its planet of origin? And the regions of space it had traveled through before arriving here?

It was clear the Lamotelokhai's discovery would be seen as one of the most significant events in human history. Bringing it out of hiding was now their chief responsibility. The Lamotelokhai, whatever it was, was bigger than Quentin—bigger than all of them. Maybe even bigger than Addison, whom Quentin had abandoned in the wilderness to die alone. And the importance of the discovery served as a rationale, a justification for this personal nightmare and the remorse that promised to haunt his remaining days.

But even as this notion took hold, a conflicting fixation was sprouting within Quentin, taking root and growing like malignant kudzu through his mind. He felt intensifying anxiety about revealing the Lamotelokhai. He could no longer convince himself it had originated on Earth. The Lamotelokhai was what it claimed to be, and it held the knowledge of a far superior race of beings.

Quentin thought of the Papuans his parents had introduced him to so many years ago. Gupy had treated young Quentin as an adult, showing him how to sharpen the blade of a bush knife while his parents weren't watching and telling him jokes about the village women. Quentin couldn't understand the words, but the jokes were evidently sexual. And Amius, with a penchant for having his picture taken, had hoisted Quentin into his lap repeatedly, knowing Quentin's mom could not resist the photographic opportunity.

But Gupy and Amius's tribe had changed in the years since Quentin's parents had studied their language and had exposed them to the outside world in the process of making a documentary. At only seven, Quentin hadn't been able to grasp the significance of Bintang beer bottles piled higher than his head outside the huts, or used needles and cigarette butts littering the ground. Quentin's dad had taken all the blame for this upon himself. It hadn't been his fault, of course. The tribe would have merged with the modern world eventually. But crushing self-reproach had destroyed his father, and therefore the event and its consequences had shaped Quentin's existence and worldview. Although the Lamotelokhai might benefit humans beyond imagining, Quentin was bringing an advanced culture's influence to his own species. He was living out his father's story on a global scale.

And so a fierce conflict grew within Quentin as he trudged, stumbled, and slid about in the mud, slowly making his way down-river with the rest of the group.

Most of the others had become quiet after the first hour of traveling. But Bobby seemed to have an endless stream of ideas and questions for the Lamotelokhai, and it distracted Quentin to listen to them talk.

"There were lots of others like you," Bobby said. "I saw them being shot out into space. Where did they all go?"

"I cannot know where."

"Did they go to other planets?"

"I cannot know. That was their purpose. It is likely some of them found suitable destinations, as I have. Others may still be searching."

"That's a long time to search."

No response.

"So you were here 245 million years ago, right?"

"Yes."

"So you saw them, right? You saw dinosaurs. Live dinosaurs."

"Yes, I encountered them."

"So you could make one to show us?"

"Yes."

"But what if it's bigger than you? How could you do that?"

"I would need other parts."

"What kind of parts?"

"The parts could come from many things."

"Could you use this tree?" Bobby patted a fig tree as he passed it.

At this point Quentin jumped in. "Bobby, that's a bad idea. Promise me you won't ask it to do that."

Bobby's shoulders slumped. "Maybe just an herbivore?"

Quentin shook his head. "Until we know more about it, don't ask it to make anything."

Eventually Bobby seemed to run out of questions, and the group pushed on in silence. Morning turned to afternoon, creating a sauna beneath the canopy's cover. Afternoon turned to evening, and still they trudged on. When the rain started, it washed away some of Quentin's sweat, but it didn't help their progress. Much of the ground had baked hard during the day, but the rain made walking perilous again. No one objected when Samuel suggested they stop.

They followed the same plan for making camp. Bobby collected fruits with help from Mbaiso, the only tree kangaroo still following them. Before long they were sitting under a new shelter, eating the fruits and the last of the khosül. Again the Addison replica sat in the open. Bobby asked it a few random questions but then lay on his side, clearly exhausted.

"Goodnight everyone," Bobby said.

Ashley and Carlos did the same. Lindsey squeezed Quentin's hand once and lay down. Samuel, at the opposite end of the lean-to, rose and moved to Quentin's end. He pardoned himself and sat next to him.

"I don't suppose you have a plan upon our arrival at a village," Samuel said quietly.

"What do you mean?" Quentin said, but he was pretty sure he understood.

Samuel eyed the Addison replica. "Quentin, in order to prevent my worst fears, we must reveal the Lamotelokhai only to those least likely to become intoxicated by its influence. You need only to think of your son Addison to know this is true."

Quentin looked at him sharply.

"I am sorry," Samuel said. After a pause he went on. "The world is no doubt full of men capable of becoming monsters, given the means to do so. It is upon us to see that the Lamotelokhai does not become the property of such men. We must reveal it to those you would know to be true of purpose. Do you believe the men of position in your home country are to be trusted with such power?"

Quentin sputtered a laugh, but then he thought about this. "Depends who we're talking about. But it'll be as safe there as in any country. Much safer than in some."

"Then that is where we should take it. But having a destination does not make the journey easy. We must have a plan for when we reach a village, for surely we soon will."

Quentin shifted in the mud and eyed the Lamotelokhai, which watched them without expression. He turned back to Samuel. "If we're lucky, the village we find will have a radio. If they do, we'll call for help and a plane will pick us up and take us to Jayapura."

Samuel looked baffled, and Quentin sighed. "I imagine we can get that far without much suspicion. After that, I don't know. They'll want to do medical exams, vaccinations, stuff like that. They're going to wonder why we're all perfectly healthy." Quentin nodded at the Lamotelokhai. "And then there's that thing."

"You are worried," the thing said. "Why?"

Quentin could see no reason to hide anything. "We want to take you to my home, the United States. We're worried that people will stop us. They will examine us to see if we are healthy. We're worried that when they examine you they'll see that you're not a real person. Then they might try to keep you and use you to do bad things."

"How will they examine me?"

"They'll listen for your heart beating. They'll take samples of your blood. Maybe they'll X-ray you so they can see your insides."

"I will make myself look real to them."

Quentin studied the thing's face. Why should he doubt that it could do this? It had made an extinct cuscus out of its own arm.

"Let us hope that you can," Samuel said. "There remains one other matter, however." He looked directly at Quentin. "If it is to be Addison, then you must call it by that name. We cannot continue to call it the Lamotelokhai."

Quentin sighed again. He turned to the figure. "Samuel is right. We will have to call you Addison." He pointed to the others one at a time. "I want you to call them Ashley, Carlos, and Bobby. They are Addison's friends. Lindsey is Addison's mother. You call her

Mom." Quentin paused. "And you call me Dad. Do you understand?"

"Yes."

Samuel lowered himself into the mud and placed both hands behind his head as a pillow. "It appears we have a plan." He closed his eyes.

"Yeah, I suppose so," Quentin whispered. He settled onto his side and put one arm around Lindsey's mud-crusted shoulder.

"Goodnight, Dad."

Quentin raised his head and stared. The thing sat motionless, watching him.

"Goodnight, Addison."

CHAPTER FOUR

"Tʜᴇʀᴇ ᴀʀᴇ ᴏᴛʜᴇʀs ᴡɪᴛʜ ᴜs."

It was the voice of the Lamotelokhai—Addison's voice. The meaning of the words took hold, and Bobby sat up, scraping his head on the rough edge of the shelter's sago leaves. The Lamotelokhai sat in the same spot from the night before. But it was pointing. Bobby's gut tightened. He looked where it pointed. Even in the gloomy morning light he saw them immediately. Three Papuan men stood there watching them.

"Look, you guys! People!" Bobby cried, louder than he'd meant to.

Suddenly everyone was awake, mumbling or staring dumbly at the strangers. The Papuans shot nervous glances at each other. Bobby could see that they were not from Sinanie's tribe. They looked old, with scars and rashes. And their bodies were thin, the skin stretched over the bones.

"Do not fear them," Samuel said. "It is a hunting party."

This was obvious. The men wore no clothing except tightly fitted penis gourds. Two of them held bows and arrows in their hands. The third man carried a shotgun on his shoulder, holding it by the fat barrel with one hand. In the other hand he held a dead tree kangaroo by its tail. Bobby stared at it until he was sure it was not the same species as Mbaiso.

Samuel approached them with his arms out. "*Nggé, gu mbakha-to-fosü le-bo?*"

The Papuans shook their heads. Samuel tried the ancient Papuans' language again. From what Bobby could tell, he was trying to tell them they were looking for a village.

The man with the shotgun spoke a long string of words. Most of them Bobby had never heard before, but he heard *lekhingga*, which he was sure meant far away. And there were some words of pidgin mixed in: *waitman*, which meant white people, and *balus*, which meant airstrip or airplane.

Bobby remembered every word of pidgin he'd learned in Wamena, so he moved to Samuel's side. Bobby said, "*Mipela laikim bilong yu helpim.* We need your help."

The man with the shotgun smiled and answered, "*Mipela nogat wailis. Mipela bringim yu long viles wantaim wailis.*"

Bobby turned to the others. "He says they don't have a radio, but they'll take us to a village that does." Everyone stared at him. "It's pidgin. I learned it in Wamena."

"Yet again you surprise me, Bobby," Samuel said. He turned to the others. "We should make haste before they withdraw their offer."

There was no breakfast to eat and no gear to pack. Mrs. Darnell and Ashley said they were going to the lady's room and went off together. While the others waited, the strangers stared at the Lamotelokhai. Even though the thing looked similar to the rest of them, there were differences. Its white skin and curly hair were clean. And there was the strange way it quietly watched everything that was happening, never really helping or taking part, but always watching.

When Mrs. Darnell and Ashley came back, the shotgun man

pointed at the Lamotelokhai and spoke to his friends. They stared at it and nodded. Samuel stepped up and said, "Very well, then. Shall we go?" He waved for the men to lead.

They didn't move. They were now looking at the trees above. The shotgun man spoke to one of the others, who raised his bow and nocked an arrow.

Bobby looked where they pointed. Suddenly his heart was in his throat. Mbaiso was climbing down the tree toward them. The tree kangaroo was very near, an easy shot for someone good with a bow.

"No, don't!" Bobby cried and rushed forward. But he was too late. The man released the arrow. Bobby turned in time to see it pierce Mbaiso. Its force tore the kangaroo from the tree. Mbaiso hit the ground with a sickening *pop*, and then lay there, not moving.

Bobby looked back at the men, who seemed surprised by his outburst. "He's our friend!" he said. "*Wantok*. Friend!"

The shotgun man held up his dead tree kangaroo. "*Abus. Kaikai.*"

Bobby ran to Mbaiso. The arrow protruded from both sides of his body, but the kangaroo's eyes were open, and they turned to Bobby as he knelt down. Bobby assumed Mbaiso could survive the arrow but feared what would happen if the Papuans got their hands on him. They might try to skin him and cut him up for food.

"Addison, help me!" Bobby cried.

The Lamotelokhai came over and knelt next to Bobby. The Papuans gathered around, apparently curious about all the fuss.

"We can't let these men have the mbolop," Bobby said to Addison. "Can we send Mbaiso back to the tree house village, like we talked about before?"

The Lamotelokhai grabbed the arrow, snapped it in half next to Mbaiso's body, and then pulled it out from the other side.

Bobby glanced at the Papuans, worried they would be mad about the broken arrow. The men watched but didn't interfere.

Addison grabbed Mbaiso's arms and lifted him onto his haunches. He sat like that for some time, looking into Mbaiso's eyes. Finally he let go. Mbaiso scampered back to the tree and climbed to the first horizontal limb. After looking down at them for a moment, he then moved higher to where the branches meshed with other trees. Soon he was out of sight, moving upstream, back the way they had come. Bobby stared at the spot in the trees, and he realized he would never see Mbaiso again.

"*M wé! Mayokh, gu laléo-lu!*" cried one of the Papuans. All three of them stared wide-eyed at Addison. If they weren't suspicious about him before, they definitely were now.

This could ruin everything. Bobby rose to his feet, thinking furiously. He spoke to the Papuans. "*Bilong balus.*" He then used his hand to show how their airplane fell from the sky, and he made a crashing sound. "*Mipela lus. Bilong tumbuna kam helpim, luk mbolop.*" The men didn't respond and Bobby tried to say it differently by rearranging words. What he wanted to say was, "Our plane crashed, we were lost, and our ancestors came to help us, looking like tree kangaroos."

The men frowned at each other, probably because they weren't buying the story. The forest sounds seemed to grow louder to fill the uncomfortable silence that followed. Finally the man with the shotgun said something to his friends, and the Papuans turned and walked away. No one else moved. When the men realized they weren't being followed, they stopped.

"*Bihainim!*" one of them called out, and waved for them to come along.

DESPITE THE PAPUAN HUNTERS' bedraggled appearance, they forged ahead relentlessly, showing no signs of fatigue. Quentin hadn't seen the river for some time, and there was no visible trail, but the men seemed to know exactly where they were going. After perhaps three hours of walking, in which Quentin estimated they'd covered only three miles, the terrain began to change. The relatively flat lowlands of the river valley gave way to more densely vegetated hills, slowing their progress even more.

The Papuans showed considerable patience toward the slower Americans. Quentin lost track of the number of times the men stopped to wait for them. They would sit cross-legged on the ground, smiling at the stragglers as they caught up. When everyone was assembled they would rise to their feet and say, *"Viles no longwe,"* which meant, *the village is not far*. And the walking would start again.

This continued through the morning and into the afternoon. And still the village was *'no longwe.'* Progress became agonizingly slow. At any given time they were either climbing a hill or descending one. They had not eaten or drank all day, and this was showing its effects. Finally, Lindsey insisted that they take a break.

"We're tired and thirsty," she said to the men. "We need to rest."

They didn't respond, so Bobby spoke up. "Um, *plis. Les. Malolo. Kaikai. Wara.*"

The men exchanged some words and then seemed to reach an agreement. They set their weapons down. The Papuan with the shotgun held up his tree kangaroo. *"Mipela kaikaim mbolop. Wara."* He motioned for them all to sit.

"Thank you," Lindsey said.

One of the hunters produced a knife and began skillfully removing the skin from the kangaroo's haunch. Bobby and Carlos moved closer to watch. The two other hunters cleared a depression in the ground for a fire. Samuel left to find fruits, mumbling his doubts of success without the tree kangaroos.

The Papuans apparently had no matches to start the fire. They found two branches as thick as Quentin's wrist and laid one of them flat on the ground. They set the second branch so that its end was propped up by the first. One of them gathered an armful of tree bark. Using his teeth, he pulled toothpick-thin fibers from the bark and placed them on the ground until there was a pile resembling a bird's nest. He bit into the bark and with some effort pulled loose a much heavier fiber, about as thick as a pencil. He shoved the bird's nest of fibers into the gap under the propped-up branch and then pushed the larger cord through the gap so that he could hold the ends of it on either side. He pulled up on the cord while resting one foot on the top branch to hold it down. He pulled first on one end of the cord and then the other, like he was trying to saw through the branch with it. The sawing became faster. There was no smoke, but the man didn't seem discouraged, and he worked at it with practiced skill.

Quentin's fatigue was catching up with him. Lindsey and Ashley were already resting on the ground, so he joined them.

Ashley lay with her arms crossed over her face, and she spoke in a muffled tone, "I don't suppose they told you how much farther it is."

Quentin had to hold his breath to cross his stiff legs. "I'm sure they know what they're doing."

Lindsey raised her brows at him as if questioning this. She then patted Ashley's ankle. "He's right, Ash. You'll be with your family in a few days."

"You live on a farm, don't you Ashley?" Quentin said.

Ashley didn't move her arms from her face. "We have horses, but it's not really a farm. Lori and Brent aren't the farming types."

"Lori and Brent?"

"My parents. They don't like to get dirty. They have a guy who does all the work."

"They'll be thankful to learn you're alive," Lindsey said.

Ashley laughed. "I bet a bunch of people will be. They've probably filed a butt-load of lawsuits."

Quentin and Lindsey exchanged glances. They had avoided discussing this.

Ashley seemed to sense their uneasiness. She sat up. "Don't worry, they won't blame you two. They'll probably blame the school, and maybe the airplane company. What about you guys? You have families that are worried, too, right?"

Lindsey smiled. "Yes, Mom and Dad and my brother."

"Do they live in Newton?"

"In Columbia. I grew up there. My folks own *The Real Macaw*."

"Seriously? Lori and Brent love to eat there! They like the cowboy room. What's that one called?"

"The Tucson room," Lindsay said. "I grew up in the *Macaw*. I worked there when I was your age, all the way through college."

Quentin had not eaten at *The Real Macaw*—named for the scarlet macaw, Aristotle, Lindsey's family kept in the sitting room—until he had met Lindsey. The first floor of the Victorian home had been converted into a restaurant. Four restaurants, actually—four different dining rooms, each with a different theme. Lindsey's parents, Tucker and Rita, had converted the place before she was born, and she had grown up living in the upper floor.

They talked about the restaurant for a few minutes, and then Ashley said to Quentin, "What about you, Mr. D?"

A vivid memory flooded Quentin's mind: his father, sitting at the dinner table, pushing his food around with his fork but not eating. Since returning from their family trip to revisit the Papuan tribe, his skin had started to sag on his cheeks and his eyes seemed larger. Only a boy then, Quentin had been terrified that his dad was transforming into a stranger—someone who hardly ever spoke. Quentin's mom asked how Quentin's day was, and she listened with tight lips as he gave his obligatory report. Quentin eyed his dad as he talked, but his dad never looked back at him. This was the last time the three of them had eaten together at the table.

Quentin realized Ashley was watching him, waiting. "My mom lives in Springfield," he said. "I imagine she's concerned."

Ashley paused. "I heard your dad…" She trailed off, obviously regretting going that far.

Quentin glanced at Lindsey and she shrugged pensively.

"My dad decided he had made a mistake. He was the kind of guy who, when he decided something, that was it. And he was prone to dark moods. He and my mom brought the outside world to a remote Papuan tribe—thought they were doing something good at the time. Nine years later, they found out otherwise." Quentin shifted his stiff legs. "The tribe had changed. I guess my dad believed he was responsible for that."

"How did the tribe change?" Ashley asked.

"For the worse. Or for the better—depends who you ask." Quentin shook his head. He had said enough. He turned away and saw Bobby and Carlos watching every slice and hack of the Papuan's knife. Addison—the Lamotelokhai—sat to the side, appearing every bit as human as the rest of them. A tendril of smoke and an orange glow came from the nest of fibers as one of the Papuans blew on it.

"They got it going!" Bobby said, actually clapping his hands with excitement.

Quentin gave Bobby a thumbs-up.

"You know what I'd like to know?" Ashley said. "Why haven't we seen search planes? When a plane goes missing, doesn't someone try to find it?"

Quentin sighed but didn't answer. A string of confounding events tugged at his consciousness: Samuel's attempts to alter time, one talisman that was now two, Bobby's assertion that he'd seen another plane; and the total absence of search aircraft. A sudden desire to share these thoughts gripped him. Maybe Lindsey and Ashley could point out something he was missing, something that would make it all seem coherent and innocuous. But he remained silent. There was no reason to burden them with worrisome—and probably unrelated—matters.

Ashley lay back and covered her face again. Then she said, "I guess the other Ashley just died, didn't she? According to that thing, Addison, I'm not even the same person. She drowned. For her, everything went black and turned to nothing. Miranda believed in heaven, but I know there's no heaven or hell. There's just nothing. And now I'm here, but that other person doesn't even know I exist. She's gone."

Quentin and Lindsey exchanged a glance.

Lindsey said, "I don't know, Ash. I have a hard time thinking you're not still the same person."

Ashley didn't respond to this, and Quentin sensed she was trying not to cry. To avoid further discussion, he turned his attention to the Papuans. The fire was now blazing, and the men had enlisted the help of the boys, having them hold strips of kangaroo meat skewered on sticks over the flames. Bobby and Carlos held a stick in each hand while Addison, whom the men had not asked to help, watched.

Samuel returned empty-handed. There would be no fruit to help quench their thirst.

As the meat cooked over the fire, one of the men stuffed a handful of leaves into his mouth and chewed until they were pasty. He then motioned for the boys to move the cooking meat in his direction. He pulled the green paste from his mouth, smeared it gingerly over the sizzling meat and then pushed the sticks back over the fire. After a few more minutes of cooking, he pulled the meat strips from the sticks and placed them on a large leaf. The man butchering the kangaroo handed over more raw strips, still smeared with blood and bits of fur. The whole process was repeated until there was an impressive pile of cooked and seasoned meat on the leaf. Only when they had prepared all the meat from the thick tail and one haunch of the kangaroo did they offer some to be eaten.

Before handing out the food, they motioned for everyone to sit in a circle around the fire. This was somehow reassuring. It seemed these men were going out of their way to treat them as equals or guests.

They all stared at the pre-chewed green glaze on the meat. Bobby was first to take a bite. He muttered something enthusiastic, and that was all it took. They tore into their portions like starving dogs. The meat was surprisingly tender and agreeable. The Papuan men pointed at them and smiled, obviously pleased.

The Lamotelokhai didn't eat. Instead it sat motionless, watching the rest of them. This did not go unnoticed by the Papuans. They glanced at Addison a few times, but then looked away, apparently unwilling to make an issue of it.

Mbaiso steadily increased his distance from the Creator, moving from tree to tree on his journey back to the village. The Creator's information—its presence—had been fading, and soon it would disappear altogether.

Mbaiso traversed a heavy vine into the lower levels of a plum pine and then stopped, panting from exertion. The tree kangaroo was aware that he would soon be alone for the first time in nearly ten thousand years. He had always been within communication range of the Creator.

He nestled his belly against the limb, allowing his legs to hang over either side. His panting gradually slowed. He closed his eyes and listened. Faint snippets of information were still coming to him, barely detectable—fragments of conversation the Creator was having with the human called Bobby; contemplation over how to express ideas verbally; swift reviews of possible consequences of actions. And occasionally there were peculiar flashes of emotion, as if the Creator were experimenting with such concepts as joy, pity, and sadness. But the incoming information was becoming weaker even now as Mbaiso rested his sore body.

He let out a long grunting sigh. It would have been easy to fall asleep. But there was much distance yet to cover. In spite of the increased risk, he would have to move to the ground where travel would be faster. He scratched his ear with a forepaw and pushed himself off his belly and onto his feet. But then he froze, listening.

Information intended specifically for Mbaiso was coming from the Creator. Usually, the information would come in packets. Each packet would contain a fully formed concept, and when Mbaiso would open the packets, the concepts would simply be there, in his consciousness. Often the concepts would be visions, showing Mbaiso the actions or the consequences of the actions he was expected to perform. But this time the information was different.

Mbaiso absorbed the incoming packets. Cognitive fingers within his consciousness pried the packets open one at a time, revealing information in forms the Creator had not used before. Instead of containing visions, these packets contained information more like words, although no words were spoken nor heard. One packet revealed that the Creator was aware Mbaiso would be on his own soon, too distant to receive information. The next one showed that the Creator was aware that since the arrival of the man, Peter Wooley, Mbaiso had begun developing independent ideas and plans. Another showed that the Creator also knew of the tree kangaroos' encounter with the crocodile and why Mbaiso had sacrificed Tripela. The Creator did not object to these decisions. Mbaiso's plans were consistent with the Creator's purpose.

Finally, there was one packet left. Mbaiso probed the packet, releasing the information, allowing it to infiltrate his awareness. It contained an array of directives—tasks to be completed. He examined the tasks one at a time and found them to be reassuring. They involved giving assistance to the villagers, which had been his primary purpose for his entire existence. And it was clear that the collective outcome of the directives was that the villagers would eventually live without his assistance. This made Mbaiso wonder if his current plans were not his plans at all, but instead had come to him from the Creator undetected.

Mbaiso examined the last of the directives. After considering it for a moment he tilted his head to one side, in case that might help with his understanding. He tried pulling back from it conceptually, to examine it as a whole. He teased it apart, looking at its components, and turned them at various angles to make sure he was not missing some veiled implication. But the task was what it was—nothing more or less. And it was to be carried out after all the others were completed.

Mbaiso shook his head in a brisk circular motion to clear the cognitive clutter. He then descended to the ground and continued his journey. The crocodile was undoubtedly far ahead of him, and it would soon require his help.

"How far away is the planet you're from?" Bobby asked.

Addison was walking beside him. "I cannot know the distance. The distance changes."

This was like most of the answers he had given Bobby. They were not really answers or they were too hard to understand. But Bobby kept asking questions because it took his mind off his thirst. He had eaten four hotdog-sized cuts of tree kangaroo meat—enough to stop his hunger—but his thirst was getting to where he could hardly think of anything else. Since they had started walking again, Bobby had asked dozens of questions. But the answers just led to more questions.

Bobby, Carlos, and the new Addison were lagging behind, but not so far that they lost sight of the others. After miles of hills, the forest flattened out again. They were now on a well-worn trail, so Bobby figured they were getting close to a village.

After being silent for some time, Carlos spoke to Addison. "I need to ask you something before we get there. When Miranda died, you talked about making another Miranda just like her. When Ashley drowned, you *did* make another Ashley. And she's just like the old Ashley. How do you do that?"

Addison explained it again, about how he could have reconstructed Miranda's body with parts he could get from the forest, and how he reconstructed Ashley's body mostly from the parts that were already there in her old body. From Carlos's look, Bobby sensed what he was going to say next.

"My brother Roberto died when our plane crashed. I want him to be alive again. I don't care what the others say about asking my parents first. I don't want my parents to know he died at all. I just want him back. Can you do that?"

"Roberto was killed before I could know of him," Addison said. "I do not have the information to do what you ask."

"But you dissolved his body, right? Didn't you get information about him then?"

This hadn't occurred to Bobby.

"Yes. Information came to me then. I could make the body of Roberto the way that it was at that time. Is that what you want?"

"No," Carlos said. "But I could tell you the rest of what you need to know. I can tell you what he was like when he was alive, like all the things he would say, and what he did."

Bobby considered this possibility. But then he thought of Addison's reincarnation. He pictured Roberto's broken, stinking body trying to walk and talk. This was a really bad idea.

Addison stopped walking. "There is much you would have to tell me."

"I've known Roberto all my life," Carlos said. "I can tell you everything about him."

Bobby felt panic coming on. Carlos was serious, and so far the Lamotelokhai seemed to do everything he was asked to do.

Carlos said, "I'll tell you everything. Can you do it now, before we get to a village?"

Addison looked around him like he was checking for ingredients. "Yes."

"No!" Bobby said. "You can't do that!"

Carlos looked at Bobby like he had been slapped in the face.

"Think about it, Carlos. I'm sure he can do what he says, but think about Roberto's body when he dissolved it. That's not what you want." Bobby looked to the new Addison for help with this, but the thing just gazed at him.

"I can tell him the rest, Bobby!"

Addison said, "It is not likely that you could tell me what I need to know to make Roberto as he was. It would take much talking. There is information I would need to know that you could not tell me."

Carlos frowned. "But you just said—"

Addison actually interrupted him. "But it is not likely. You have memories of Roberto. But they are not enough. It is likely there were things about Roberto you do not know. Others who knew Roberto may know these things. They would have to tell me what they know. And it is likely there were times when Roberto was with no others. There would be no memories of Roberto at those times."

Carlos exhaled slowly. He rubbed his previously injured hand.

"I'm really sorry," Bobby said.

Carlos shot him an angry look. "You don't even *have* a brother, Bobby." Then he turned and ran ahead to catch up with the others.

Bobby looked at the Lamotelokhai. "Did you help me out on purpose?"

"I saw that you had doubts about Carlos's request. Your doubts were correct. And so I helped you."

Bobby stared. The new Addison stared back without blinking.

"Addison wouldn't have done that," Bobby said.

THEY REACHED the village late in the afternoon. The trail abruptly opened to a vast clearing. Quentin shaded his eyes with his hand. The clearing had been hewn from the forest, and it was longer than it was wide—an airstrip. At the far end were thatched huts. From one of the huts rose a steel latticed tower with an antenna at its tip. Hopefully this meant they had a radio. The Americans stared at the site as if they had stumbled upon a lost city of gold.

Their Papuan guides stood before them, smiling. One of them held his shotgun and what remained of the tree kangaroo over one shoulder. With his other hand he pointed at the huts. "*Viles,*" he said.

Then the men abruptly turned back the way they had come. As they walked past Addison, each of them stared intently at him, but they said nothing.

"They're leaving," Ashley said. "Why are they leaving?"

Lindsey called to them. "Won't you stay and introduce us to the villagers?"

The men glanced back at her but kept walking. So Bobby spoke to them in pidgin. They stopped. As they responded they shook their heads, pointing to the village.

"They don't get along with these people." Bobby said. "They fight with them."

"This is not surprising," Samuel said. "It is the way of most of the indigenes I have come to know."

Again the men turned to go. But suddenly the Addison replica spoke to them—a combination of pidgin and their own tribal language. The men stared at him. Addison held out three small gray objects cupped in his hand. After some encouragement from him they each took one. Addison motioned for them to eat. They glanced at each other. Addison's words became soft, reassuring, and he smiled at them.

One of the men pressed his object between his fingers. It was pliable. He sniffed it and then took a small bite. He mumbled something to his companions and then took another bite. The other men gave in and ate theirs. They nodded to Addison, apparently thanking him for the peculiar food. They turned away and a moment later they were gone.

Quentin was almost afraid to ask. "What was that, Addison? What did you do to them?"

Addison smiled, the same reassuring smile he had given the Papuans. "I gave to them the same gift I gave to you, Dad."

Quentin waited but no explanation came. "And what is that?"

"The first effect is repair of those conditions that need it."

Ashley said, "You made them healthy?"

"Yes. And after that will come improvements of functions, and then information about how I came to be here and about my creators. As I have done for you."

"Why did you do that?" Quentin asked.

"To help them understand what I am. Didn't it help you understand my purpose?"

"Yes," Quentin said. "But if you give this gift to everyone we see, the people here may never let you leave. We want to take you to where we are from. We believe the leaders there will not use you to do bad things. But here—we're not so sure."

Addison's smile was gone. "I understand. You wish for me to give no more gifts until we arrive at the place where you are from."

Quentin felt a pang of guilt. Who was he to dictate the use of such a gift? How could he possibly know the right thing to do? He had to remind himself of the logic of their plan. He placed a hand on Addison's shoulder. "Your knowledge is a gift for all, not just a few. To be sure you benefit everyone, we believe we should take you to where we come from."

After a brief pause, Addison's smile returned. "I will help you with this."

"It appears that we have been discovered," Samuel said. He pointed to the far end of the airstrip.

A naked child stood at the edge of the village watching them. They all walked from the shadows onto the airstrip. Lindsey waved. The kid turned and ran for the nearest hut. A moment later, other villagers emerged. By the time they reached the end of the airstrip, at least a dozen Papuans waited for them. Some wore little more than penis gourds or reed skirts, but others wore ragged t-shirts and shorts. They held no weapons. The child, who Quentin now saw was a girl, broke away from the others and ran to greet them. Other kids followed her, wide-eyed and talking. They seemed fascinated by the visitors' pale skin and Samuel's vest of spider silk. The girl, who was perhaps six, pulled at Quentin's khaki pants and spoke the same phrase several times. All the others had lost their clothing when the plane had dissolved, and she seemed to wonder why he was the only one with pants.

The adults greeted them with similar warmth and curiosity, and soon the crowd grew. It was evident that the villagers had their own tribal language, but they interspersed words of pidgin. Bobby tried to explain that their plane crashed and they were lost.

Quentin pointed at the radio tower. "You have a radio. Can we call for help?"

"*Wailis*," said one of the villagers, also pointing to the tower.

Bobby said, "Yes, wailis. Plis wailis. Plis."

The villagers fell silent as a short Papuan man pushed through the crowd. He wore a faded t-shirt with a Cooper's Beer logo on it, and he spoke with a thick Australian accent.

"I'm the bloke you're looking for, then."

THEY WERE LED to a shelter at the center of the village. It was no more than a flat roof of sticks supported by corner posts, but it blocked the searing sun. It reminded Quentin of the picnic shelters in city parks back home, and it seemed to serve the same purpose. A woman brought them brown-tinted water in a battered plastic gallon jug and they accepted it gratefully.

The man who'd claimed the radio waited patiently until the water jug was on its second round. "Call me Obert," he said. "You cobbers look to have seen some trouble."

Quentin briefly described the plane crash and the deaths. He skipped everything about the Lamotelokhai, the tree house village, and the murder of the villagers there. He said they had wandered for days until they came upon this village.

As he listened, Obert looked from one of them to the next. His eyes stopped when they met Samuel's. "And what's your story, then?"

Quentin answered for him. "Samuel is a biologist. He was doing research in the area where our plane went down. He found us and helped us out."

Obert considered this. "He had no radio?"

A moment of silence followed. Quentin could not think of an answer, but Lindsey spoke up. "Samuel has had his own troubles. He got separated from his research team and ended up lost, without any of his equipment."

Obert studied Samuel, no doubt taking in his strange vest and his clean-shaven face. "How long you been out there, mate?"

Samuel hesitated only a second. "It is difficult for me to say. I am sure that it seems to me much longer than it has truly been."

Obert's frown relaxed. "Right, then. I'm guessing there's folks who'll be happy to hear you're breathing. One of you come with me to call this in. They'll want specifics."

"Quentin will go," Lindsey said.

Obert's hut was dark and smelled of gasoline and animal feces. As Quentin's eyes adjusted, he saw two dogs lounging in the middle of the floor. They raised their heads but didn't get up. Machines and gadgets cluttered the hut. Most looked to be broken or disassembled, as if in the middle of a repair job. There were several lawn mowers and a weed eater, all gas-powered, and some kind of drill that looked like it could be strapped to a person's back. Quentin counted four generators, but only one appeared to be intact. Red plastic gas containers lined one wall. Leaning against one of them was a battery-powered metal detector.

The radio sat upon a knee-high wooden box. Obert motioned for Quentin to kneel on the dirt floor next to it. There were no chairs. In fact, other than a mattress set on palettes, there was no furniture at all. Obert went to the only intact generator, fiddled with a few settings, and yanked the pull start. The thing coughed a few times and jumped to life. At first the noise of the engine was almost overwhelming. Quentin had heard no such unnatural clatter in many days. Obert adjusted the throttle, and the engine smoothed out. A cloud of exhaust filled the hut. Obert ignored it and knelt with Quentin.

The radio looked modern enough. It resembled a home audio receiver, with a digital display and a variety of knobs on the front. A handheld microphone was attached to it with a spiral cable. Obert switched it on, punched the channel button a few times, and spoke into the mic.

"Navera IC74 to Sentani IC9. Obert, Navera IC74 to Sentani IC9."

A voice came back. "Obert, *apa kabar*. Anton, Sentani IC9."

Obert smiled at Quentin. "That's Anton." Then he spoke into the mic, "Anton, *kabar baik*. I've got me an emergency, bloody oath! Got some Yanks here. Say they've been lost for days. Their plane crashed. You hear me? A plane crash. We need the tall poppies."

There were several clicks at the other end, the microphone being jostled about. Obert spoke to Quentin. "Gave him a bit of a jump, I reckon. He'll get someone on that matters."

After what seemed like a long wait, another voice came on. "Sentani IC9. Navera, I understand you are reporting a plane crash. Is this correct?"

"Deadset, Sentani, I swear it. Americans. They've been in the bush for days. Some have died."

There was a muffled, "Bloody hell!" and then another pause. "Navera, I have no knowledge of a plane going down. What are the names?"

Obert looked at Quentin, brows raised.

"Quentin Darnell and Lindsey Darnell—and some of our students. And there was an Indonesian couple on the plane. We didn't know them or the pilot. It was ten days ago, I think."

Before now Quentin had allowed himself to hope that his suspicions were wrong. But now it was confirmed—they were never missed. The implications of this flooded his thoughts, but the man on the radio had more questions. Where did they come from? What plane were they on? Did anyone need immediate medical treatment? Finally he said it was too late in the day to send a plane, but one would arrive in the morning, first thing.

QUENTIN AND OBERT returned to the shelter with the news that they would be picked up in the morning. The others' reactions were surprisingly subdued. Initiated by Lindsey, there was a round of restrained hugs.

Before long, some villagers led a pig to the shelter. One man carried a bow and an arrow. After lashing the pig to one of the shelter's corner posts, the man readied his bow. The villagers fell silent.

Lindsey pleaded with Obert, "Please don't do this on our behalf. This is too much."

Obert nodded but made no effort to stop it. "Visitors are a rare thing, ma'am. Especially those who've survived a plane crash. You cobbers are lucky to be alive. A bit of celebration is in order. You are hungry, no?"

"Yes we are, but..."

Obert grinned. "She'll be right, then. Wouldn't be fitting to send you away with no tucker in your gut."

The pig squealed when the arrow pierced its side. It pulled at the rope as the man yanked the arrow back out and casually nocked it again. Obert invited them all to sit on the ground. In minutes the pig was dispatched, butchered, and transferred to foil packets that were placed into the embers of a fire. From their huts villagers brought sweet potatoes, breadfruits, bananas, and a variety of other fruits and vegetables.

For Quentin, it began to sink in that they would actually make it back. It hadn't occurred to him that this realization would be difficult. But it was. They had endured days of tragedy and violence. At some point a switch had turned on in Quentin. He had learned to see the potential threat in everything, the darkness behind the eyes of every human being. And now he struggled to turn the switch off. There was no reason to think these villagers would harm them— that they might kill them as they slept. There was no reason to think that the plane would fail to appear in the morning, or that it would crash on the flight to Sentani, killing them once and for all. But these were Quentin's thoughts. And even if they survived the flight tomorrow, what would happen then? It seemed that the remainder of his life would hold only threats.

Obert and another Papuan brought out two cardboard boxes containing bottles of beer. This surprised Quentin, although he wasn't sure why—if the villagers could get lawn mowers to maintain the airstrip, they could certainly procure beer. Obert offered a bottle to each of them, including the students. Ashley snatched the opener and popped hers open without a word. She took a long swig of warm beer and then let out a sigh, holding her eyes closed.

Bobby and Carlos looked stunned. Ashley tossed them the opener. They both turned to Quentin and Lindsey. Quentin just shrugged.

"They're our students, Quentin," Lindsey said.

He smiled and gave her a pleading look.

She gazed at the boys. Finally she nodded and turned away.

In unison, the boys said, "Yes!" They opened their bottles and drank deeply, not to be outdone by Ashley. They both frowned at the bitter taste.

Obert chuckled. "Watch you don't get yourselves stonkered, lads."

The opener was passed around and they all drank a beer, except for Addison, who just gazed curiously at his bottle and its South Pacific Lager label.

"It has been some time since I have had the occasion to drink beer, Obert," Samuel said, holding up his half-empty bottle to salute their hosts. "You can scarcely imagine how refreshing this is."

THE VILLAGERS INSISTED that Lindsey and Ashley sleep in a long hut at one end of the village. Obert explained that the long hut was where all children and unmarried women slept, and that arrangement was expected of all female guests. Quentin began to protest, but Lindsey assured him they would be fine.

Quentin, Samuel, and the boys were taken to the hut of one of Obert's friends, a man named Seri. Seri had a wife and daughter, but apparently his wife preferred to sleep in the long hut. Once they had settled into Seri's hut, other villagers brought them sleeping mats.

Quentin was relieved to find that Seri's hut didn't smell as bad as Obert's. But before long, Seri started a fire. There seemed to be no thought given to ventilation, and soon the smoke hung thick in the air. Seri did not speak English, but he chattered to them constantly, oblivious to the cloud of smoke. There was less smoke near the floor, so Quentin followed Samuel's lead and lay flat on his sleeping mat. He told the boys to do the same. Bobby and Carlos did so, but Addison continued sitting up, watching Seri bustle about the hut.

The entire village had witnessed Addison's refusal to eat or drink anything, so they were already curious about him. It would not do to have him sitting up all night.

"Addison, please lie down and at least act like you are sleeping," Quentin said.

Addison complied. "Goodnight, Dad," he said.

"Goodnight, Addison."

Eventually Seri stopped talking and settled in for the night. The hut became silent. An animal scuttled across the floor, followed by more of them. One even crawled over Quentin's legs, pausing to sniff his pants. Quentin heard chewing only a few feet from his head. Rats. The hut was alive with rats. They were probably harmless, otherwise Seri could not ignore them the way he did. But the thought of them inspecting every inch of his body as he slept would not make it any easier for Quentin to rest. He wondered if Lindsey and Ashley were dealing with the same issues. But then exhaustion overcame him.

QUENTIN AWOKE to the roar of an airplane passing low over the village. It was already daylight. Bobby and Carlos were still sleeping. Addison was not, and when he saw Quentin stirring, he sat up without a word. Seri and Samuel were not in the hut.

Quentin inspected his clothing and skin. No rat bites, although several brown pellets fell from his shirt as he rolled to his side. He crawled to Bobby and Carlos and they woke up as he inspected them.

He said, "You ready to go home? The plane is here."

They emerged from the hut to find most of the villagers already waiting by the airstrip. Standing with them were Lindsey, Ashley, and Samuel, talking to Obert.

"You ladies sleep as soundly as we did?" Quentin said.

Lindsey forced a smile. "Our hosts were very kind."

Ashley leaned in and whispered, "There were rats! Loads of them!"

Obert overheard this and smiled. "Our rats help keep our humpies clean. And they eat up the centipedes." He held his hands up about a foot apart, apparently showing the size of the centipedes. "Better rats than centipedes. Deadly, those are."

After circling the village, the plane straightened out and approached the airstrip, which now seemed absurdly short. But the pilot landed skillfully, and the plane bounced to a stop at the end of the airstrip. It was another Twin Otter, identical to the one in which they had crashed, right down to the blue Merpati Air logo on its side. Two Indonesian pilots hopped out of the cockpit and walked back to the hatch behind the wing. They lowered it to the ground, allowing access to the stairs built into the back of the hatch. A white man who looked to be about forty emerged from the cabin. In his polo shirt and khaki shorts, he looked like he'd just stepped off a cruise ship. He jogged the twenty meters from the plane and extended his hand.

"Mr. and Mrs. Darnell, I presume?"

Mbaiso crept forward, placing his paws on the narrow limb with extreme caution to avoid shaking it. It was an unusually dark night, but his eyes were well suited for darkness, his body having been patterned after the living tree kangaroos of the coastal region where he had been created. The *poupa*, a bird Samuel called the crested berrypecker, was now only a tail-length beyond Mbaiso's reach. It was roosting for the night, but one overly eager step would alert the bird to his presence and it would flutter away. With measured precision, he moved two steps closer and then lunged. He caught the poupa in his jaws before it even opened its eyes.

Mbaiso's diet consisted mainly of leaves and fruits, but he had traveled all through the day and most of the night. The bird would replenish his shrunken energy reserves. He bit off the poupa's head first, then quickly consumed the rest of the body, leaving nothing but a few blue and green feathers that turned in gentle spirals as they drifted to the ground.

The hanging village was not far now. There would be much to do when the morning light came. Mbaiso looked down at the forest floor. This was an excellent place to rest. He backtracked on the limb and settled into a comfortable position where it joined the main trunk. He then shifted his body until he had an unobstructed view. He belched out a contented grunt and gazed at the extraordinary sight below him. The ground was speckled with a sea of glowing green *maselop*. Samuel referred to them as luminescent mushrooms. There were hundreds of them, but in the blink of an eye Mbaiso accurately counted those he could see and statistically estimated the number he couldn't see due to obstruction from vegetation. But the Creator was gone—the central database was out of range—so Mbaiso deleted the data from his consciousness. He allowed his mind and muscles to go loose, and as his energy stores gradually replenished, he simply observed the mesmerizing luminescent scene.

Eventually the morning light overpowered the glow of the

maselop, making the forest floor below Mbaiso look no different from any other area. Rejuvenated, he stretched, descended to the ground, and then traveled the remaining distance to the area of the hanging village. Before searching for the villagers, he made his way along the bank of the Méanmaél, watching with his eyes and listening for information. He found what he was searching for at a place where a sandbar extended out from the shore. Mbaiso also detected Tupela's presence. He spotted her sprawled in a tree, warily eyeing the sandbar. Satisfied, he turned away from the river. He took to the trees. Before long he was within the boundaries of the village. He stopped in the lower canopy of a eucalyptus tree. The unusually tall tree was characteristic of the area, which was in fact the reason the village had been built here. He held his small ears erect, listening. The hut that had housed the Creator was nearby, but there were no sounds indicating it was occupied. He made his way to one of the sleeping huts, and then to another, but they were empty. Although Samuel had lived in his own hut, the indigenous humans had a number of huts that were used by all the villagers. They would sleep or prepare food in the hut that most suited their needs at the time.

Finally, he heard the villagers talking in the distance. The sounds led him to Samuel's abandoned hut. He entered the opening in the hut's floor and watched them. The human called Addison had recently killed and disaggregated many of the villagers, and now all of the survivors were here. They were inspecting and discussing the strange variety of objects and furnishings Samuel had created.

Sinanie was the first to notice the tree kangaroo's presence. He hissed at the others. The villagers became quiet and watched Mbaiso as he moved his forelimbs, signing to them. The Creator had provided Mbaiso with many ways to communicate, but the villagers had always preferred the language of gestures.

When Mbaiso finished signing, he crawled through the opening, descended to the ground, and waited. Sinanie clambered down the rope ladder first, followed by Matiinuo, Ambep, and Willok. When it was clear the others were not coming, Mbaiso led the four tribesmen to the river. They followed without speaking, although it was a long walk, and Mbaiso did not pause to sign to them. The tribesmen were surprised he had returned, and they undoubtedly had questions regarding the Lamotelokhai's whereabouts and progress. But that could wait.

When they arrived at the sandbar, Tupela was still there keeping watch. Sinanie immediately pointed to the sandbar, where two reptilian bodies basked like beached logs in the morning sun.

"*Semail*," Sinanie exclaimed. This was their name for crocodiles.

While the tribesmen remarked on the size of the semail and the rarity of seeing two at once, Mbaiso hopped to the edge of the river where the vegetation ended and the sandbar began. He considered walking out onto the sandbar, but the presence of the second crocodile made the possible consequences unacceptable. So he sat on his haunches and focused on the information coming to him. The information indicated that Tripela's sacrifice and subsequent actions would likely result in the desired outcome. The semail was primed to carry out its function.

The night before, during his journey back to the village, Mbaiso had created the last few information packets needed for his plan. He now concentrated on the packets, verifying their precision and integrity. In the same way he had always released data packets to the Creator, Mbaiso released the packets to the semail.

The larger of the two crocodiles turned and began lumbering toward the shore. It crawled directly over the back of the second crocodile, provoking a disapproving grunt. The tribesmen stopped talking when they saw what was happening, and they began backing away when the creature pushed through the tangled vegetation on the shore, headed in their direction. But then the semail stopped. Mbaiso approached it, resulting in excited words from the men. He signed for them to come closer, but they were reluctant.

The crocodile began to change. Its body developed folds, which grew deeper until they actually pinched the entire body into smaller portions. Before long there were nine masses of reptilian flesh squirming on the ground. The uneasy tribesmen came closer, whispering wishes of good fortune to their ancestors to appease them. As they watched, the masses transformed into nine smaller crocodiles, each the size of a large man's leg. When the transformation was complete, all but one of the crocodiles crawled to the river and disappeared. The last one lay before the men, not moving.

Mbaiso purred to draw the attention of the fascinated men. He then signed to them. Matiinuo signed back, and Mbaiso signed again. This went on for some time. Still the crocodile did not move.

Finally, Matiinuo nodded. He walked away and returned with a rock the size of a breadnut fruit. With both hands he raised it above his head and brought it down with considerable force, crushing the crocodile's skull.

Matiinuo and Sinanie each grabbed a hind leg and together they hefted the reptile up between them. The four men smiled approvingly. The creature was large enough to supplement their diet with animal meat for many days. And as Mbaiso had explained, the eight remaining semail would stay in the area. In fact, they would passively crawl out of the river whenever they saw members of Sinanie's tribe. The tribesmen were to spare at least one of the semail, which would grow large and then split again into smaller semail. And this would continue, cycle after cycle.

The tribesmen understood. They spoke personal praises to Mbaiso. Finally, they turned and headed back to the village with their generous supply of meat.

Mbaiso gazed after the men until they disappeared. He reexamined the array of tasks the Creator had given him, then he designated one of them as completed.

CHAPTER FIVE

———————

WHEN THE PLANE came to a stop and the pilots lowered the passenger door, vivid details of the plane crash Bobby had survived ran through his mind. He felt a stab of dread.

But his fear began to fade when an American man appeared. The guy had an easy way about him, and he smiled a lot. He carried a silver coffee mug with him like it was perfectly normal to drink coffee while getting off an airplane.

"Mr. and Mrs. Darnell, I presume?" He laughed at this like it was a joke. "The name's Gregory Stamper. Are you or any of your party injured or in need of medical help?"

Mr. Darnell said no, that everyone was fine.

"Damn good thing, because I don't know the first thing about medicine." He laughed again. "But I was the only American handy when they heard about you last night. They asked me to hop on this flight so you'd have a friendly face to talk to. So, here I am!" The guy smiled broadly and drank from his silver mug. Bobby decided he liked Mr. Stamper.

They had nothing to pack, and there was no reason to wait. So they said goodbye to Obert and the other Papuans. Before boarding, Samuel walked around the plane, running his hand over the dirty white surface, looking closely at every detail. Unlike Bobby, he seemed excited at the prospect of flying.

Without thinking, Bobby took the same seat he had on the first Twin Otter. In fact, of those who were on the other plane, Addison was the only one who did not sit in the same seat as before. Instead of sitting next to Carlos across the aisle, Addison sat in the single seat behind Bobby. Samuel was alone in the back of the cabin, and Gregory was in the front, taking up the two seats where Roberto and Russ had been crushed.

The pilots brought the engines to a full deafening roar before the plane started moving, and then suddenly it shot forward and picked up speed. At the last second it lifted off the ground, just in time to clear the trees where Bobby's group had stood looking at the village the previous evening.

As soon as they were on their way and had adjusted to the noise of the engines, Gregory spoke. "I'm from Boston University, but I regularly work with the International Environmental Rapid Assessment Program. We've been conducting a survey of the Mamberamo River Basin for a few years now. I happened to be at the airport when your call came in."

Mr. Darnell introduced all of them.

Gregory looked at them and waited, like he expected more. "What exactly happened to you folks?"

Mr. Darnell gave him the same story he had given Obert, including the lie about Samuel getting lost from his research camp and helping them out.

"I haven't heard about a field biologist going missing," Gregory said to Samuel. "What project are you with?"

"My story is more complicated than that, I am afraid," Samuel said. "I have no wish to deceive you, sir, and so I must ask that you do not inquire further."

Gregory looked from one of them to the next. He let out a long whistle and then spoke aloud to himself, "Stamper, what have you gotten yourself into now." He shook his head. "I have to be honest with you people. I've been with you only twenty minutes and I can see something is out of whack. The folks at the airport are already suspicious, and I can confidently say it's going to get worse when you arrive. They say they have no knowledge of any missing planes. Plane wrecks are normally big news around here." He gave them a serious look. "Do you hear what I'm saying, folks?"

"How can they not know our plane is missing?" Mrs. Darnell said.

"No idea," Gregory said. "Listen, I know what happens to people who are lost in the bush with no first aid supplies and no tent to keep the insects off. You people look to be perfectly healthy. Personally, I don't care what you're up to. But the Indonesian security personnel you are about to face—I promise you they care. You seem like good people. If there's something you're hiding, maybe I can help."

The hum of the engines seemed to get louder as he waited.

"We have to tell him," Bobby said.

Mr. Darnell shook his head. "We land in less than half an hour. How can we explain?"

"We don't have to explain," Bobby said. "Addison can show him."

"He's right, Quentin," Mrs. Darnell said. "We have no choice. Bobby, you talk to Addison." She turned to Gregory. "Mr. Stamper, we have something to tell you. It's important—more important than you can imagine. We have to bypass the red tape in Sentani and board a flight to the United States immediately."

Gregory frowned. "Ma'am, that's not likely to happen."

Bobby turned his back to them. "Addison, we need Gregory to know what you are, and we need him to know right now. Can you help?"

Briefly, Addison's eyes shifted to golden yellow. "Yes," he said.

Without another word, he unbuckled his seatbelt and got up. He held something out to Gregory. "This is a gift," he said. "You should eat it."

Gregory looked surprised. "Thank you, son, but I'm not hungry."

"It will not harm you," Addison said. "If you eat it, you will understand."

"What is it, a drug? You guys aren't in some kind of cult are you?"

"It's not a drug," Mr. Darnell said. "I'm not sure how to tell you this, but we have found something." He put his hand on Addison's shoulder. "This boy is not what he seems to be. Look, there just isn't an easy way to explain it. But you must understand how important it is that we get him to the United States. We can't tell you; we have to show you. If you eat that, you will see."

Gregory let out a nervous laugh. "You want me to eat it?"

"Gregory, please look at me," Mrs. Darnell said. When he turned to her, she went on. "I give you my word. It will not harm you, and you will not regret it. Please."

Gregory took the thing from Addison. "If this makes me sick, I'm having all of you locked up in Jayapura." He popped it in his mouth, chewed a few times, and swallowed.

"Do not be afraid," Addison said, and he returned to his seat.

For a few minutes Gregory just looked at them. Then his face went blank. Suddenly he moaned and folded up, dropping his head onto the seat next to him.

The pilot on the left side of the cockpit leaned his head through the door to the cabin and shouted in Indonesian at Gregory, who didn't answer. The pilot called someone on his radio while the other rose from his seat and moved to Gregory's side. He shook Gregory and spoke to him. Gregory's hand shot up and pushed the pilot away.

"He'll be fine," Mrs. Darnell said.

The pilot ignored her and remained by Gregory's side. For some minutes Gregory just lay there, curled up in the two seats. The plane began to descend. They were approaching Sentani.

Bobby turned to Addison, "It's going to be too late."

Addison pointed forward and Bobby turned back around. Gregory was sitting up, his eyes wide, tears streaming down his face.

Mrs. Darnell said, "Are you okay?"

His eyes darted to her. "Hell no! Do you have any idea what I've seen?"

"What the rest of us have seen, I assume," she said. "The planet where it was created, and how it got here. And we hope you saw something about why it is here and what it can do."

The plane dropped lower, approaching the airport. Gregory persuaded the pilot to return to the cockpit, and then he asked bursts of questions. Between the questions, he held his head in his hands and spoke to himself, saying things like "Stamper, you're going to wake up," or "Just breath, Stamper." At one point, he said to Addison, "Do you understand me?"

Addison smiled. "Yes."

"When we land, there will be questions," Gregory said. "I think you are going to have to show them what you showed me."

Bobby gripped his seat and closed his eyes as the plane dropped to the runway. But the landing was smooth. Before the plane even stopped rolling he looked out his window and saw men approaching. Some wore white shirts with ties, but others were Indonesian police with brown uniforms and guns on their belts. There was no way all these men would agree to eat chunks of Addison's body.

The pilots lowered the door, and then the men were waiting for them just outside. Gregory's hands were shaking, and he wouldn't stop talking to himself. It didn't look like he would be much help.

One of the white-shirt men boarded the plane. "My name is

Natsir Santoso, of the Ministry of Foreign Affairs. I am told you people are survivors of an accident. Is this correct?"

"That's true," Mr. Darnell said. "Our plane crashed on its flight from Wamena on July twelfth. We would like an immediate flight to the United States."

The man frowned. "Of course you will be transferred to your original destination. But there are protocols that must be followed."

Gregory spoke up. "Mr. Santoso, could I have a few minutes alone with these folks? They have suffered a terrible ordeal and their situation is, um, very complex. I was just making progress with them when we landed."

Santoso's frown grew even deeper. "Mr. Stamper, my understanding is that you are not trained in trauma counseling. These people must talk to qualified professionals."

There had to be some way to convince these men to help them get home, or at least to buy some time to come up with a better plan. Suddenly Bobby had an idea. He turned to Addison and spoke quietly.

"There's something I want you to do."

<hr>

QUENTIN COULD ALMOST SMELL the tension in the cabin. An Indonesian security guard entered the plane and stood by the hatch, his presence menacing. Quentin stood up. "Mr. Santoso, please try to understand. We have lost three of our students, and we've survived in the wilderness for ten days. Gregory here understands our situation and our distress. We wish to speak with him and only him at this time."

The man's expression did not change. "We do not wish to appear unsympathetic. Of course Mr. Stamper may remain with you. But there are some discrepancies we are trying to resolve. We have no records of a carrier missing en route from Wamena.

It is important we understand the source of our faulty data. You will all come with us now. You will receive proper clothing and food."

Suddenly Bobby cried out, "He's hurt! Can't you see that? We need to get him to a hospital now!"

It was Addison. He had a huge gash on his left shoulder and arm. The flesh had been torn away and the humerus bone was visible, looking strangely white and clean amidst the surrounding blood and torn tissue. Blood flowed freely from the wound and covered his lap.

Gregory gasped. "What the hell?"

"He needs a hospital now!" Bobby said.

Santoso's face changed to alarm. "Mr. Stamper, I understood there were no injuries."

Gregory stammered, "Yes, well, this boy clearly needs medical attention."

Quentin looked at Bobby, and their eyes met. "What's going on, Bobby?"

"Don't you see? We have to get Addison to a hospital right now!"

Quentin understood. It was crazy, but now there was no turning back.

Lindsey caught on, too. "We need you to take us to a hospital, and we demand to see an American doctor. We're wasting time!"

A few minutes later a woman who apparently had EMT training hurriedly wrapped Addison's wound, and then they were in a minibus on their way to a hospital in Waena on the outskirts of Jayapura. Santoso and his security men followed closely behind. Bobby had managed to buy them more time, but Quentin had no idea what to do next.

Gregory had gone along with the ruse of Addison's injury, but now his confusion was catching up to him. As the bus turned onto the Jalan Sentani Chimera, the road to Jayapura, he said, "Alright, what the hell is going on? He's not really hurt, is he?" He nodded at Addison, who was now bandaged from shoulder to elbow.

The EMT had not spoken any English, so Quentin assumed she didn't understand, but Gregory's tone obviously concerned her.

"I asked him to do that," Bobby said, as if this explained everything.

This was not how Quentin had pictured things going. He had hoped they might simply convince the Indonesians to let them fly immediately to the United States.

Gregory continued, "But it looks real. The blood—"

Quentin held up his hand. "We can't waste any more time. We need to figure out what we're going to do." He turned to Gregory. "Do you have a cell phone?"

Gregory closed his eyes for a moment. "I'm sorry. This is happening so fast. Yes, I have a phone." He pulled his smartphone from his pocket.

"Can you call the U.S. from here?"

"Generally, yes." Gregory kept looking at Addison as if worried he might disappear.

Quentin snapped his fingers in Gregory's face, the same way he would with a distracted eighth grader. "Do you agree with us that this discovery," he nodded at Addison, "should be taken to the U.S.?"

"I have no idea what to do with it!" Gregory held one hand to his cheek, covering one eye. "Yes! Yes, I suppose that's the thing to do."

"Then please make a call to the States. To anyone who can help us."

Gregory ran his hand over his eye and into his hair. "Phil, Stamper. Call Phil." He punched some buttons on the device and then stopped. "Country code. Oh God..."

"Zero zero one," Lindsey said. She glanced at Quentin.

Gregory finished dialing and waited. A moment later he sat up straight. "Phil. Gregory Stamper here. Can you hear me?" A pause. "No, no, I'm still in Jayapura. Please listen to me carefully, Phil. Something big has happened. I'm going to ask you to trust me, because I don't have time to elaborate. I'm with some Americans now. They have found something that is monumentally important. It's a matter of national—no, global security." Another pause. "No, not a nuke—much bigger than that. I'm asking you to trust me, Phil. I simply cannot explain. We're on our way to the hospital in Waena. We need help from the American government." A pause. "That's right. We have to get them to put us on a flight to the U.S. now. Yes, now." A longer pause. "I swear to God this is real, Phil. Thank you. I'll contact you again as soon as I can." Gregory cut off the call and pocketed the smartphone. "Phil Bollinger is the head of my department. He has a lot of connections, so he'll contact someone who can help."

"I want to call my parents," Ashley said. "Gregory, can I use your phone?"

Gregory looked at Quentin and Lindsey.

Quentin felt a sudden wave of apprehension. He started to protest but couldn't come up with a reason that he thought would sound rational. Instead he shrugged.

Gregory punched the screen into cell phone mode, entered the country code again, and handed it to Ashley. "Just the area code and the number."

Ashley appeared surprised that her request actually worked. With white knuckles she tapped out her number. The seconds passed, and a lump grew in Quentin's throat. He turned to stare out the window. They were now passing by shanties instead of unbroken forest. They were entering Jayapura.

Ashley stiffened. She'd gotten through. Then her shoulders slumped. "Voice mail," she said.

A moment later she left a message. "Hey, guys. It's me, Ash. I know you've been worried to death, but I'm okay. We're still in

Papua, but we're coming home." She paused as if considering how much to say. "And also, we're bringing something with us. It's something important, like the most important thing ever. I just thought you should know. I love you guys. See you soon."

She hung up and gave Gregory the phone.

"I understand what you say." It was the EMT. She glared directly at Gregory. "You are trying to hide something."

Gregory looked stunned. "Ma'am, we just want to get to the United States."

Her eyes narrowed. "You talk about taking something with you. Are you stealing something from us?"

"No, it's not like that. You can see we have no possessions." Gregory looked to the others for help.

Lindsey spoke up. "It's actually Addison, the boy you are treating." She rose from her seat and kneeled in the aisle next to Addison and the EMT. "What is your name?"

The woman eyed Lindsey and her features softened slightly. "I am Arina Rohadi."

"Arina, this is Addison. He found something in the forest. It must be something he ate, or something he touched. But whatever it was, it had an amazing effect on him. His body heals very quickly when he is hurt. *Very* quickly." Lindsey spoke to Addison: "If we remove your bandages, do you think your wound could be all gone by now?"

"Yes, if that is what you would like."

Lindsey tilted her head toward Addison. "Arina, go ahead and remove his wrap."

The EMT looked from her to Addison and back. "You play a game?"

Addison began unwrapping the wound himself.

"Let me do that!" Arina snatched the unwrapped portion from his hand. She spoke rapid Indonesian as she unwrapped the wound, perhaps cursing. As she peeled away the last layer, she suddenly stopped talking. Addison's wound was gone. Even the blood was gone, although the bandaging was stained red. Arina ran her hand over Addison's arm, pressing the flesh between her fingers. "You play a game?" she said again, much louder this time. "I saw this lesion. I touched it!"

"This is what I meant," Lindsey said. "Addison's body has been changed by something he found in the forest. Whatever it was, it is still out there. We don't want to steal it. We just want to get Addison safely home. The United States has well-equipped research facilities. You know that, right?"

The woman was trembling. "We must find the source. To find it we need your help." She touched Addison's arm again, as if she couldn't trust her eyes. "Yes, this is important."

The minibus came to a stop. They were at the hospital, a low two-story building with a slanted red roof. It resembled an American motel one might see along any interstate highway.

Without warning, the EMT bolted. She threw open the door and ran directly to the minibus that was pulling up behind them. As Santoso and the others piled out, she accosted them, waving her hands as she spoke.

Samuel sighed loudly. "That young woman's reaction, I fear, is what we must expect from those we encounter. I must say, Lindsey, you told an impressive story. Let us hope it has the desired effect."

"Listen, everyone," Quentin said. "We all stick with Lindsey's story. Addison ate something in the forest that makes him heal quickly. Addison is a real person. He's our son, and we just want to get him and ourselves home. Is that clear?" There were nods all around. The driver watched them in his mirror but showed no sign that he understood.

Santoso and several of his guards walked to the door of the minibus. He leaned in. "Let me see the boy's injury," he said, dropping all pretenses of being cordial. He moved to where Addison sat and looked closely at his shoulder. He turned him roughly and looked at the other shoulder and then straightened up. "You told me that this boy was injured. I had no reason to doubt you, and it appeared to be so. But I see that he is not hurt after all. Miss Rohadi is hysterical. She seems convinced that you have found a medical miracle in the bush. You have said that you were involved in an airline accident, and yet we have no information about a missing carrier. We have contacted the Los Angeles International Airport, and they informed us that there has been no group of passengers missing on return flights from Jakarta."

Santoso paused, letting this sink in. "You people puzzle me. I have seen foreigners smuggling narcotics. I have seen men who buy airline tickets for our young women, with the intent of selling them into slavery. Once I talked to a woman attempting to leave here with three infant children. She claimed that she gave birth to triplets while on holiday here. Such is the world today." He looked at Addison. "Now I will have a new story to tell, no?"

Santoso gazed out the minibus window at the hospital. "But first we must understand. There will be questions. Trust me when I say that it is in your best interest to answer them with truth. Our doctors will examine you, to be sure that you do not carry malaria or other diseases. And then, when we fully understand your situation—but certainly not before then—we will make a decision about the next course of action." He flashed a seemingly genuine smile. "Let us hope that involves sending you to your home country."

Santoso turned to leave. "You will come with me now." He then turned back like he had forgotten something. "Mr. Stamper, I understand you have a cellular phone in your possession. May I please have it?"

Gregory frowned. "It's really not necessary to take my phone."

Santoso waved to one of the guards. The guard pulled his pistol from his belt, leaned in, and pointed it at Gregory's face. Gregory's features hardened as he handed it over.

Santoso smiled. "At this time we do not know what is necessary, do we?"

THEY WERE SPLIT into groups as they entered the hospital. Bobby was taken to a room with Carlos and Addison. Mrs. Darnell and Ashley were put in a room across the hall, but Bobby didn't see where the Indonesians took Mr. Darnell and Samuel.

The room was almost bare except for two patient beds against one wall. There was no medical equipment. The room smelled like it had been scrubbed, but the floor and walls were faded with age, making them look dirty. A policeman stood inside the door until the EMT named Arina got there. She came in with a woman doctor and one of the men with white shirts. The policeman stepped out the door, but Bobby saw that he didn't leave.

The white-shirt man introduced himself and said that he worked with Mr. Santoso. Arina pointed at Addison and spoke in Indonesian to the doctor. She still looked nervous.

The doctor spoke English to Addison. "I am Dr. Semedi. What is your name?" Her voice was relaxed and friendly.

"Addison."

"Well, Addison, you have some explaining to do, no? You have upset Miss Rohadi. She believes that you had a serious cut that disappeared. But you and I know that is not possible, don't we?"

"I saw it," Arina said.

Dr. Semedi ignored this. She looked at each of them and frowned at their filthy bodies and scraps of clothing. She spoke to Arina. "Please go and get some clothes for these boys. One of the nurses will help you find what you need."

Arina hesitated for a moment but then left the room.

Dr. Semedi faced them again. "Addison, why did you deceive Miss Rohadi?"

Addison said, "I was asked to."

Bobby tensed up. This was not the plan.

The doctor raised her brows. "Who asked you to do this?"

Addison nodded at Bobby. "Bobby asked me to."

Bobby tried to make himself smaller as she turned to face him.

"And why would you ask him to do this?" she said.

Carlos spoke up before Bobby could answer. "We just wanted to get home. These men showed up and they had guns. We thought it would be better to come to a hospital and talk to someone like you instead."

She eyed Bobby. "Is that correct?"

Bobby nodded.

Dr. Semedi spoke to the white-shirt man. "Would it be possible for me to talk to these boys alone?"

The man simply shook his head no.

She sighed. "Very well. Addison, Miss Rohadi is a medical technician. She has treated many injuries. How is it that you could deceive her in such a way?"

Addison said, "Would you like me to show you?"

Again Bobby tensed up. But before he could protest, Addison did it. He grabbed the skin on his shoulder and ripped it away. The sound of it made Bobby gag. Blood started pouring down his arm, and shiny white bone could be seen in the wound.

In the corner of his eye, Bobby saw the white-shirt man step back against the wall. Dr. Semedi froze, staring at the wound.

Addison smiled at her. "It is a deception."

Dr. Semedi grabbed the loose skin and muscle that hung from Addison's shoulder and pressed it back into place. "This is no deception. You have hurt yourself." Still holding the shoulder, she yelled at the man against the wall. "Please, I need help." The man looked a little sick, but he nodded and left the room.

Addison still smiled. He put his hand on hers. "It is a deception," he said again. He pulled her hand away. The flesh stayed in place and the wound no longer bled. Her eyes grew larger as she stared. The skin was moving. The torn edges closed up. And then the last of the blood seemed to soak into Addison's skin and disappear.

Dr. Semedi stared at the shoulder without speaking. Footsteps echoed in the hallway. The door burst open and some doctors and nurses came in, followed by the white-shirt man. They examined Addison and shook their heads like they were upset about being disturbed for nothing. They all spoke Indonesian, and some were yelling. Dr. Semedi finally threw up her arms and with some effort she shooed them all out of the room, even the white-shirt man. She paced back and forth until Arina came in with three pairs of plastic flip-flops and a stack of hospital-blue shirts and pants that looked like those the nurses wore. Arina handed over the clothes and then left the room.

Bobby asked Dr. Semedi to turn around. He and Carlos peeled off the filthy remains of their clothes and put on the shirts and pants. Bobby told Addison to do this too. The clothes were too big, but the clean cotton felt nice against Bobby's skin.

At last Dr. Semedi stopped pacing. "I do not know what I saw, but Miss Rohadi saw the same thing, so I did not imagine it."

"It was a deception," Addison said. "As I said, Bobby asked me to do this so that we would be brought to this place."

Dr. Semedi inspected Addison's shoulder again. "How did you do that?"

Bobby saw a possibility to stick with their planned story, and he spoke before Addison could answer. "We told you, Addison ate something he found in the forest, maybe a flower or a mushroom or something. It was something that makes him heal really fast."

Dr. Semedi looked like she wasn't buying this. "That doesn't explain what I saw. There is no substance which can make a body heal wounds in such a way."

Addison stepped forward. "That is not true." He pushed his

hand up under his new shirt. "I have what you want." He pulled his hand out, and it was now holding a plant. The plant looked to be alive, even though the bare roots hung there in the open air. It had tiny oval leaves, and between the leaves were brown seedpods the size of peas.

Dr. Semedi stared at the plant. She then eyed Addison for a moment. She turned from Addison to Bobby, and then to Carlos. Finally she took the plant from Addison's outstretched hand.

SANTOSO TOOK QUENTIN, Samuel, and Gregory to a stark room and posted a guard inside the door. It appeared they were prisoners. Quentin asked why they'd been separated from the others. Santoso assured him that it was to facilitate medical examination. More likely, thought Quentin, it was to identify discrepancies in their stories.

"Please, gentlemen, make yourselves comfortable," Santoso said. This was a token sentiment, because the room contained nothing more than two bare hospital beds.

Gregory said, "Are we accused of a crime, Mr. Santoso? If we are, I would like to call the American Consulate. Perhaps you could return my phone?"

Santoso smiled and dismissed this with a wave of his hand. "Of course not, Mr. Stamper. We merely wish to understand the circumstances regarding your American friends." He turned to Samuel. "I know Mr. Darnell's name, but you I have not yet met."

"My name is Samuel Inwood."

Santoso raised his brows. "Are you British, Mr. Inwood?"

"Indeed I am. But I have been a resident of New Guinea for a rather long time."

"New Guinea? This is Papua, Mr. Inwood. A province of the Republic of Indonesia."

Samuel cleared his throat and stood straighter. "When I came to this land, it was known as Dutch New Guinea. And this particular settlement was known as Hollandia."

Santoso paused before speaking, as if calculating. "A very long time, indeed. I assume that you have the proper papers?"

Samuel looked to Quentin for help, so Quentin spoke for him. "Samuel has been lost in the bush also. He was very generous to us when we found him. But like us, he has nothing."

"I see," Santoso said. "Very unfortunate events."

An Indonesian doctor entered the room, brushed past the guard, and spoke quietly to Santoso. Santoso's body stiffened as the doctor spoke. He glanced fretfully in Quentin's direction and then left the room. Minutes later he returned, still visibly agitated.

"It seems the American authorities have taken an interest in your situation," he said. "Your telephone call has captured their attention."

Quentin felt a rush of relief; finally some good news.

"Then you will allow us to fly to the United States?" Gregory asked.

"By no means will you leave our country until you have had medical examinations and we are satisfied that you have not broken our laws. But this will now be a joint effort between your people and ours. You will remain here until some Americans arrive from your Consulate in Jakarta."

"And when will that be?" Quentin asked.

"Before the day is over, I am told." Santoso opened the door to leave. "I will see that you are fed and provided with clothing. It would not do, after all, for your American friends to think we are not gracious hosts."

Dr. Semedi stared at the plant. "Where did you get this?"

"You will find there the substance you want," Addison said.

The doctor turned the plant over in her hands. "Did you have this with you when you came into the hospital?"

Addison did not reply.

The doctor looked doubtful. "How can you know this is the specimen of importance?"

"You will find there the substance you want," Addison said again.

The door burst open and Mr. Santoso called Dr. Semedi out into the hall. They stood outside the door talking, but Bobby couldn't make out their words.

"What did you give her?" Bobby said to Addison.

"She is interested in healing wounds. So I gave her what she wanted. This is consistent with the deception you asked me to create."

Dr. Semedi entered the room again. She pulled the plant from where she was hiding it under her lab coat. It was now starting to wilt.

"It seems that responsibility for your health is now out of my hands," she said. "I do not know what it is I have seen here today. I do not know if you tell me truth or lies. But please tell me, if I examine this specimen will I waste our time and resources? We have little to spare."

Bobby answered, "You won't be sorry. It's real."

"It is the fruits," Addison said. "You must eat them."

She looked at the plant. "The fruits."

"Do not try to understand the substance of the fruits," Addison said. "You will not succeed. Instead, use the fruits to grow more plants, so that you will have more fruits."

Dr. Semedi turned toward the door. Mr. Santoso opened it for her and waited. She turned back to them and spoke quietly. "I am not to question you further. In case there is any truth to what you say, I will keep this safe." She tucked the plant back under her lab coat and left the room. Mr. Santoso glanced at each of them, and then he followed her, leaving them alone.

QUENTIN, Samuel, and Gregory were confined to their room well into the afternoon. Quentin requested to see Lindsey and the students, but was told to wait. Gregory asked endless questions about the Lamotelokhai and its capabilities and origins. But finally he seemed to reach cerebral overload, and he lapsed into silence. He was taking it pretty well, Quentin thought, considering all he'd been forced to absorb in a single day.

Samuel passed the time by asking his own questions, mostly regarding the various devices he had encountered since leaving the forest: radios, smartphones, and the hospital intercoms that interrupted them every few minutes with announcements in Indonesian. He never passed up a chance to physically touch anything unfamiliar to him, including the glass window and its plastic frame in the door of their hospital room.

It was late afternoon when Santoso led two Americans into the room. One stepped forward and extended his hand. He wore a gray suit and was tall and thin, perhaps sixty, with almost-white hair impeccably combed straight back.

"Gentlemen, Sterling Hess, Regional Security Officer, U.S. Embassy Jakarta. This is Dr. Paul Saskia." The other man appeared Indonesian, though he was dressed in an American-cut suit almost identical to Hess's. They shook hands all around and gave their names.

Hess sat in a folding chair. The man had a relaxed but commanding way about him, and he seemed to consciously ignore Santoso, as if he had already decided he was tired of dealing with him. He pulled a digital tablet from his black bag. "There is some confusion over your situation," he said. "The first order of business is to clear that up." He tapped his way through some screens. He stared directly at Quentin for a moment and then looked at something on his screen, frowning. "Where are the others?" Hess asked Santoso. "Mrs. Darnell and the other passengers of the flight?"

Santoso answered, "We have put them in other rooms in order to facilitate their medical examination."

Hess addressed Quentin. "Do you wish to be separated from your wife and the others at this time, Mr. Darnell?"

"No, I don't."

Almost before Quentin finished speaking, Hess boomed, "Then this is bullshit. You are isolating these guests of your country against their will. Please bring the others here. Now."

Santoso's face reddened, but he nodded to someone outside the door. Within seconds Lindsey entered the room, followed by the students, including Addison. They all sported the same shirts and elastic pants that had been given to Quentin and Samuel. Quentin introduced all of them. He presented Addison as his son, which was easier than expected.

Hess looked back and forth from his tablet screen to each of them. "Roberto Herrera, Miranda Henry, Russ Wade," he said. "Do you know the whereabouts of these people?"

After a few uncomfortable glances, Lindsey said, "They were killed when our plane crashed. Along with the pilot and two Indonesian passengers."

Hess hesitated a moment. "I'm very sorry to hear that." He then stood up. "If you will forgive me, there is something I must clear up right away. Dr. Saskia here is an American doctor. After what you have endured, you must surely have some use for his services."

Hess stepped into the hall but did not close the door. Dr. Saskia smiled at them and approached Ashley first. Santoso motioned for one of the Indonesian doctors to stay close and observe Dr. Saskia's activities. Quentin tuned them out and listened instead to Hess.

"Cameron, Sterling Hess here. There's been a major gaffe. I'm here with the people now and have confirmed their identities." A pause. "Cameron, they were standing right in front of me." Another pause. "Well, they're quite obviously wrong." A longer pause. "I don't know that yet. Yes, I'll find out. I'll get back to you. Oh, and Cameron, they say three Americans were killed. Students, in their teens. Along with three Indonesians. Yes, indeed it is."

Hess re-entered the room. "Who was it that called the United States earlier today?" He glanced at his tablet screen. "The call was made to a Dr. Phil Bollinger."

Gregory raised his hand.

Hess motioned to the door. "I would like to speak to you alone."

Santoso looked as if he might interfere with this, but then he let them leave the room.

"You're wasting your time," Ashley said to Dr. Saskia. "You won't find anything wrong with me or any of the rest of us."

The doctor appeared to be flustered. Clearly this was not what he had expected.

"These people claim to have discovered a remarkable curative agent," Santoso said, without hiding his skepticism. He pointed at Addison. "Perhaps that boy is the one you should examine first. The boy somehow fooled us, making it appear that he was injured."

Dr. Saskia approached Addison with a warm smile and urged him to move to one of the patient beds. Addison was soon lying on his back with his shirt off. The Indonesian doctor hovered near as Dr. Saskia asked Addison questions and palpated his abdomen. Quentin held his breath, trying not to show his apprehension.

Hess entered the room, frowning. Apparently Gregory's words had done little more than irritate him. Gregory followed behind him. His eyes met Quentin's, and he shook his head.

Hess spoke, obviously trying to keep his voice calm. "I must say, I can scarcely imagine what motives you people have."

"I assure you," Quentin said, "we have something that must be taken to the United States right away. You simply need to trust us."

Hess glared, a darkness gathering in his eyes. The man truly had an imposing presence. But before he could speak, Dr. Saskia's voice filled the room.

"What in God's name?" The doctor's hands were on Addison's knee and thigh. Even from where Quentin stood, he could see that the leg was moving, as if the bones were shifting beneath the flesh. The doctor gaped at the leg. "How did you do that?" he said.

Addison did not answer. Instead he looked at Hess and smiled.

Hess said, "Paul?"

The doctor's face had gone white. "I don't know. I have no way to explain what just happened."

Hess eyed Addison for a moment, as if trying to make a decision. Then his features hardened, and all signs of hesitation were gone. "Mr. Santoso, we are no longer willing to share this investigation with your doctors. It is clear that these American citizens have medical conditions that can only be addressed in a fully-equipped American facility, staffed by American doctors." He approached Addison. "Son, can you walk?"

"Yes."

Hess turned to Santoso. "We will immediately transport these people to the airport, and they will be flown to the U.S."

Santoso appeared frozen in place. Dark veins pulsed in his forehead. Suddenly he spoke to the two guards standing in the doorway. One of the men yelled down the hall, presumably to other policemen, and the two men entered the room with their hands on their side arms. Within seconds several more armed men blocked the door.

Santoso turned back to Hess. "It seems we are at odds, Mr. Hess. Perhaps you wish to rethink your decision."

Hess pulled his smartphone from his belt and punched in a sequence of numbers. The guards looked to Santoso for instructions, but he shook his head, allowing Hess to make the call.

Hess spoke loudly. "Cameron, Sterling Hess. We have just

been forcibly contained at the hospital. I don't have details at this time, but there may be something to the communications intel intercept we discussed. We need these people in American custody pronto." He paused, and his brows shot up as he listened. "You're kidding me. Why are they interested? It's just a mistake at Qantas." He listened. "Good God. I hope it's worth it. Make sure they know we're on the first floor, north wing. It doesn't look like we're going anywhere." He returned the phone to his belt. "Calvary's almost here already. They were sent before I even called."

"Why?" Quentin asked, but Hess had already shifted his attention to their captors.

"Mr. Santoso, you are minutes away from having an international relations incident on your hands. You and I are diplomats. Let's talk this out before things escalate."

Heavy footsteps clattered in the hall, and more Indonesian police appeared outside the door. Quentin heard others in the building, shouting curt commands to each other. It sounded like they were positioning themselves for an attack. The whole situation seemed surreal.

Santoso now sweated profusely, his face still red. "Yes, Mr. Hess. We will begin with you explaining exactly what it is that you are so eager to take from our country."

"We wish only to get our citizens back to their home where they can receive proper medical treatment. Please have your men stand down and let us pass. You have no legal course for holding us. I have been informed that a United States Special Operations Forces unit will be on site very shortly. A hospital is no place for a confrontation."

Santoso's expression was venomous. "We have no intention of using force. We merely wish to know the truth. If force is used, it will be a result of your people's eagerness for violence. Perhaps you should use your phone again and put an end to this nonsense."

A cacophony of sounds suddenly poured in from outside the

hospital: vehicle tires screeching, men shouting and running, an unintelligible bullhorn voice. Santoso's eyes grew wide. He started to speak but then thought better of it and left the room. Indonesian policemen now formed a semicircle outside the door, their pistols drawn and held pointed at an upward angle against their chests.

Hess stepped toward the door but was repelled by the guards. He wheeled around. "What exactly in the hell are we risking so much to protect? It damned well better be important."

Quentin said, "It's more important than you can imagine, but this is a mistake. We can work together—."

Suddenly there was a gunshot from outside the hospital, and then another.

Hess shouted, "Jesus Christ!"

Quentin and Lindsey forced the students into the corner of the room and onto the floor. Angry yelling from outside the hospital was now constant. But then suddenly, as if it were orchestrated, things quieted down. Only the garbled bullhorn could be heard, but shortly even that stopped. Quentin looked at the nearest policeman, and their eyes met. The man forced a nervous smile. He was visibly shaking. A single gunshot rang out from the street, and the man's smile faded. For a moment following the shot there was total silence, and the man's eyes seemed to plead with Quentin. Then the silence was torn apart by a scream of anger from outside. Before the cry ended, gunshots filled the afternoon air. It sounded like someone had lit a whole strand of firecrackers in the street, and for a moment Quentin could almost convince himself that this was all it was.

Santoso stormed into the room. "Do you have any idea what you have done?" he managed to scream in a mix of Indonesian and English. Two policemen followed him into the room, their pistols drawn and eyes wild. "And for what?" Santoso cried. "A boy and his tricks?" Spit flew from the man's mouth as he spoke, and

Quentin realized they were in immediate danger. Santoso had been driven over the edge.

From the corner of his eye, Quentin saw Bobby lean over and whisper to Addison. This was not the time for another brash idea. Quentin started to warn Bobby, but Santoso yelled at them, "Maybe you are not worth it, no?" He motioned for the policemen to point their weapons at Addison. They glanced at each other, but then complied.

"If you are so valuable," Santoso cried, "then perhaps we should put an end to this!"

Addison rose to his feet. He moved toward the men. This had an almost calming effect on Santoso. He stopped talking and watched Addison approach, as if mesmerized by this unexpected behavior. Both policemen's guns were pointed at Addison. Addison took another step, until the nearest gun pressed against his neck. The man holding the gun muttered what could have been either a curse or a prayer. Addison stepped directly in front of Santoso, pushing the policeman and his gun back a step. The room was quiet, although sporadic gunfire could still be heard outside.

Barely above a whisper, Lindsey pleaded, "Don't shoot. Please don't shoot."

Addison deliberately lifted a hand and grasped the policeman's wrist. With his other hand he reached for Santoso's hand. He held them, smiling gently. The policeman seemed to relax, and his gun moved away from Addison's neck. Quentin's eyes were drawn to their hands. Where Addison's skin touched the men, it appeared to flow into them like liquid.

"Do not be afraid," Addison said.

Santoso and the policeman looked down at their hands. Both men tried pulling free, but Addison held tight. The policeman's gun fell and clattered on the floor. Santoso's eyes grew wide as he watched his own arm change shape, becoming shorter. He babbled something unintelligible and tried desperately to free himself. The policeman simply stared at his arm, silent but horrified. The other men looked on helplessly. Santoso's arm was no longer even recognizable, and his babbling had turned into pleading screams.

Abruptly the nearest policeman stepped forward, raised his pistol, and shot point blank at Addison's face.

The pistol's crack was deafening in the stark room, and it was followed by silence. Even Santoso's screams stopped. Addison did not fall. The bullet had torn a gaping hole under his eye and out the back of his head. But he stood erect, still smiling. The policeman who had fired lowered his pistol, and it hung limp in his hand as the hole in Addison's face closed upon itself.

Santoso's screams resumed. Addison disengaged his own hands from the men's arms, which had become no more than bulges on their shoulders. The policeman tried to scream too, but his cries turned to sputtering grunts. Both men collapsed onto the floor. The guards from the hall were now in the room, but all they could do was watch in horror as the two bodies fell silent and transformed into amorphous blobs of flesh. The clothing on the bodies seemed to disappear as it was integrated into the shifting forms. The two bodies then merged together into one larger mass.

Quentin moved to where Bobby stood. "What have you done, Bobby?"

Bobby looked at him, his face ashen, and then turned back to the transforming monstrosity as if he might miss something. "I told Addison to make something to scare them away, so we could get out of here. I didn't think he'd kill them."

The mass on the floor began taking shape. Pink fleshy skin turned leathery, and bumps formed on its surface. Wrinkles in the skin appeared, growing deeper until folded limbs were apparent. The mass of tissue shuddered, and then it rolled over and expanded. Everyone stepped back. Two legs shot out to their full length, and a snake-like neck uncurled from beneath the arms. Each arm was fringed with red feathers and ended with three impossibly long fingers tipped with hooked claws. Upon the neck was a head the size and shape of a deer's, but instead of a muzzle, the creature bore a thick beak. The beak sprang open, and a piercing cry filled the room, like a dozen parrots screeching in unison. The creature was on its side, but the head righted itself, revealing another fringe of red feathers that stood out from the back of the head. Oversized marble eyes gazed about the room as if studying each one of them.

After a surreal moment of silent observation, the thing kicked wildly and twisted its body. And then it was upright on two legs, its head nearly touching the ceiling. More long red feathers spread out in a fan from the tail. Thick muscles twitched under the leathery skin, and now that it stood fully erect it was obvious that the body was built for power and speed. A dinosaur of some kind—it had to be. It was a terrifying hulk, and Quentin shrank back to the wall, pulling Lindsey and Ashley with him. One of the policemen ran from the room, but the others seemed too confused to take action.

And then the creature attacked.

Without a sound, it lunged at the men in the doorway. Clawed feet skidded on floor tiles and it went down, slamming into the open door and knocking it from its hinges. The creature managed to grab one of the scattering policemen. The heavy beak clamped onto the man's thigh. Even as the thing scrambled to right itself, it shook its head violently, tearing through trousers and flesh and flipping the man to the ground like a doll. One of the other men stood his ground and fired at the dinosaur. It charged out of the room after him.

There were more gunshots and screams and ripping flesh. The injured man lying in the doorway stared dumbly at his ruined leg. Quentin rushed over to help him, but then he stopped. The bloodied leg was changing, pulling itself up into the torso, just as Santoso's arm had done. The man was being transformed.

Screams and gunfire now came from elsewhere in the hospital, followed by the piercing call of the rampaging creature. The man on the floor tried to speak, but was pitifully weakened by sheer panic. The guy's body was becoming something else, probably just as menacing as the dinosaur. Only this time there was no one else in the room for it to attack. They had to get out. Lindsey and the students seemed to know this and were already stepping over the broken door. Quentin followed, and urged Hess and Saskia to come. But they were frozen in place.

"I don't know what's happening," Hess said. The doctor just stared at the changing man on the floor.

"Later," Quentin said, "but now we have to go!"

Hess snapped out of his trance. He grabbed the doctor's arm. "Paul, we're going."

In the hallway they immediately ran into three more fallen men. The bodies were already changing and were beginning to merge. One of them was still conscious, and he pleaded to them. But the lower half of his body had already become a shuddering mass and was flowing into the others.

Quentin started for the front doors, but then he spun around and confronted Addison. "This has to stop. If everyone that thing attacks turns into another one, we'll have an epidemic! Can you stop it now, before it kills more people?"

"The creatures are living things. I cannot—"

Addison was interrupted by a stabbing screech. A second feathered dinosaur rushed out of the room they had just left. This one was smaller, formed from the body of only one man. It ran headlong into the much larger third one that was just rising up on two massive legs. The larger creature staggered and lifted its head. Its neck became entangled in a hanging fluorescent light fixture, which broke and fell in pieces around it. It then snapped at the smaller animal that had run into it. The two fussed at each other for a moment and then stopped, as if realizing they were the same species. Together they turned and faced Quentin and the others.

Oh shit. Quentin shot a glance down the hall. The front doors were too far away. They would have to make it to the nearest room.

As if reading Quentin's thoughts, both creatures charged. Quentin turned to run and abruptly collided with Hess. Hess fell hard, and Quentin stumbled over him onto the floor. He looked back. The creatures' feet skidded on the tiles, but they were quickly building speed. Quentin jumped up, scrambled to the nearest door and slammed into it. It didn't open. He tried turning the knob but felt resistance. Through the narrow window a doctor stared back at him, his face stricken with fear. He was holding the knob. Quentin pounded on the door and screamed at him, but the man shook his head and held on.

And then it was too late. Before he could turn around, Quentin heard the clicking of claws on the floor, mixed with the cries of the students as they fell over each other to get away. Quentin turned. Dr. Saskia was helping Hess onto his feet, and the dinosaurs fell upon them first. The larger one grabbed Hess's arm in its beak, and the smaller one latched onto Saskia's shoulder. The doctor swung at the creature and ripped free of its grip. He stumbled away. The dinosaur then turned to Hess, who was helpless on the ground, and grabbed his ankle. Both creatures began shaking and pulling.

"No!" Hess's voice warbled as the creatures shook his body.

Suddenly, deafening blasts obscured these sounds. The smaller dinosaur's neck was severed and its body flopped on the floor next to its head. The larger creature dropped Hess and turned to face the source of the noise. Three men in black fatigues crouched inside the front doors, their rifles trained on the dinosaur. They all fired at once. The creature's legs splayed outward, and the body collapsed with a loud bestial grunt. It didn't move again.

One of the men swiveled and waved to others outside the doors. He then bellowed, "Are you people Americans?"

"Yes," they all shouted back.

The men approached cautiously. Behind them, others began

working their way toward the far end of the hall. They wore riot gear and bulletproof vests. The men approached and then stood staring at the creatures they had killed. Hess cursed as Dr. Saskia examined his wounds. Addison was at Hess's side, too, resting his hands on him. Quentin hoped he was preventing Hess from transforming into another raging beast.

A stocky, gray-haired man walked in the front doors and made his way straight for them. He wore a green uniform, and the men in black fatigues moved out of his way as he brushed past them. He looked at the dead dinosaurs and then faced them.

"I'm Colonel Roger Richards, Defense and Army Attaché, U.S. Embassy Jakarta." His eyes glided confidently from one of them to the next. "Folks, I'd like to know what in God's name is the cause of this goddamn cluster fuck."

CHAPTER SIX

"Why were you in Wamena?"

"Where did your plane go down?"

"Do you have identification?"

"What have you told the Indonesians?"

They had been hustled into a green military truck with no windows, and the truck now roared through the streets of Jayapura. Bobby didn't want to talk to these men. The horrified faces of Santoso and the policemen as they watched their own bodies morph into something else flashed through his mind over and over. Their screams of terror rang in his ears. Bobby had killed them all. He had asked Addison to do something without thinking it through, and now the men were dead. There wouldn't even be bodies for their families to bury. Instead, the dinosaurs would probably be taken somewhere to be dissected and studied.

"Tell us your full names, one at a time."

"Why were you taken to a hospital?"

"What the hell were those animals?"

The questions kept coming, but Bobby ignored them. His mistake had killed people, and he couldn't stop thinking about what this meant. How was he any different from the Addison who had killed Miranda and the Papuans? At least Addison had the excuse of being brain damaged.

The truck's engine grew louder as it accelerated. Bobby decided they must be leaving the city, maybe going back to the airport.

"Have you contacted anyone in the states?"

"Where are your passports?"

During all of this, Ashley and Carlos sat quietly staring at the plastic hospital flip-flops on their feet. The men weren't asking Addison any questions directly; obviously they didn't know he was what this was all about.

Eventually the truck slowed down and made several turns before coming to a stop. There were shouts and then a metal door shutting. When the back of the truck opened, they were inside a large building, like an airplane hangar. They climbed out of the truck. Other soldiers worked at various jobs around the hangar, and they stopped what they were doing to stare. Colonel Richards took them to one end of the hangar where there was a narrow hallway with doors, and they entered one of the rooms. Small tables had been pushed together to make one large table in the middle of the room with metal folding chairs around it.

They sat around the table, and some men brought pitchers of water and a stack of paper cups. One of the men said that restrooms were in the hall, but no one got up to use them. Colonel Richards sat at one end of the table, between two other men in green uniforms. One of them turned on a voice recorder and placed it on the table.

Richards cleared his throat. "Folks, I appreciate the fact that you have suffered an ordeal, but we've got a situation on our hands, and you people have made it worse."

Mr. Darnell shifted in his seat. "A situation?"

Colonel Richards frowned at him. "You were in Wamena when

it started, were you not? On July twelfth? Flare-up between the OPM and Indonesian forces. Some indigenous Papuans were shot. Nothing new. But Washington, in its infinite wisdom, decided we should get involved. That didn't go over well. Things have been hairy around here since. Washington realized the mistake in short order, and we've toned it down." Richards waved his hand. "This facility is a temporary base for conciliation measures. The climate had become almost quiet—until today. We get orders to pull you folks out, bring you stateside pronto. We show up. Tempers are short at the get-go. Recipe for a Charlie Foxtrot, which is exactly what we got."

Bobby didn't know what a Charlie Foxtrot was, but he got the idea.

Richards rose from his chair and leaned forward with his hands on the table. "Now I need some straight answers. It seems your flight out of Wamena was part of the evacuation fiasco, correct? And you say your plane went down in the jungle?"

They all nodded.

"Folks," Richards said, "we're working up a scenario for getting you back to the States without inciting a war. I don't know yet how that's going to shake out." He paused. "The circumstances are atypical. We've got a firefight that started for God knows why and didn't end well for two Indonesian police. We've got Indonesian personnel who are missing. We've got doctors claiming you possess something that belongs here with them. And we've got three dead animals in a public hospital. I'm no expert, but they look like goddamn dinosaurs. You're not going to tell me those things live here in the jungle, are you?"

"No, we're not," Mr. Darnell said.

Colonel Richards nodded his head at this. "And so, here we are."

AFTER PROVIDING HOPELESSLY confusing answers to some of Colonel Richards's questions, Quentin suggested they simply tell their story from the beginning. This time they told everything. They even described the hanging village and the ancient Papuans who lived there. Samuel resisted this at first, but Quentin explained that these were representatives of the United States, that the village would be safe. Samuel was dubious but conceded he would have to trust Quentin's judgment.

Throughout the inquisition, Colonel Richards's face was granite. Even as they explained their dreams revealing the Lamotelokhai's origin, and that Samuel had lived in the forest for a century and a half, his face showed nothing more than mild interest. He didn't even take notes, apparently relying on his memory and the recorder to document the entire conversation. There was no telling if he believed a single word of their story.

The interrogation continued into the evening. Quentin eventually explained Bobby's attempts to communicate with the Lamotelokhai using the rules of Kembalimo. At this, Richards frowned.

"Kembalimo? You mean the language software?"

Quentin glanced at Bobby, who nodded. "I thought it was just a game," Quentin said.

Richards leaned forward on his elbows. "It's much more than a game. How could this thing buried in the jungle understand Kembalimo?"

Quentin shrugged. "Good question."

Richards grunted. "It appears Peter Wooley may have some explaining to do."

Samuel had been silent for some time, but suddenly he spoke up. "Bobby has told me of this Peter Wooley. I believe that I have known the man."

All eyes turned to him.

Richards said, "If you've been living like an ape in the jungle for a hundred and fifty years, how could you know Peter Wooley?"

"Who is Peter Wooley?" Quentin asked.

Richards spoke without taking his eyes off Samuel. "Developer of Kembalimo."

Samuel put his palms on the table. "Sir, could you tell me more about this Peter Wooley?"

"Brilliant man, supposedly. Developed the software algorithms that make Kembalimo work. Folks say it may change the way we all communicate. Wooley is head of SouthPacificNet. He's damn rich, but oddly enough, not from Kembalimo. He's an eccentric. Won't allow Kembalimo to be sold. Wants everyone to use it for free." Richards scrutinized Samuel as if waiting for an explanation.

"Samuel?" Quentin said. "This isn't the Peter you told me about is it? The one who came to the village?"

Samuel leaned back in his chair. "The evidence seems to suggest it, though I was a witness to his death. Peter was killed before my eyes."

"That is correct," Addison said. It was the first he had spoken since they had entered the room. "The villagers killed Peter. But Peter asked me to help him."

"But I saw it. He was beaten beyond hope of repair."

"You are correct. Peter was reconstructed."

Bobby said, "You mean like you reconstructed Ashley?"

Addison nodded. It was a gesture Quentin hadn't seen the Lamotelokhai use before.

A smile formed on Samuel's face. "Then it is he. It is indeed Peter."

"What the hell are you talking about?" Richards said.

"It is he," Samuel repeated. "That is how he has created this Kembalimo you speak of. It must be. Even the name itself—Kembalimo—this is a word used by the indigenes. Its literal meaning is, *to return.*"

Quentin pushed away from the table and stood up. He paced the room, pondering this revelation. The man who had stumbled upon the hanging village over forty years ago was the very same man who had created Kembalimo. Peter Wooley must have learned to communicate with the Lamotelokhai using the same symbols Bobby had used. When he had left the village, he took this knowledge with him.

Richards eyed Samuel intensely. "You're telling me you've personally met Peter Wooley, even though you've been hiding in the jungle since men fought with muskets?"

Samuel's eyes sparkled as he spoke. "Colonel Richards, for a short time Mr. Wooley was a guest in the village of my indigene hosts. I considered him a friend, although I have doubts he would say the same of me. Until recently, I believed him to be dead."

Richards shook his head and let out a grunt that may have been a laugh. "Very well, then." He waved his hand for Quentin to be seated. "Please continue."

As Quentin continued the story, the men on either side of Richards frequently left the room. After talking on their phones in the hall, they would return and whisper to Richards before sitting down, only to repeat this a few minutes later. Finally, Quentin asked what they were doing.

"We are currently involved in a diplomatic dance with the Indonesians," Richards said. "Lives were lost today. They want restitution. And frankly, they want you people."

Quentin considered this. Perhaps it didn't matter if Richards believed them or not, as long as he was willing to get them safely to the United States.

Lindsey spoke up. "Colonel Richards, we would like to have access to a telephone." She nodded toward the cell phone held by one of the men. "The students' families deserve to hear from them and know that they are alive."

Richards exchanged a glance with the man next to him and

rubbed his chin. "We have been ordered to restrict your communication until things are ironed out. There are unanswered questions."

"What questions?" Lindsey asked.

"Questions such as those we are exploring now. Shall we move on?"

And so the talking continued. With difficulty, Quentin told of Addison killing the villagers and then killing Miranda. Richards looked at Addison warily.

"Don't worry," Quentin said. "My son Addison is no longer with us. This is not really Addison."

"Then who is he?" Quentin found a little satisfaction in the look of genuine confusion and alarm on Richards's face.

Samuel spoke up. "What you see before you is the Lamotelokhai itself. It has disguised itself so that we could bring it to those in your home country who would use it with wisdom. A great moral responsibility is upon you, sir. We trust that you will act accordingly."

The colonel's next words were low and commanded their attention. "You want me to believe this boy is not human, that he is some kind of computer sent from an extraterrestrial civilization?"

Lindsey placed her elbows on the table. "This morning, would you have believed that you would be killing dinosaurs in a hospital?"

Richards just stared at her.

"It's true, sir," Gregory said. "I didn't believe it either, but the boy gave me some sort of drug and I had these incredible visions—." Gregory then seemed to realize this didn't sound the way he had intended. He spoke to Addison. "Maybe you should show him, too."

Gregory was right. Richards would need proof. Quentin looked at Bobby and their eyes locked. But instead of jumping at the chance to help as he had so many times before, Bobby just lowered his gaze. Quentin felt a pang of guilt for expecting so much of him. Bobby no doubt felt responsible for the bloody scene at the hospital.

"What do you want me to do?" Addison said.

Lindsey said, "Colonel Richards needs to understand what you are."

"But don't do anything that will hurt people," Bobby added.

Addison reached under his hospital shirt and pulled out a brown lump like the one he had given to Gregory. As he walked around the table, the men next to Richards stiffened. He held it out to Richards.

The Colonel glanced at Gregory. "Is this the drug you took?"

"I don't know if I would call it a drug. But yes."

Richards took the object and handed it to the man on his left. "Get this to our doctors and have them figure out what the hell it is." The man took it and left the room.

Addison spoke without expression. "The purpose of the substance is to help you understand. You should eat it."

Richards grunted. "Like hell I should." He pointed across the table. "Please take your seat, son."

Addison looked at Bobby.

"Show him in a different way," Bobby said, "but don't hurt him."

There was no detectable delay between Bobby's last word and what happened next. Colonel Richards was simply gone. There was a loud pop where his body had been as air rushed in to fill the vacuum. A wisp of water vapor swirled in the air briefly and then vanished. Quentin blinked. The remaining man who sat next to Richards was so startled he practically toppled over in his chair.

"What the hell?" It was Richards. The voice came from outside the door, in the hallway. The door burst open and Richards stepped in. His face had gone white.

The man at the table said, "Sir, are you alright?"

Richards looked around him, and then down at his shaking hands. "What was that?" he said to Addison.

"It would take time to fully explain. Working together, the parts of my body are able to change some properties of the area near me, such as properties of space and time. What I did to you was simple. The spaces in this room and outside the door are known to me. I did this to help you understand. It is a capability I have that you might find useful."

Richards put his hands on his chest, as if making sure he was in one piece. Then he looked up and said, "Can you do that again?"

There was another pop and a thin cloud where his body had stood. The rest of them simply stared at the spot, speechless.

Another cry came from the hall, this time a burst of delight. The door flew open again, and Richards entered the room. He gaped at Addison. He then pulled his eyes away and leveled his gaze at Quentin. "I may be slow, but I'm not stupid," he said. "I'm starting to get the point. Lumenick!" he barked at the other man. "I don't care what it takes, but see to it that the negotiations get wrapped up. We're taking these people stateside, and we're doing it now."

The man stood. "Yes, sir!" He nearly stumbled over his own feet to get out the door.

Bobby didn't get it. Addison makes someone disappear and then appear on the other side of a wall, and now Colonel Richards seemed—finally—to believe them. Seeing live dinosaurs wasn't enough for him, but getting zapped through a wall was.

Colonel Richards ordered all the soldiers to drop whatever they were doing and guard the building. The group was taken to a bigger room with tables at one end and sleeping cots at the other. Green curtains hanging on metal frames separated the cots into sleeping cubicles. Men and women with guns stood near the doors, and more talked and yelled outside. Colonel Richards said he had to go talk to the Indonesians, and he asked if Addison needed anything special like electricity, or some other power source. Bobby grinned at this. Addison told him no, he would be fine.

And so they finally had a chance to clean up and get some rest. There were two bathrooms, and Bobby took his first shower since they had left the losmen in Wamena, thanks to hoses rigged from the pipes below the sinks to the tops of metal curtain frames. To Bobby it was the best shower in the world. Water splattered his skin and ran onto the floor, brown from grime and dried blood. Bobby gazed down at his naked body. It looked strange, like it belonged to someone else—someone older, more grown up. His pubic hair was thick and dark, and there was a shadow of fine black hairs from there down the inside of each of his legs. After scrubbing the dirt away, Bobby realized his skin was now darker. Even though they had spent most of the time in the forest's dim shadows, somehow he was tan, except around his groin where his pant scraps had been tied. He ran his hand over his chest, feeling the scar from the tribesman's spear. He was glad the scar hadn't disappeared completely.

Bobby turned off the water from below the sink, dried off, and slipped back into his blue hospital clothes and flip-flops. Except for Addison, the others had showered before him, and now they were gathered around a table piled high with packages of junk food.

Carlos shot him a look as he approached and said, "Dinner." The single word came out around a mouthful of orange cheese puffs.

Bobby salivated as he inspected the pile. It looked like someone had emptied an entire snack machine on the table. There were candy bars, pretzels, oatmeal cookies, animal crackers, and all kinds of chips—a grand mountain waiting to be conquered.

Bobby guessed it was dark outside, but he had no way to know. In spite of being tired he didn't want to miss whatever might happen next. The others must have felt the same way, because they sat around the table even after they were too full too eat. Colonel Richards came into the room occasionally to check on them. The third time he came in, he asked Gregory to go with him. Within minutes Gregory came back, frowning.

He stood looking at them for a moment. He pulled one of the chairs from the table and sat. "It's funny—I only just met you folks this morning, but in one day you have turned my life upside down." He tried to smile, but it looked forced. Then he said, "Just spit it out, Stamper! It seems my role here is no longer important. I have been asked to go on about my business."

After some uncomfortable silence, Mr. Darnell said, "You've been a great help to us, Gregory. I hate to think of where we might be now if you hadn't been there."

Gregory got up and shook Mr. Darnell's hand. "I would like to believe I've played a role in this, despite how small it may have been. At this moment, I am one of the few who know the world is about to change." He reached out to shake Mrs. Darnell's hand, but she hugged him instead. He then moved around the table to shake everyone's hands.

When he got to Addison, he said, "I hardly know what to say to you. In spite of what you may see from some of us, please know you are welcome here. I hope you can help us learn to use your knowledge wisely."

The Lamotelokhai eyed him curiously. "If there are others like you where we are going, that should be easy." Addison then shook Gregory's hand, mimicking what the others had done.

Quentin wasn't convinced it was safe for Gregory to leave the compound, but Richards assured them Gregory would have protection until he caught his flight to the interior, where he would join his research team. And so Gregory left.

PERHAPS AN HOUR PASSED before Richards entered the room again and instructed Samuel to come with him. They returned a short time later. Richards and half a dozen men stood by the door as Samuel approached Quentin and the others.

Samuel sighed deeply before speaking. "It seems that your countrymen and the officials here have come to an accord. To put it to few words, all of you are to be allowed free passage if I remain here."

A flurry of protests filled the air. Samuel held up his hands to silence them. "I have agreed."

There were more protests. Lindsey's voice rose above the others. "Samuel, why would you do this? You wanted so badly to return to your home."

Again Samuel raised his hands. "Please understand. For many years I have endeavored to hide the Lamotelokhai from the world, believing that its powers had no place in the hands of men who think themselves civilized but often act to the contrary. But I have always known, as the indigenes have known, that one day there would be no choice. You have convinced me that transporting the Lamotelokhai to your home country is a just and reasonable action, and I now have one last opportunity to assist the endeavor. The Indonesian officials believe we have discovered a plant bearing remarkable healing qualities. Sensibly, I am the one who could lead them to the place where the plant grows." Samuel nodded toward Addison. "They do not know of the Lamotelokhai, and so they will allow you passage if I stay and guide them."

"But there is no plant," Quentin said. "When they find that out, they won't be happy."

Samuel raised only a finger this time. "If Addison will provide me some suitable substance that I might keep hidden until the proper time, perhaps I can give them what they believe exists." He looked at Addison.

"Yes, Samuel, I can do that."

Samuel smiled. "There, you see?" This was followed by dubious silence, so he continued. "As for my wishes to return to England, please know that this was a wish to return to the England I once knew, where the people I left behind still waited for my return. My colleagues. My father, Solomon Inwood, and my mother, Charity. And my beloved—" Samuel looked directly at Lindsey. "Her name was Lindsey. Lindsey Ennis. Did Quentin tell you this?"

Lindsey started to speak, but then she just shook her head no.

Samuel went on. "But of course she is long dead. I once thought I might visit her grave should I ever return. But she is surely buried beside a husband whom she loved for many years after I was forgotten. And the graves of their children will no doubt lie next to them. And perhaps their grandchildren. I feel no great calling to return there now. Besides, from what I have seen since we have left the forest, I do not believe I would recognize the places I once knew. The world is now filled with marvels beyond my understanding. If the medicinal effects of the Lamotelokhai on my body do not yield, I will still have ample time to grow accustomed to such things. I have even thought of returning to the village of my indigene friends."

Richards was pacing by the door. "Mr. Inwood, we don't have the luxury of long goodbyes."

Quentin glared at Richards. This was too much of a compromise. Samuel had studied the Lamotelokhai for a century and a half. His knowledge would surely be important. Besides, he had become a personal friend. It didn't seem right to use him as a pawn.

But Samuel seemed okay with this, and he quietly conferred with Addison, undoubtedly getting what he would need to placate the Indonesians. Addison handed him something that Samuel tucked away in his vest. Samuel headed for the door, but then he turned around. "Quentin, I would speak to you alone, if you would allow it."

Quentin raised a finger to Richards to give them a minute and then moved to the far corner of the room. Samuel followed him over.

"This is a mistake," Quentin said quietly. "We're going to need you."

"It is decided," Samuel said. "But I must speak of my concerns. Perhaps it is too late to undo what has been done, but I must beg you to be diligent in protecting the Lamotelokhai. You have assured me that men in your country will be fitting caretakers, but I must say that those we have encountered have not given me great confidence. Colonel Richards seems an honest man, but I rather doubt he shares the same morals as you and I."

As if he overheard this, Richards cleared his throat loudly and pointed to his watch.

Samuel put his hand on Quentin's shoulder. "I have grown to respect you, Quentin, but I fear we may have made a mistake. If you find reason to agree with me on that, please take whatever action you must—before the Lamotelokhai is removed from your stewardship."

Quentin figured it was already too late for that. He looked Samuel in the eye. "I understand what you and the villagers have sacrificed, and I'll do my best."

Samuel gave him a simple nod and then headed for the door.

Before following Samuel out, Richards turned back to them. "We had to bargain to accomplish our goal. But I guaran-goddamn-tee you this: Mr. Inwood will not be forgotten. Once we deliver you folks stateside, we have every intention of extracting him. He seems to think he can deliver what the Indonesians want. After he does that, I'm sure they will negotiate further." He glanced at his watch again. "Gather what belongings you have. We've commandeered a commercial carrier to take you to L.A. It won't be stopping in Jakarta. I'll accompany you on the flight." He nodded and left.

Within minutes they had boarded a truck and were trundling toward the waiting jet. It was now dark, but Quentin could see that military vehicles packed with armed men flanked them. Richards wasn't taking any chances. When the truck stopped, they were far out on the tarmac rather than at the terminal. A massive intercontinental Qantas jet loomed over them, blocking the backdrop of stars.

"Now that's a *real* plane," Ashley said as they piled out of the truck.

Bobby stood still, gazing up at the vast aircraft. "I wish Samuel could see this."

The men escorted them up the wheeled staircase. They passed through the lavish first class into a much larger economy section. The sheer size of the cabin was unsettling. Without seats, the area would be large enough for a game of kickball. And there were no regular passengers, only a small cluster of people surrounding a gray-haired man in a black suit.

As they entered, the man introduced himself as Cameron Weis, Ambassador, U.S. Embassy Jakarta. He had personally come to see that they were being treated well. He had gathered several doctors who were available on short notice, including a man in a khaki uniform, Captain William Kessel, Commanding Officer of the U.S. Naval Medical Research Unit. Also there was Dr. Saskia, who had been at the hospital with Sterling Hess and had witnessed the horrific events there. Dr. Saskia seemed to have recovered from his dinosaur bite, and Quentin wondered if Hess had been so lucky.

As the students filed into a row of seats, the men seemed unable to keep their eyes off of them. Apparently Hess or Saskia had told them at least some of what they had seen.

Ambassador Weis cleared his throat, and the men quit staring. "We honestly do not know what your situation is, folks," he said. "Only that one or more of the students with you has a most extraordinary condition. Dr. Saskia is here because he has firsthand experience with the student. Our primary objective at this time is to transport you safely to the States, to an adequately-equipped facility with qualified staff. A team of experts is assembling as we speak, although it is difficult to recruit specialists when you have little idea of the nature of the situation." The ambassador spread his hands to indicate the group of men. "These good doctors will examine each of you. We must be diligent with regard to pathogens."

Quentin noticed that a row of seats next to them was piled high with metal cases that probably contained medical equipment.

Ambassador Weis continued. "Do you mind telling us which of your students Colonel Richards might have referred to when he used the phrase, *a boy, but not really a boy?*"

"His name is Addison." It was Richards himself. Quentin had not seen him enter the cabin behind them. Richards pointed at Addison. "And I did not claim he wasn't a boy, only that these people claimed he wasn't. I do know he may be more valuable to our country than you can possibly imagine. Let's get this tub in the air."

Quentin didn't like Richards's tone. It was time to say something. "I want to make sure everyone here realizes why we brought Addison to you. We believe the U.S. is where he should be, but only because we believe the U.S. is likely to understand that his gifts are meant for everyone on this planet. They are not for the benefit of one nation, or any one group of people. Do you agree?"

Dr. Saskia nodded, but Ambassador Weis gazed at Quentin dubiously, as did most of the others. They obviously didn't believe that Addison was anything more than a boy.

"I'm certainly no expert," Richards said. "And I can't imagine anyone else here is—not after what I've seen. So let's focus on the task at hand. When we get you folks stateside, the true experts can determine a sound course of action." Richards then made his way to where Addison sat and began asking him questions.

Quentin's emotions churned as he watched Richards speaking eagerly to the Lamotelokhai. Quentin was still trying to accept that he would never see Addison again. And now he realized that once they got home he would also lose this replica of Addison. Suddenly he was overcome with the notion that he was making a colossal mistake.

BOBBY hardly even noticed when the plane took off. It was nothing like a Twin Otter, and it seemed impossible that anything could go wrong. Ambassador Weis did not stay with them. Even the soldiers that were there left the plane before it took off. Maybe they figured once the plane was in the air, they were safe.

Bobby wanted to sleep, but the doctors weren't finished with them. They were stabbed with needles to draw blood. Before the plane crash, Bobby had been afraid of needles, but now he hardly noticed. They all had to pee in cups, and then they had to spit into more cups. Long cotton swabs were pushed into their throats, noses, eyes, and ears. Bobby even had to go behind a curtain and strip down so a doctor could examine every inch of him.

The doctors wore masks and rubber gloves, like they were afraid of catching a disease. But of course they wouldn't. And Bobby was pretty sure they wouldn't find diseases in the blood, urine, or anything else taken from their bodies.

During all of this, Colonel Richards kept speaking to Addison. When it was Addison's turn to be examined, Richards stayed right there with him, repeatedly asking the doctors if they saw anything unusual as they wiped Addison with swabs and stuck him with needles. Mr. Darnell tried telling them this was a waste of time, but Colonel Richards told the doctors to do it anyway. Then Mr.

Darnell told Addison to show them the trick of tearing open his shoulder and then fixing it. Addison did this without even blinking an eye, and again it made Bobby a little nauseous. The men got quiet, except for Dr. Saskia, who said they all should have believed him in the first place.

So finally Colonel Richards said, "Due respect, gentlemen, but I think this is beyond your expertise. Let's hold off until we know what the hell we're dealing with." Then he took Addison back to where they were sitting before.

Ashley yawned loudly. "Well, this flight has been a blast so far. Time to sleep." She then shuffled toward the front of the plane.

Colonel Richards spoke up. "Miss Stoddard, it would be best if you all stayed together."

Ashley turned with an irritated look. "The plane is empty. No one is in first class. And you guys are making too much noise figuring out what we already know." She waved her hand at the cabin wall. "Do you think I'm going to run away?" Then she pushed through the curtain and was gone.

Richards gazed at the curtain for a moment. "Kid's got spunk," he said.

Mrs. Darnell said, "You boys should get some rest too."

Bobby and Carlos headed for first class. Before passing through the curtain, Bobby turned. "Colonel Richards, you should be careful."

Richards looked at him, and so did the doctors.

Bobby swallowed and went on. "Be careful what you ask him to do, because bad things always happen."

Richards said, "Duly noted, son. Your name is Bobby Truex, isn't that correct?"

Bobby nodded.

Richards smiled at him. "There's something I'm curious about, Bobby. You were the one who told it—the Lamotelokhai—to change itself to look like the son of Mr. and Mrs. Darnell. Correct?"

Bobby glanced at Mr. Darnell and then nodded.

"Why Addison?" Richards said. "Why not ask it to look like one of the others?"

Bobby didn't know how to answer this.

"Or why not ask it to look like someone famous? Maybe Abraham Lincoln, or Clint Eastwood? Why specifically Addison Darnell?"

Mr. Darnell spoke up. "Colonel, Bobby was making a legitimate point. You should thank him, rather than question—"

Addison was sitting next to Richards, but suddenly something wasn't right. Bobby immediately saw what it was, and his senses became numb.

"I can answer Roger Richards's question," Addison said. But it wasn't Addison. The gasps from the doctors seemed faint, like Bobby was hearing them through ears clogged with water.

Sitting next to Colonel Richards was Bobby himself.

Richards turned to look. He stared. He turned to Bobby, and then turned back to the other Bobby.

Bobby wanted to look in a mirror to make sure he was still himself. Instead he looked at his hands. He then pushed past the doctors and stood at the end of the row where Richards and the other Bobby sat. It looked like him in every single way he could see.

The thing spoke to Richards. "I cannot form myself into a creature or object I do not have knowledge of. Bobby knows this. Bobby asked me to form myself into Addison Darnell because he believed he was responsible for Addison going away. Bobby believed it would comfort Quentin Darnell and Lindsey Darnell if I formed myself into the body of Addison." The thing paused like it was waiting for a reaction. "Do you feel that your question has been answered, Roger Richards?"

Colonel Richards's eyes narrowed, but the corners of his mouth smiled a little—a look Bobby found disturbing. Richards said, "Yes."

Addison went on. "Bobby is correct, you should be careful. I was created to share with you some of the achievements of my creators. You must decide what you do with my creators' achievements. If you harm yourselves, then those who eventually replace you may learn from your mistakes."

"Do you understand what he is saying?" Mr. Darnell said. "He's been here for over half a billion years. You could use him stupidly and destroy the entire human race, and he wouldn't try to stop you. He wouldn't even care."

Richards glanced at Mr. Darnell. His face still had the same smirk.

Bobby couldn't help but stare at his duplicate. Now the resemblance was less than perfect. In fact, the more he stared, the more obvious the differences became. He realized the thing was changing. The straight brown hair was transforming into longer corkscrew curls, and the eyes were closer together. Before long he was looking at Addison again.

Bobby suddenly felt very tired. He stared at the colonel for a moment, but Richards wouldn't look at him. He shuffled back to the curtain where Carlos waited, and they both passed through it.

First class was much nicer than the rest of the plane. Each seat was actually a booth, the size of four regular seats, and Ashley had already figured out how to turn her seat to the side so it stretched out flat into a bed. She was lying on her side, but she lifted her head when Bobby and Carlos settled into booths across the aisle from her.

"Definitely first class," she said.

Bobby checked out his space. There was a flat TV screen and connectors for plugging in smartphones, laptops, and other gadgets. Headphones were tucked into a cubby, and for the first time in days Bobby wished he had his smartphone so he could fall asleep to music.

Ashley said, "I tried using the phones, but they must be turned off."

A stewardess appeared and offered them sodas. They each took one and chugged them down like they were dying of thirst. The stewardess showed them how to control the personal lights in their booths, and then she turned off the overhead lights. She left them alone in the dark. Within a minute Bobby heard Carlos snoring.

Ashley crushed her empty can and said, "I was thinking. Since we're going straight from Sentani to L.A., it should take about sixteen hours. Papua is sixteen hours ahead of L.A. That means we'll get there at the same time we left."

Bobby considered this, but what really interested him was why Ashley had even said it. On the flight to Papua all those days ago, she would never have talked to him like this. In fact, she hadn't talked to him at all. In the darkness he heard her sigh. She must have thought he was asleep. He wanted her to keep talking, so he said the first thing he could think of. "Addison turned into me."

"Why in the hell would he want to be you?"

"Well, I think he was trying to answer a question that—"

"Jesus, Bobby, it was a joke. I watched you guys through the curtain. Two Bobbies—damn scary."

Bobby sensed that she was smiling, even though it was too dark to see for sure. "Yeah, I was kind of scared."

After some silence, Ashley said, "I'm afraid to go home."

Bobby's seat now lay flat, but he pushed up on one elbow to look at her. His eyes were getting used to the dark, and he saw that she was sitting up. "I know what you mean," he said. "Everything's going to be different."

Ashley pulled her legs out of the narrow space and turned her seat forward. "We're safe now, but they won't let us call home. Why?"

Bobby didn't know the answer to this. "I bet you miss your friends from school, huh?"

"Miranda was my best friend. She's dead."

"What about your boyfriend?"

Ashley was silent for a moment. "Not so much."

She then slid across the aisle and sat on the floor in the space left open by Bobby's swiveled seat. Her face was only inches away, and Bobby felt a tingle through his body.

"What about you? Do you have a girlfriend?" Ashley talked softer now. The low roar of the engines seemed to fade away to nothing.

Bobby felt his face flush and was glad for the darkness. "No, no girlfriend at the moment." In truth, Bobby had never had a girlfriend.

"Saving yourself for the right girl, huh?"

Bobby knew she was teasing him, but he seemed to have lost the ability to talk. He struggled for anything to say other than the thought that was in his head. The seconds were passing by. It was no use. "Actually, I kind of wanted to ask you to be my girlfriend."

Ashley froze. Bobby dug his fingernails into his thigh and cursed himself silently. Why was he such an idiot? But she wasn't laughing at him or cussing him out. Instead, it was like she was thinking. What if she said yes? What would he do then? He had no idea.

And then Ashley did the last thing he expected. She reached out and grabbed his head, leaned over him, and put her mouth on his.

Bobby had never kissed a girl before, although he had practiced against the mirror with the bathroom door locked. Ashley pressed her mouth hard against his. And then he felt the tip of her tongue. He did not dare move his tongue, and she didn't do it again—just that one quick flick of her tongue into his mouth. And then she pulled away.

Bobby watched her. "You kissed me." It was a stupid thing to say.

"If you were a few years older, I'd do it again."

"You're only three years older than me."

Ashley sighed. "You're what, fourteen? You know what will happen when we get home. I'll have my senior friends. You'll have your freshmen friends. I'll say, 'Hi Bobby' when we pass in the hall, but that'll be about it."

She was right, of course. Ashley flopped her head against the side of the seat, and Bobby could smell the hand soap she must have used in her hair in the makeshift shower in the hangar.

"You know, it's funny," she said. "I can't have you for my boyfriend. But if any boyfriend I've ever had were on this trip instead of you, I think we might all be dead."

This didn't seem very funny to Bobby. "Why did you kiss me?" he asked.

She shrugged. "Why did you ask me to be your girlfriend?"

"Because I like you."

"Well, that's why I kissed you. But if you tell anyone, I'll just deny it. Who do you think they'll believe?"

Bobby felt the tingles in his body slipping away, replaced by tension. Best to change the subject. "Do you think we made a mistake, bringing Addison with us?"

She looked at him without answering.

"I'm afraid of what they'll do with him when we get home," he said.

Still she didn't answer.

"He could do something awful, like destroy the whole world."

"I guess we have to trust them to do the right thing," she said.

"I thought I trusted myself to do the right thing, but look what happened at the hospital."

Ashley pulled her leg in from the aisle and sat on her foot. "Maybe we won't even need hospitals anymore. It seems like things can only get better, since the world is so screwed up now."

"Yeah, I guess so." Actually, Bobby didn't think the world was screwed up at all. He had heard people say that, but he'd never understood why.

As Carlos snored in the next booth, they talked about Miranda and Addison and Roberto and Russ. They talked about Samuel and the hanging village and the Papuans who still lived there and the ones who had died. But they didn't talk about home again. Or school. Or boyfriends and girlfriends.

Finally, Ashley yawned and went back to her own booth. Bobby rolled over and closed his eyes. He touched his lips lightly, thinking of the tip of her tongue.

* * *

Mbaiso had labored through the previous day and then had traveled through the night and into the morning. Traveling was slow, because the human following him could not keep up. The man was sluggish and had difficulty negotiating hills and thick undergrowth. But they had finally reached their destination. The tree kangaroo crouched low and peered through a gap in the leaves. Before him was a village with several small huts. A much longer hut stood beyond the smaller ones. Three human women sat around a fire pit between the huts, talking and performing some task with their hands. Five smaller humans laughed and chased each other around the women. Mbaiso watched them playing. In all the centuries of his existence he had rarely seen small children in the hanging village. The villagers there almost never died, and there had been no need for new children to replace them.

Mbaiso turned around and waited for the man to catch up. Finally, he saw movement. As the man plodded slowly up a slope, the array of green lorikeet feathers in his hair could be seen bobbing back and forth. Sinanie came to a stop after nearly tripping over Mbaiso. He looked down at the tree kangaroo with vacant eyes. He said nothing, because he was not capable of speaking.

Mbaiso moved to the side. Sinanie then walked past the tree

kangaroo, pushed through the vegetation, and emerged into the village clearing. Mbaiso remained hidden and watched.

The children saw Sinanie and immediately began yelling and pointing. The women rose to their feet and also began yelling. Other villagers emerged from the huts, mostly men. The tribesmen wore caps of human skin, and their upper bodies bore rows of swollen scars resembling crocodile skin. Several of them carried sharpened spears.

The men gathered around Sinanie. They spoke forcefully to him in their tribe's language.

Sinanie stared at them, but he could not speak.

The tribesmen spoke louder. One of them slapped Sinanie's face but got no response. They turned him and pushed him toward the forest, but Sinanie simply turned back around. One of the men struck Sinanie's head with the side of his spear, knocking him to the ground. Sinanie gathered his feet under him and slowly stood up.

The tribesmen spoke to each other. Abruptly, the men who had brought spears with them turned on Sinanie, thrusting their spears with full force at his neck and face.

Sinanie fell to the ground. The tribesmen stood over him watching until his body stopped moving.

Again the tribesmen spoke to each other. Two of them grabbed Sinanie's body by the ankles and dragged it across the dirt to the edge of the fire pit. The women went to one of the huts and returned with sharpened wedges of bamboo. By this time the entire village had gathered around and they began butchering the body, preparing for an unexpected feast.

Mbaiso was nearly exhausted, but he had no desire to rest so close to these villagers. So he began his journey back. It had taken him most of the previous day to create a copy of Sinanie developed enough to convince the cannibal tribe it was real. There would be enough flesh to feed the entire tribe. And soon after being consumed, the flesh would carry out its intended purpose. The villagers would no longer have any memory of a hanging village that existed only one day's travel up the river.

After moving a good distance away, Mbaiso paused in the lower branches of a fig tree to eat some of its fruits. Again he examined his last array of directives from the creator, and he designated another of them as completed.

CHAPTER SEVEN

Quentin felt someone shaking his shoulder.

"Mr. Darnell. I must speak with you."

Dr. Saskia stood in the aisle next to him. Quentin rubbed his eyes. It felt like he'd been asleep for a very long time. He looked around. Lindsey slept curled up in the next seat. It was still dark outside the windows, but they were descending. Was it possible he had slept longer than twelve hours? He shook his head to clear it. "What is it, Paul?"

The doctor looked at Lindsey and hesitated.

Quentin pulled himself up and moved to another row of seats against the bulkhead separating this area from the larger cabin where most of the others had settled in for the night. Quentin heard Colonel Richards's voice coming from beyond the bulkhead.

Saskia frowned at him. "I woke up some minutes ago, after having the most extraordinary dream. It was a dream, but not a dream, if that makes any sense."

"Yes, it does. Did you move through space and then come to Earth?"

Dr. Sakia blinked. "That is precisely what happened."

"We've all had that dream. That's how the Lamotelokhai explains how it got here. Did your dream end up in a tree in the rainforest?"

"It was in a tree, yes. But it didn't end there. The dream showed you and your friends with it there, and then bringing it to civilization."

Quentin smiled. "I guess that means we're an important part of the story."

Saskia did not smile. "Mr. Darnell, I have always looked at dreams as merely a physiological curiosity. But this dream was unlike any I have ever had. I was entirely lucid."

Quentin considered this. "Paul, you were at the hospital. Addison put his hands on you when you were hurt. Whatever the stuff is that he's made out of got into your system. That's why you had the dream. And there will be more. Just wait until you wake up tomorrow. Do you see why we're trying to get Addison safely to the U.S.?"

"I do, which is why I have come to you now. Colonel Richards has not slept. He talked to Addison all night. He doesn't seem himself."

"He's still at it?" Quentin got up and went forward to the larger cabin. Saskia followed. The other doctors were scattered about, all of them apparently asleep. Richards and Addison still sat where Quentin had last seen them. But the area around them had changed. Some seats were missing, and a few were grotesquely mangled. Bizarre objects were scattered about: a metal watering can, a stack of paper currency at least five inches tall, a large shapeless mass that appeared to be gold, an antique phonograph player, complete with a horn speaker, and several devices that looked like weapons from a science fiction movie. As Quentin stared at these last objects, alarm began constricting his chest.

In the midst of all this sat Richards, talking frantically, his voice now hoarse. Addison patiently listened. Richards glanced up as they approached, but he just went on talking.

"... the extent of my knowledge of the mechanism. But I'm thinking you can fill in the gaps so that we end up with a functional device. Do you think that's possible?"

Addison's face was expressionless. "Yes. But the device then may not be what you desire it to be. My own ideas for design are different from yours."

Richards waved his hand in exaggerated dismissal. "That doesn't matter. Once it is functional, we'll deconstruct it. Then we can make them ourselves."

"What's going on here?" Quentin asked.

Richards turned. "I thought you were sleeping."

Saskia was right; Richards was not himself. There was no sign of his typical self-control.

"We were. We slept a long time. Dr. Saskia says you've been at this all night." Quentin waved at the strange objects. "Colonel, what is all this?"

Richards looked at the area. "I have learned a great deal about the capabilities of this young man." He looked at his watch. "And there is precious little time before we touch down."

As if on cue, an electronic ding came from above, followed by the pilot's voice announcing that they were approaching LAX and they should move to their seats. Richards turned back to Addison.

Quentin picked up one of the peculiar science fiction devices. It was heavy and solid in his hands. "Colonel, this looks like a weapon. Please tell me you didn't ask Addison to make these. That's not at all why—"

Richards swung around to face him. "I'm trying to learn what is possible here. If you honestly think that all possibilities will not be explored when the experts get their hands on him, then you are goddamn naïve. Put that down before you hurt yourself."

Quentin couldn't believe what he was hearing. Richards had ignored all their warnings. After staring at the colonel for a moment, Quentin looked at the weapon in his hands. Suddenly it became clear beyond any doubt that Samuel had been right. Men like Richards were simply not equipped to deal with the Lamotelokhai. Perhaps no one was. Quentin's fingers trembled with anger—anger at himself and anger at Richards for so brazenly proving him wrong. Richards glared, looking from Quentin's eyes to the weapon. Quentin realized Richards was afraid. This had to mean that the weapon was real, which only intensified Quentin's disgust. He had to do something.

Quentin fumbled with the weapon and found a trigger. He raised the thing and pointed it at Richards. "Colonel, your time with Addison is over."

Richards shifted in his seat like he was preparing to lunge at Quentin. But he sat tight. Dr. Saskia stumbled into a row of seats and crouched against one of the windows.

Richards started to speak, but Quentin cut him off. "I said you're done! You can sit over there until we land." Quentin nodded toward the far side of the cabin.

Richards closed his eyes as if trying to calm himself. "You're making a mistake, Darnell. Place the weapon on the floor now."

Quentin took a threatening step closer. The device felt warm in his hands now, as if responding to his intentions. "Addison, please move away from Colonel Richards. I have reason to believe he should not be allowed to talk to you."

Addison stood up and moved away.

Richards's face grew dark with anger. "You have goddamn nerve, Darnell, I'll give you that. But your behavior is ill advised. I've made progress here. Can't you see that?" He pointed to the odd assortment of objects around him. "Did you know your son could change common materials into just about anything? Even gold!"

Quentin still pointed the weapon at him. "As a matter of fact, I did know that. But compared to his other abilities, that's not important. And it's not important compared to what he knows. He has been here for half a billion years, and he has collected—"

Quentin stopped. Something wasn't right. Richards's eyes had shifted to the side, looking over Quentin's shoulder. And then his head nodded almost imperceptibly. Before Quentin could turn, he was hit from behind. Two arms shot around his shoulders, grabbed the weapon, and pulled it up over his head. Quentin fought to hold on to it.

"Release the weapon, Darnell!" The voice was inches from his ear. It was William Kessel, the Navy medical officer.

Quentin pulled the weapon back down to the level of his face. He let go with his right hand and thrust his elbow into Kessel's gut. The man grunted and doubled over, forcing his hand to pull hard on the weapon. Quentin felt the trigger move.

There was a low pulsing sound that Quentin felt more than he heard. For a brief moment that sound was all he was aware of. And then the world around him exploded. Deafened by the roar of rushing air, Quentin watched in disbelief as loose items flew upward and out a massive hole in the ceiling. Kessel's arms were now around Quenton's waist, holding on to him instead of the weapon. Quentin looked at Richards. The man seemed confused as the debris around him was sucked upward. His eyes met Quentin's, and then he was lifted off the floor. His head struck the edge of the opening, and his body flipped over and shot straight up and out the hole. Quentin watched it rise through an upper cabin he didn't even know was there to a second hole above that. Then the rushing air above the plane ripped the body from view with terrifying force. Quentin stared at the gaping hole. For a brief moment he actually saw stars in the night sky where Richards had disappeared.

The suction threatened to pull Quentin off his feet, and he suddenly realized the only reason he still lived was that Kessell now held his legs tight against one of the seats.

Bobby sat up and banged his shoulder on the wall of his booth. Something was terribly wrong. The plane shook like it was falling apart, and a deafening roar hurt his ears. Emergency lights now cast a red glow throughout the first class cabin, and Bobby saw that Carlos and Ashley were sitting up too. Ashley tried to say something, but he could barely hear her.

Bobby leaned over and looked out the window. Instead of the solid black of night, he saw an ocean of yellow lights below them. They were over a large city and were dropping fast. The stewardess ran by them, her wide eyes emphasized by the red light of the cabin.

Bobby made his way toward the rear of the plane. The floor shook so much that he had to clutch the booths to stay on his feet. He entered the larger cabin and squinted against the brightness of the lights that were still on. At the far end the ceiling was torn wide open, and air gushed through the hole, carrying all kinds of debris with it.

The plane suddenly pitched, dropping even faster. Bobby lost his balance and tumbled backwards, hitting the floor. As he gasped for breath, he realized the air in the cabin was very thin. He pulled himself up. The plane's motion had jarred some of the overhead storage bins open, and now blankets and pillows flew out the hole in the ceiling.

Most of the doctors were there, clinging to seats and staring at the hole above, but the teachers were gone. And then Bobby spotted Mr. Darnell, directly under the hole, trying to get through a doorway, holding on to whatever he could. Mr. Darnell turned and saw Bobby. He yelled something. Bobby couldn't hear the words, but from the look on his face he knew it was: "I'm sorry." And then Mr. Darnell went through the doorway and was gone.

The plane lurched again and Bobby fought to stay on his feet.

Ashley grabbed his arm from behind and yelled, "You need to come back and buckle in!"

Bobby nodded. "Go! I'll be right there."

Their eyes met. She was terrified. They were going to crash and Ashley knew it.

"I have to find Addison!" Bobby yelled. "I'll be there in a second."

Ashley nodded and released his arm.

Bobby turned around and scanned the cabin. He spotted Addison, sitting against the outer wall. He was alone, and he looked very small amidst the violence around him.

Gripping seats hand over hand, Bobby made his way to Addison and crouched beside him. He looked past Addison out the window and saw rows of airport runway lights. But the plane was dropping far too fast. It was literally falling toward the lights.

"We're going to crash," Bobby cried into Addison's ear. "Please help!"

"I cannot stop this," Addison said.

Bobby felt faint. "Can't you fix the plane?"

Addison glanced at the huge hole above. "Not in time to stop this."

Bobby looked out the window. Addison was right. There was no time.

"I don't want to die, Addison! I wanted to help you do what you came here to do!"

Addison's face showed no expression, but his eyes shifted to a now-familiar golden yellow. He seemed to be thinking. He let go of the seat and held Bobby's shoulders. "I cannot stop this. But perhaps you can have what you want."

Bobby blinked away tears that were filling his eyes. What did that mean? Suddenly everything went gray. The noise of the plane was gone, and he felt nothing but peace and quiet. But then the earsplitting rush of air was back, and with it his fear.

Addison was smiling. "Do not be afraid."

Bobby took his last look out the window and raised his arms to protect his face.

CHAPTER EIGHT

Nine minutes earlier

With Dr. Saskia behind him, Quentin approached Richards and Addison. Some of the seats around them were either missing or oddly deformed, and Quentin stared at a strange assortment of objects scattered around. Among the objects there was money, and even gold. And there were several long devices that looked like futuristic weapons. Obviously Richards had used Addison to create these. What the hell was the man thinking?

Richards talked frantically to Addison and hardly noticed as they approached. It sounded like he was discussing plans for creating some kind of device. Richards seemed almost frantic, speaking rapidly with a voice hoarse from overuse. Dr. Saskia had been right—Richards was not himself.

Quentin stepped closer, preparing to say something, when suddenly he had to steady himself against one of the seats. His vision went gray, as if he were about to faint, but his thoughts were still coherent. There was simply an absence of senses. No sight, no sound, just awareness. It was actually serene. But the moment passed, and the disturbing scene was back.

"What's going on here?" Quentin asked.

Richards turned to them. "I thought you were sleeping."

"We were. We slept for a long time. Dr. Saskia says you've been at this all night. Colonel, what is all this?"

"I've learned a great deal about the capabilities of this young man, Mr. Darnell. And there is precious little time left."

An electronic ding sounded from above, followed by the pilot's voice saying they were approaching LAX.

Quentin picked up one of the weapon-like devices. "Colonel, this looks like a gun. Did you have Addison make this? This is not why he's here."

Richards's sighed loudly. "You're being naïve if you think such possibilities won't be explored. Put the weapon down. You have no idea how to handle it."

Quentin did not put it down. His anger threatened to consume him. How could he have been so wrong? They should have never tried to bring the Lamotelokhai to the United States. He turned to Saskia. The doctor shook his head, unable to offer any help. But his eyes flitted nervously to the weapon in Quentin's hands. Quentin looked around the cabin, hoping some kind of solution might suddenly appear. Most of the doctors were still sleeping. But the Navy doctor, William Kessel, was sitting up, watching them with interest.

Struggling to contain his anger, Quentin examined the device in his hands. He was disgusted that Addison had been used to create such a thing. He found the trigger, then tightened his grip on it and pointed it at Richards.

Before Richards saw the threat, another ding came from above, and then the pilot's voice. "Folks, due to a situation on the ground at LAX, we are being re-routed to Long Beach Airport a short distance to the south. We'll be changing course momentarily so please fasten your seatbelts."

Quentin relaxed his grip on the weapon and placed it on the floor. What could possibly force such an important flight to change course? The plane tipped to one side, shifting its direction. Quentin looked out the downward-facing windows and saw the vast expanse of lights that was Los Angeles, and the parallel runway lights of LAX below. And then he saw it. Sprawled amidst the lights was the carnage of a catastrophe. Patches of fire and flashing lights illuminated scattered wreckage.

"Sweet Jesus!" It was Richards. He had moved to one of the windows next to Quentin.

A stewardess brushed past them, her face etched with concern.

Richards stopped her. "Ma'am! What happened down there?"

"We don't have details yet, sir." She rushed off toward the rear of the plane.

Quentin turned back to the window. The wreckage was scattered over a huge area, as if a plane had literally splashed onto the ground.

"It was our airplane."

They turned to face Addison.

"What are you talking about?" Richards demanded.

Addison looked at Quentin. "The airplane that crashed was this one, Dad. You pointed the weapon at Roger Richards. You wanted him to stop talking to me. William Kessel tried to take the weapon from you. The weapon was activated. This damaged the airplane, and the airplane crashed."

A hollow numbness grew in Quentin's gut.

"That's nonsense!" Richards said. "We're still here, aren't we?"

Addison's voice was calm. "Before the airplane crashed, Bobby asked me to fix the damaged airplane. I could not. He convinced me to do something else instead. So I made a change in the space near the airplane. The change made a second airplane, from an earlier moment in time. I did this so that Bobby might still exist to do what he wanted to do." Addison gazed at Quentin. "You have experienced such a change before."

"Yes." The numbness in Quentin's gut turned into an icy chill.

"Who was on that plane?" Richards said, pointing out the window.

"We were on it," Addison said. "It was the same airplane. You were ejected from the airplane before it crashed. The weapon you asked me to create damaged the airplane, and you were almost certainly killed."

"Sweet Jesus," Richards repeated.

Out the window, the burning wreckage slipped from view. Quentin struggled to grasp the meaning of Addison's words. They were all killed?

"We can't land at another airport," Richards said. He seemed to be talking to himself, but then he turned to Quentin. "There was a team of doctors and other specialists waiting for our arrival, not to mention a Special Forces unit to provide security. We'll be vulnerable if we land anywhere else." Richards pulled his smartphone from his belt and started to punch in a number. "We need to mobilize them."

Quentin stepped up and placed his hand on the phone. "Colonel, consider what just happened. We were killed. I fired the weapon that caused the crash, but you're the one who had Addison create it in the first place. The point is it happened. And it will happen again. People get intoxicated with what the Lamotelokhai can do. Your team of experts won't be immune to that. You told me yourself they would use Addison to make weapons. You don't honestly believe this gift was sent for that reason, do you?"

"I have no evidence your son's capabilities are a gift of any kind, nor that he is an extraterrestrial."

Quentin refused to give up. "You'll see evidence of that soon. You'd know it now if you'd slept during the night. But my point is that you now know what can happen. You saw the disaster at the hospital, and now your own mistake has caused the deaths of everyone on this plane."

"We are not dead," Richards said.

"We're just copies of ourselves!" Quentin struggled to control his voice. "Tell me, Colonel—this team of experts—do you believe they have plans to immediately share Addison's gifts with the rest of the world so that everyone can make decisions about its use? Or will they confine the investigation to a group of people who might first consider the benefits to the United States?"

Richards seemed to actually think about this. "Your second assumption is likely."

Quentin lowered his voice. "Addison is capable of shifting time and space, for God's sake. Think of the chaos he could create if the wrong people control him."

Richards studied Quentin's face for a moment. "Alright, Darnell. What do you suggest?"

BOBBY AWOKE to the pilot's voice—something about landing at a different airport. He'd slept through most of the flight. The cabin lights came on, and he squinted against the brightness. Carlos and Ashley were stirring, too. Ashley mumbled something he couldn't understand, and then their late-night conversation came back to him. And so did the kiss.

"We can't be there already," Ashley said.

Carlos headed for the restrooms, leaving Bobby alone with Ashley.

Ashley gazed at him. "Let's agree not to act weird about things, okay?"

Bobby was relieved that she brought it up first. "I'll pretend nothing happened if you keep thinking about what I asked you," he said. "Maybe someday you'll change your mind."

Addison came in and stood in the aisle between them. "Something has happened. Roger Richards asked me to create things. I did. One of the things was a weapon. Dad did not like this. He picked up the weapon and William Kessel tried to take it away. The weapon was activated, and it damaged the airplane. Bobby, you asked me to repair the damage, but I could not repair it before the plane crashed to the surface. Before it crashed, you asked me if I could do something that might allow you to continue living. So I did. What I did created a second airplane. The first airplane crashed. This probably killed everyone on that airplane. But on this airplane you may live to accomplish what you want."

Addison had spoken clearly, but Bobby struggled to understand. Perhaps his brain wasn't awake yet. He turned to Ashley for help, but she looked just as dumbfounded. Slowly, Addison's words sank in and Bobby's skin began to prickle.

Carlos came back in and stopped when he saw their faces. "What's going on?"

"Plans are being made," Addison said. "You should come with me now." He turned and walked away.

"Addison made a copy of our airplane, and the other one crashed," Bobby told Carlos. "We all died." Bobby turned away from Carlos's baffled gape and followed Addison.

QUENTIN WOKE Lindsey and did his best to explain the events. As she listened she nodded a few times but then held up one hand and shook her head as if unwilling to hear any more of it. Quentin sat next to her and waited patiently.

A few minutes later she said, "I want to be strong. I do. For you. For the students. But I don't know if I can handle any more. How am I supposed to respond to this? I died—we all died—in a plane crash? What the hell, Quentin?" She turned away and stared out the window.

Quentin had no answers. So he simply sat with his hand on her knee as the plane descended toward the Long Beach Airport. Minutes later they touched down. Lindsey turned back to Quentin and silently motioned for him to get up. They joined Richards and the doctors in the main cabin.

Colonel Richards seemed genuinely disturbed by the turn of events, and he now freely revealed what he knew. As he talked, Quentin became aware of the magnitude of their mistake in bringing the Lamotelokhai here. Richards admitted that government officials were planning to keep everything a secret until they fully understood what they were dealing with, which Quentin assumed would be a very long time. The Jayapura hospital conflict had been reported as an unfortunate skirmish, with no mention of dinosaurs or anything else out of the ordinary. The only ones who knew about their flight to Los Angeles were the hastily assembled homeland security officials, government doctors, and armed security men awaiting them. But the plane this team waited for had crashed. To Quentin, the ensuing confusion represented a window of opportunity—a chance to somehow correct his mistake. And Richards now seemed to agree.

"We have to make the general population aware of Addison, before he is sequestered into secrecy." Richards said.

Quentin nodded. "You're willing to help us do that?"

"I told you before, I'm slow but not stupid. It's not every day a man responsible for killing himself and those around him has the chance to reflect on it postmortem." He glanced at his watch. "Let's assume what your son says is true. An exact copy of our plane and our own bodies are smeared over the LAX tarmac. You can be damn sure the homeland security folks are going ape-shit. Those boys will be up our asses in a few minutes—fifteen tops. We have to get you off this plane and to a public place."

"Why a public place? Shouldn't we just hide out somewhere until we figure out what to do?"

Richards shook his head. "You stated yourself that you don't want your son controlled by only a few individuals. So hiding out with him is a bad idea, unless you feel you are the only ones qualified to work with him."

"No," Quentin said. "We don't think that."

"Then what you want is a media blitz in a public place—show the whole world. If everyone knows about your son, it'll be a hell of a lot harder to secretly misuse him."

"He's right," Lindsey said. "Everyone needs to know."

Addison and the students emerged from the forward cabin and joined them as the plane lurched to a stop. Quentin looked out the windows. They were on the tarmac rather than connecting to a gate. Airport vehicles with flashing yellow lights rushed here and there, but he saw no military or police vehicles approaching their plane.

"We have to get off the plane," Quentin said.

The Navy doctor, Captain William Kessel, had approached them as they talked. "There's no reason to leave this plane now," he said. "A team of specialists will arrive momentarily. They'll transport you and provide anything you need."

"Pardon me, Bill." Richards pushed his way past Kessel from behind. He was carrying one of the weapons Addison had created. In his other hand was a large stack of bills. Richards ignored Kessel and spoke to Quentin. "We may need these."

Quentin wanted nothing to do with the weapon. "Please leave that here. In fact, it should be destroyed."

Richards knotted his brows, but then he nodded and handed the weapon to Addison. "Your father would like you to disable this device. And the others, too, if you would."

Addison took the weapon, but he did not move away until Bobby nodded at him.

Kessel said, "Colonel, what exactly are you planning to do?"

"Bill, there are portions of this story you don't know, and I have no time to explain."

Kessel pulled out his smartphone and started punching in a number.

"There's no point in trying to stop him," Richards said to Quentin. "They're on their way here anyway. We have to go." Richards moved to a hatch marked *Exit*. He gripped the handle.

Kessel paused his phone conversation. "Colonel, we have orders to wait on this plane until a team arrives. Please don't touch that hatch."

The pilot's voice came from above. "Folks, there seems to be a large scale security alert due to an incident at LAX. We'll have to sit tight for a spell. Shortly, security personnel will board the aircraft for what we hope is a brief inspection. Due to the specialized nature of this flight, I assume this is merely a formality. Until then, though, the plane will be locked down. Please make yourselves as comfortable as possible."

Richards leveraged his full weight against the hatch's handle, but it didn't move. They were stuck.

Quentin thought of the colonel's words: '...*a media blitz...show the whole world at once...*' Richards was right, and he seemed willing to jeopardize his career to help. If there was to be any chance of making the Lamotelokhai public, they had to act now. Quentin signaled Bobby to follow him down the aisle to where Addison knelt by the weapons, which were now malformed masses of metal and plastic. Quentin bent down and nodded for Bobby to do the same. He kept his voice low. "Addison, we need your help again. It is important that we get you off this plane and take you somewhere else. But the doors are locked."

Addison gazed at him with no indication that he understood.

"Bobby, can you explain?" Quentin said.

"I don't know what you want him to do," Bobby whispered.

"I don't know, exactly. Maybe he could do what he did to Colonel Richards yesterday."

Before Bobby could answer, Addison spoke up. "I moved Roger Richards to a space that I knew of because I had walked there. I do not know of the space outside this airplane."

Quentin glanced up at the others. They were focused on Kessel's phone conversation. "Do you think you could know the space outside by looking out the windows? We really have to go now!"

"Yes. But it will be safer for you if I know of the area by walking there."

Then Addison was gone. Quentin was so close that he felt the air whoosh through his hair as it filled the vacuum with a loud pop. He blinked. But before he fully understood what had happened, Addison was back.

"Now I know of the space outside the airplane," he said. "It will be safer for you."

Bobby touched Addison's arm. "Whoa!"

"Mr. Darnell?" It was Kessel.

Quentin looked up. The doctors stared directly at him, apparently alerted by the popping air of Addison's departure. But their view of Addison was at least partially blocked by seats. Quentin hoped they had not seen Addison reappear. Quentin grabbed one of the mangled weapons and held it up for them to see. "Looks like we don't have to worry about these any longer."

The doctors seemed to buy this, but Richards knew something was up. He moved to their position and knelt with them as if he were inspecting the weapons. "In minutes we're going to be neck deep in personnel," he said.

Quentin looked at Addison. "Can you do it?"

"Yes."

Quentin stood and faced the others. Lindsey was listening to Kessel's conversation, but she eyed Quentin warily. He motioned for her to grab Ashley and Carlos and join them.

"What's going on?" Lindsey said when they were all together.

"Addison thinks he can—" Quentin stopped. There was no need to finish the statement. They were already on the ground. Quentin's ears popped as they adjusted to the different air pressure. The roar of idling jet engines assaulted his senses. He gasped and his lungs filled with the warm, coastal night air of Los Angeles. He looked up. They were directly beneath the belly of the massive jet.

"Sweet Jesus, he did it!" Richards cried. He grabbed Quentin's shoulder and shouted, "Follow me!" He pointed to the terminal and waved for them all to follow.

As they moved away from the plane, Quentin turned to look up. Staring at them through one of the jet's windows was Dr. Saskia, a broad smile on his face. In the window next to him was the face of Captain William Kessel, wearing a look that was as far from a smile as it could have been.

Getting teleported somewhere wasn't what Bobby thought it would be. There was no tingly feeling, just the sudden noise from the planes. And the air was different. It smelled like oil and pollution.

But there was no time to think about this. They were running, following Colonel Richards. The colonel understood now how dangerous the Lamotelokhai was. Bobby was starting to wonder if anyone would be able to use the Lamotelokhai without killing people.

As soon as they entered the terminal, an airport security guard stopped them. The guy stared at them, and Bobby realized they must look pretty strange. Except for Colonel Richards, they all wore the plastic flip-flops and blue shirts and pants from the hospital. They looked like mental patients on a field trip.

Richards took charge. "I'm Colonel Roger Richards, from the U.S. Embassy, Indonesia." He opened a wallet and showed an ID. "These civilians I am escorting have suffered an appalling ordeal, and it has been rendered worse by a diversion to an alternate airport. I'm procuring a rental vehicle and getting them the hell out of here."

The guard asked to see everyone's identification.

The colonel scowled. "As I said, these people have just been through an ordeal. They've lost their possessions and have been transported back to the States on a military-sanctioned flight. There are special circumstances involved." Richards glanced at his watch and looked around the terminal. "Look, son. We're taking your valuable time. You obviously have a situation on your hands here. Here's my card." He pulled a white card from his wallet. "Feel free to confirm my objective, but I've got to get these people to their destination." Richards then nodded at them to follow him. The man stepped aside and let them go.

Soon they were out the front doors. They following the *Ground Transportation* signs and headed across a street lined with waiting taxicabs. They stopped briefly on a divider and then darted across another three lanes and into a parking lot filled with rental cars. They approached the glass-fronted building. "We're not in the clear yet," Richards said. "We need to secure a rental before the place is overrun."

At that moment, screaming sirens filled the air. Police cars pulled up in front of the terminal on the far side of the street. Behind the police cars was a string of black SUVs. If they had crossed the street only seconds later, they would have been directly in the cars' headlights.

"Time's up," Richards said.

They entered the rental building and moved to a row of seats hidden from the front windows by one of the counters. Richards stood at the counter and rented a vehicle. Bobby peeked over the counter to watch the activity across the street. Men piled out of the vehicles and ran into the terminal. Four men in suits waited outside with the vehicles, but then one of them pointed across the street. They started walking toward the building.

"Colonel Richards!" Bobby hissed. "Those men are coming."

Richards pushed a paper across the counter and snatched up a key that was lying there. "Please take us to our vehicle," he said to the woman behind the counter. "We're late."

They left through a door on the side of the building just as the men finished crossing the street. They were led to a red minivan. The rental lady started doing some kind of inspection, but Richards hastily signed a clipboard and waved her away. As they piled into the van, the four men came out the side door of the building and one of them spotted Colonel Richards. The man pointed at them and yelled something.

Richards mumbled a curse. "I'll have to talk to these boys. As soon as I get them out of view, you get the hell out of here." He dumped some things that Bobby couldn't see onto the driver's seat and tossed the key to Mr. Darnell. "Remember, a media blitz. Whatever it takes, make it happen." Then he closed the door and walked toward the men.

Mr. Darnell climbed into the driver's seat, moving the things Richards had put there under his seat. Mrs. Darnell and Ashley still stood outside the sliding door, and they quickly got in.

Richards tried guiding the men back to the building, but it didn't work. They continued toward the van. Richards waved his arms for them to drive away. Mrs. Darnell slammed the sliding door shut as the van backed out of its slot. Then the men were there, just outside, looking in. The locks popped down as one of them reached for the door.

"Sir, please open the door," the man said.

For a second, Mr. Darnell looked like he might unlock the doors. But Colonel Richards was waving like mad. The van leapt forward.

Bobby turned around. The men were running after them. They almost caught up as they turned a corner at the end of the row. But then the van sped up and bounced through an exit onto a street. They made a few more turns and then merged onto a ten-lane highway.

For several minutes everyone sat in silence. They were running away from the government, probably the FBI. There would be APBs and roadblocks, maybe even helicopters.

Ashley finally broke the silence. "Okay, now what?"

* * *

"I IMAGINE it's too late to go back and apologize," Lindsey said as she moved up into the empty passenger seat.

Quentin shook his head. "Richards was right. We have to let everyone know. He probably gave up his career to help us do this. We can't go back now."

"Then what do you suggest?" Lindsey said. "Those men have already called for help. They know what we're driving. We'll be stopped in no time."

"Lindsey, please," Quentin said. "I just need some time to figure this out." He stared at the road before him and tried to focus on the problem. Richards had suggested a media blitz, but it would take time to arrange that. Even if they managed to convince a TV station to interview them, one station could be suppressed. The story may never get out. It would have to be an organized event, where multiple TV stations would be willing to broadcast live. In order to arrange an event like that they needed ideas and they needed time.

"We go home," he said at last. "We arrange a media event in Newton."

There was a moment of silence.

"How are we going to get all the way to Missouri?" Lindsey said.

Quentin had no idea, so he didn't bother answering. But if they stayed on the interstate, they would be spotted. He exited onto Westminster Boulevard. According to the compass on the van's console, they were headed east. Quentin did some calculations. Los Angeles was at least 1,700 miles from Missouri. That was close to thirty hours of continuous driving, more if they were cautious and took minor roads.

"Quentin?" Lindsey was still waiting for him to respond.

"We're driving to Missouri," Quentin said. "We'll take the back roads. It will give us time to arrange a media event there, something so big that no one can do anything about it."

"Why can't we arrange something like that here?"

Ashley spoke up. "Just have Addison make a T-Rex, or have him make a skyscraper disappear or something like that. Then you'll have your media event."

"We can't," Bobby said. "We've killed too many people already. It happens every time."

Everyone was silent. Bobby was right. Based on their previous experiences it would be reckless to ask the Lamotelokhai to do anything spectacular, particularly in a densely populated area. After privately stewing over discrepant events of past days, Quentin had made a reluctant conclusion about what waited for them in Newton. If he was right, and if they showed up there on live television, it would draw serious attention without blindly requesting another ill-advised action from Addison.

In his mirror Quentin saw Addison sitting quietly in the back of the van, gazing out the window like a normal teenage boy. By itself the Lamotelokhai was passive and posed no threat. It simply granted any request. But the minds of humans made it a horrifying menace.

"Taking it to Newton is the best idea we have," Quentin said.

Lindsey gazed at him. "Alright, then. We're going to need road maps and clothes for everyone. We don't exactly blend in with these clothes. The most immediate problem is that they know what vehicle we're in. I suggest we get another one."

Carlos spoke up. "Maybe we can change this one's color. I bet Addison can do that."

"Jesus," Quentin said. "Have you guys done this before?"

He stopped at an all-night convenience store. It would take time to initiate a large-scale search, so it was best to make a stop now. The gas tank was nearly full, but Quentin wanted to top it off anyway. He peeled some bills from the stack Richards had given him. They were all twenties. Once inside the store, he found a rack of t-shirts and grabbed six of them. There were no road maps to be found, but he loaded his arms with drink bottles and snacks and dumped everything in front of the bulletproof glass that protected the gray-haired man behind the counter. Quentin pulled the bills from the pocket of his hospital pants and inspected them. They looked real enough. He thumbed through them. *Oh crap.* They all had the same serial number.

Quentin glanced at the cashier, but the man was busy ringing up the purchase. He casually wrinkled several bills so they wouldn't look so similar. As he waited, three teenagers entered the store. They eyed Quentin's hospital clothes for a moment then laughed and mumbled to each other. Quentin silently willed the cashier to hurry.

The total was over eighty dollars. Quentin slid six bills under the glass, telling the cashier he wanted twenty dollars worth of gas. He held his breath as the guy thumbed through them, counting, and then finally stuffed them into the register drawer. Quentin got his change, scooped up the items, and left. The van took only eight dollars of gas, but he drove away without going back in.

They drove for another half hour, making their way northeast using the van's compass. Lindsey turned on the radio and flipped through some stations. Disembodied voices described the LAX plane crash. All those on board the unscheduled flight from Indonesia were killed. Beyond that, the voices had little more to say. The number and identities of passengers were still unknown. The purpose of the flight, unknown. The cause of the crash, unknown. No mention of a duplicate plane or a search for fugitives. Hearing reports of their own deaths was unnerving, so Quentin switched the radio off.

It was now midnight, and they had not yet made it beyond the suburbs of Los Angeles. If the police had been notified, it was only a matter of time before they were stopped. The van had no GPS, so Quentin stopped again to get a road map. This time he found a larger store—a truck stop—and parked the van in the shadows behind the main building.

Lindsey and Ashley had to use the toilet. They put on t-shirts from the previous stop. Both displayed a gold logo for Cuervo tequila. With their hospital pants and flip-flops, this hardly improved their credibility. Quentin gave them a wad of bills and warned them about the identical serial numbers. Then they walked around the corner of the building and were gone.

Unable to think of anything else, Quentin counted 470 seconds until they returned. They had a handful of state highway maps and pairs of shorts for everyone.

Ashley tossed the shorts into the van. "The guy said we're only a block from Pomona Freeway, which goes east to Interstate 10. That will take us all the way to Arizona."

"Bobby?" Lindsey said. "Do you think you can get Addison to change the van's color?"

"You can ask him yourself," Bobby said. "He's right here."

Lindsey hesitated. "Okay. Addison, can you do that?"

Addison stepped out of the van. He held his hand against the red paint on the sliding door. "Yes," he said. "What color would you like it to be?"

Lindsey looked around. She pointed at the building's cinderblock wall. "I'd like it to be white like that wall."

Addison stared at the wall, his hand still on the van. The paint under his hand changed. Slowly an asymmetrical area of white began spreading. He pulled his hand from the van and looked at Lindsey, expressionless.

She shook her head. "I guess I shouldn't be surprised."

When the others were in, they closed the sliding door. Quentin pulled the van onto the street. By the time he merged onto Pomona Freeway, he could see the white color expanding across the vehicle's blunt hood.

THEY DROVE by the San Bernardino Mountains, but it was too dark for Bobby to see much. Eventually, flashing lights lit up the night ahead. A roadblock. They exited onto a smaller road before being trapped. They didn't know if the roadblock was for them, but the Darnells didn't want to take the chance.

Several hours later, Mr. Darnell stopped to get gas again. After filling up, he headed to the restroom. No one else had to go. But a minute later Bobby changed his mind. He left the van and passed through rows of bright candies and chips and automotive stuff until he found the restrooms in the back.

As he entered he heard a voice from one of the stalls. "It was four years ago, the first day of spring break. That's exactly how she said it. You remember." There was a pause. "Like I said, because I was there."

It was Mr. Darnell's voice. Bobby stepped up to one of the urinals, trying to be quiet.

"All I ask is that you have an open mind," Mr. Darnell said. "Think about what I've told you. I could go on, but I don't have time. We should be there sometime tomorrow, maybe thirty or so hours from now. We're coming, regardless." A pause. "Please don't do that. That might create results you really don't want. If anyone calls or comes there before we do, just claim that you don't know anything about this." Another pause. "Please help us."

Bobby finished peeing and backed quietly away from the urinal. But the urinal detected his movement and flushed loudly. The stall door popped open, and Mr. Darnell stepped out. He had a smartphone to his ear.

"I have to go now," he said. He switched off the phone and put it in his pocket. "Bobby, is everything alright?"

Bobby couldn't look him in the eye. "Yeah, it's fine. Just had to use the bathroom." Bobby went to the sink and washed his hands.

"This phone is from Colonel Richards. He gave it to me when he gave me the money."

"I didn't know you had a phone," Bobby said.

"I thought it might be best if we didn't talk about it."

Bobby pushed a lever for a paper towel. "Who were you talking to?"

Mr. Darnell opened the door and nodded for him to go on out. "Just trying to get help from someone I know."

CHAPTER NINE

The hours dragged on as they drove east. Orange clouds began to glow on the horizon ahead. Carlos was sleeping, so Bobby talked to Addison.

"What happened to the other Addison when the plane crashed? Are there two Lamotelokhai now?"

Addison stared out the window at the darkness as he answered. "No. The Lamotelokhai on the other plane allowed itself to be destroyed."

"How do you allow yourself to be destroyed?"

"By changing the properties of my parts."

"That's not a very good answer," Bobby said. "It's kind of like not answering at all."

Addison turned to him. "It would require much talking to explain. I decided that you would probably not want to do that. Was I wrong?"

"No, you were right," Bobby said. "Could you survive a plane crash if you wanted to?"

"Yes."

"Those people on the other plane—were they copies of us, or are we copies of them?"

"The other Bobby was the same as you," Addison said. "There were no differences."

"It makes a difference to me. Am I the original Bobby, or just a copy?"

"There were no differences. But now the other is dead and you are alive. That is the difference now."

"So I have to go the rest of my life thinking I'm just a copy of someone? That really sucks."

Addison's eyes glinted orange from the sky ahead. Or maybe they were shifting colors again. "Something that really sucks is a bad thing, isn't it?"

"Yeah, it is." Then Bobby said. "Why do you make your eyes change colors sometimes?"

This time, Addison's eyes really did shift to golden yellow. "My creators enhanced their talking with colors. I thought it might help you to know when I am thinking carefully about something. Would you like me to stop?"

"No. I mean I don't care. But if you want people to think you're a normal person, maybe don't do it."

Addison gazed at him with blue eyes.

"I want to know more about Peter Wooley," Bobby said. "Colonel Richards said he invented Kembalimo. Did he learn Kembalimo from you?"

"My knowledge of Kembalimo is only what I have heard in your talking. Peter Wooley talked to me using the same symbols you did when you first talked to me. He probably made Kembalimo based on those symbols."

"Why did the Papuans try to kill him?"

"The Papuans believed Peter would take me away. They did not want him to do that."

Bobby considered this. "But they let us take you away."

"Because of you, Bobby."

Bobby felt a tingle on the back of his neck. "Why me?"

"You knew how to talk to me when you came to them. Because of that they knew, and I knew, that it was time."

"Time for what?"

"Time for what is next."

Bobby frowned. "And what is next?"

"I cannot know what is next, Bobby. What would you like to happen next?"

Bobby sighed. "It's not up to me. I'm just a kid."

Addison turned back to the window to watch the growing dawn.

Bobby's thoughts returned to Peter. All those years ago he had found the hanging village and the Lamotelokhai. And after leaving —or escaping—he had created Kembalimo, one of the biggest networked learning programs ever. He didn't do it to make money, so why?

Then Bobby had an idea. "We need to call Peter Wooley," he said out loud. "Mr. Darnell, can we use the phone?"

Ashley perked up. "We have a phone?"

"Quentin, you have a phone?" Mrs. Darnell's voice was low and cold.

Mr. Darnell looked in the rearview mirror, right at Bobby. The orange sky ahead lit up his eyes. "Richards gave me the money and his phone. Yes, I have his phone."

There was an uncomfortable silence.

"I could call my parents," Ashley said. "Why didn't you say we had a phone?"

Mr. Darnell let go of the wheel and held both of his hands up, like he was surrendering. "Yes, I have a phone! I didn't say anything because I wanted to avoid this."

"My parents need to know I'm not dead," Ashley said.

"They already know you're not dead!" Mr. Darnell actually yelled, and it shocked everyone.

Mrs. Darnell kept her voice low. "How do you know that?"

He shook his head. "I didn't want to say anything before, because I wasn't sure. But now I am. They know she's alive because she isn't missing."

Everyone was quiet now.

He went on. "It wasn't a coincidence that the Twin Otter crashed. It was caused by something Samuel did with the Lamotelokhai. A copy of our plane was created. An exact copy, except that ours was damaged in the process. The other Twin Otter was fine. It didn't crash."

Again it was quiet.

"That's why there were no search planes looking for us."

"We don't know that," Ashley said. "I want to call home anyway."

Carlos was awake now. "I want to call home too."

"Actually, we do know for sure," Mr. Darnell said. "I called."

"You called who, Quentin?" Mrs. Darnell said.

He stared at the road ahead.

"Quentin!"

"I called our house. We were asleep, but I got up to answer the phone."

This was followed by stunned silence. Finally, Ashley whispered, "Oh my God."

Bobby knew Mr. Darnell's words were true. He'd seen the other Twin Otter with his own eyes. Days ago, Addison—Addison the monster—had said to him, *'you can't go there, they won't want you.'* Even Addison with his brain damage knew.

You can't go there, they won't want you.

Seconds passed and only the van's wheels on the road could be heard. Bobby's mind was numb. He needed to think about something else. "I still want to call Peter Wooley. Can I use Colonel Richards's phone?"

Mr. Darnell sighed and then pulled the smartphone from his pocket and passed it back. "You're right, maybe he can help us. If you can find a number, you should let one of us talk. I imagine an adult will have a better chance of connecting with him directly."

Bobby turned it on and pulled up the web browser. The signal was weak, but before long he was at the home page for Kembalimo. He had been there before, but only to download the app that connected to the servers and allowed him to play. After a few minutes of digging around, he was at the site of Kembalimo's parent company, SouthPacificNet. There he found some information on Peter Wooley, but no phone number. Finally he found some numbers for customer relations. One of them was in the United States, in Texas. Ignoring Mr. Darnell's request, he tapped the number to switch to cell phone mode and call it. A computer voice came on, offering him choices. He selected, *talk to a customer relations representative.*

"SouthPacificNet International Relations. How may I help you?"

Bobby sat up straight. "Uh, my name is Bobby Truex. I need to talk to Peter Wooley."

"Mr. Wooley resides in Brisbane, Bobby. He does not take unsolicited phone calls. I will be happy to help you if I can, or I could connect you with technical support."

"I really need to talk to him. It won't do any good to talk to someone else."

"I would be happy to give you an email address. Mr. Wooley often monitors email, and he's been known to answer them personally."

Mr. Darnell had been right. Bobby should have let an adult call. "No, there's no time. Is there any way you can tell him what I want to talk about?"

The woman actually laughed. "Bobby, I have never talked to Mr. Wooley, and I probably never will. But I would be happy to take your message and pass it on."

Bobby wasn't ready to give up. "I have things Mr. Wooley would want to know, I swear. Can you let him know we've been to the hanging village in Papua? We met someone he knows named Samuel. And we found the Lamotelokhai. He would want to know that."

"Bobby, what did you say? Can you please repeat that?"

Bobby repeated it.

There was a pause on the other end, and clacking on a keyboard. "What was it you said you found Bobby? Please speak it clearly."

"The Lamotelokhai. We found the Lamotelokhai."

"Oh my sweet Lord," the woman said. "Bobby, please stay on the phone. Do not hang up. In case we get disconnected, can you give me your number?"

Bobby pulled the phone away and looked at it. He wasn't familiar with the controls. "It's not my phone. I don't know the number."

"Okay, if we get disconnected, please call back. My name is Maria Navarro. Ask for me." She made him repeat her name. "I have to put you on hold for just a moment, okay?"

"Okay." Bobby heard a click. He looked up. Mr. Darnell was looking at him in the mirror. The others were staring, too. "I think she's calling Mr. Wooley for me," he said. As he waited, Bobby heard several beeps. Someone was trying to call Colonel Richards's phone.

At least two minutes passed.

"Bobby, you still with me? I'm going to connect you now with Mr. Peter Wooley. Is that okay with you?"

It was a stupid question. "Yes."

A click, and then another voice. "Hello, this is Peter Wooley. With whom am I speaking?"

Bobby swallowed. "I'm Bobby Truex, Mr. Wooley."

"How old are you, Bobby?"

"I'm fourteen. I know Samuel, Mr. Wooley. Do you remember Samuel?"

Peter was silent for a moment. "I know a few Samuels, son."

"This one is different. He's like a hundred and fifty years old. He said he knows you. He thought you were dead."

Another silence. "Well, I'll be stuffed. Samuel Inwood is alive and well?"

"He was when we left Jayapura. He was going to come with us, but then we had to leave him there."

"Son, where did you meet Samuel?"

"In the jungle after our plane crashed. We went to his village— the hanging village."

"And you got him to leave that village?"

"It's kind of a long story. Some bad things happened."

"I want to hear it all. But first, something very important: the customer relations folks in my company are required to memorize two words from a confidential policy document. They are instructed to call a dedicated line to me in the event that a caller mentions these words. One of the words is *Samuel*. Son, what do you reckon the other word to be?"

Bobby didn't hesitate. "Lamotelokhai."

Peter cleared his throat. "That's the one. What do you know of the Lamotelokhai?"

"I know a lot. I know you invented Kembalimo, and that's how I could talk to it at first. Is that why you made Kembalimo, Mr. Wooley?"

"Oh, dear God. Yes." Then there were some shuffling sounds, like Peter might have pulled the phone away from his face. "Yes, that is precisely why."

"Well, it worked."

Peter let out a long breath. "I wanted the next person who found it to be ready."

"Kembalimo was just the beginning. I asked it to change its shape into a person. Now it looks like Addison, one of my friends. But—" Bobby paused. "Addison's gone. So now the Lamotelokhai is Addison, and we just talk to it like a normal person."

There was another long breath. "I'll be stuffed," Peter said again. "Bobby, who else is there with you?"

"My teachers and two of my friends. We're trying to get home without getting caught."

"What do you mean, 'getting caught'?"

"That's a long story, too. We think some people might use Addison to do bad things."

"Bobby, it would seem there is some urgency to your situation. Might I talk to one of your teachers?"

As he passed the phone forward, Bobby heard the beep of another incoming call.

⸻

Quentin glanced at Lindsey. She took the phone from Bobby, but instead of talking to Wooley she held it out to Quentin with her head cocked to one side. She was angry. He should have told her about the phone—and about everything else.

He put it to his ear. "This is Quentin Darnell."

"Quentin, Peter Wooley. Can you confirm that what Bobby has told me is true?"

"It's all true." Quentin glanced in the mirror. "Bobby isn't one to lie."

"This is astonishing news. Forgive me if I am at a loss for the proper thing to say. May I ask why you called me?"

"It was Bobby's idea. We thought you might be able to help us. Peter, what exactly happened at the hanging village?"

There was a deep sigh. "That was over forty years ago. I am guessing you may know this, but I remember every detail as if I were living it at this moment. I also have not aged a day in the years since. Do you know why, Quentin?"

"I do. What do your doctors think of that?"

"I have no need for doctors."

Quentin came to a T in the road. Lindsey looked at the map in her lap, and she pointed to the right, so he turned.

"So what happened in Papua?" Quentin said. "Samuel thought you were dead."

"I was a reckless youth then, testing my own blood's worth with a self-imposed walkabout. When I stumbled upon the village, the natives wanted to kill me when they found I could not speak with the Lamotelokhai. But Samuel convinced them to wait. This allowed me to learn to manipulate the adaptive symbol mapping system used by the Lamotelokhai. I made steady progress, constructing a common language with an intelligence I had nothing in common with. It was enlightening, to say the least. But my progress was not fast enough for the natives. They decided to kill me.

"But you're alive," Quentin said.

"After they attacked, I woke up a short distance from the hanging village. My body was unharmed. So I made my way back to civilization."

Quentin recalled the conversation with Colonel Richards at the airport in Sentani. Samuel had said he had witnessed the Papuans killing Peter. 'Beaten beyond hope of repair,' he had said. Quentin knew what this meant. They had pulverized the body. That's how they made sure people stayed dead.

"Peter, do you have any idea how you survived?"

"Knowing that the natives intended to kill me, I attempted to ask the Lamotelokhai's help. So I assumed it used its curative powers to heal me after they attacked and discarded my body, thinking I was dead."

Peter was wrong. The Papuans would have been thorough. And the Lamotelokhai had said it had reconstructed him, as it had done to Ashley after she'd drowned. Peter had been created from scratch, no doubt from elements in the vegetation and the soil. Apparently Peter did not know he was a copy of his original self.

A beep sounded in Quentin's ear, an incoming call.

"Peter, I may have to end our conversation. We've got a bit of a situation here."

"Bobby mentioned you were avoiding capture. What the hell is going on?"

"You know how important the Lamotelokhai is," Quentin said. "Without trying to explain it all, we're trying to get to our hometown, where we hope to make an announcement to the whole world. This is the only way we can think of to prevent it from being used in secrecy. That's the only plan we have. We're kind of winging it."

"And where exactly are you at this time?"

This put Quentin on alert. "We're some distance from our destination."

Peter hesitated. "Quentin, I am convinced your intentions are spot-on. It seems to me you need an ally. I have a bit of influence and some resources that might prove useful. If you would rather not disclose your location, then tell me your destination. You said you wanted to make an announcement to the world. Beauty of an idea. I will help arrange that."

"So you're willing to help us?"

"I have devoted forty-two years of my life to preparing the world for what I alone knew was coming. Does that answer your question?"

It did. Quentin told Peter their destination. They agreed that

Quentin and Lindsey's house would be the location for the media event. Peter gave his personal cell phone number, and they ended the call.

Within seconds the phone chirped. A number with a 213 area code glowed on the screen, but there was no name. Quentin eyed Lindsey but her face was a blank slate. She was either dwelling on his decision to hide the phone from her, or on his unsettling motive for doing so. The phone sounded again, and finally she shrugged. So he answered the call.

"Darnell? Quentin, is that you?" It was Richards.

"Good to hear from you, Colonel. What's happening there?"

"A great deal of confusion, but the scenario is taking shape. There is a general understanding that we have transported here something extraordinarily important, and that you have sequestered it. I have explained why, but you can bet your life they're assuming the worst. There's a shit-storm building here, Darnell. Top-level personnel and resources are coming into play. Where the hell are you?"

"We have a plan, but it's going to take some time."

"Well, I'm in no position to question your judgment, but you don't have much time. Listen to me, Darnell. The media blitz we discussed, you've got to do it now. And you'd better get rid of my phone. I don't think they know you have it yet, but—"

There was a click, followed by silence.

"Mr. Darnell, please don't hang up." It was a different voice.

"Who is this?"

"My name is Darron Mesner. I represent the interests and security of the people of the United States. Again, please do not hang up. It is very important that you talk to me."

Quentin gripped the steering wheel tight with his free hand and stared at the road ahead.

"Mr. Darnell—it's Quentin, right? Please explain your situation and your intentions."

"I'm with my wife and our students. We haven't done anything wrong."

"You are not accused of doing anything wrong, Quentin. Therefore we'd like to know why you fled the airport. Is there anything you can explain that would help us to understand?"

"We have something that is very important. Our only intention is to make everyone aware of it. We believe it's here for a reason, and that reason does not involve weapons, or one country dominating another."

There was a pause. "Perhaps you can tell me what exactly you are referring to."

"It's a gift—for all of us. But we've seen that it can be very dangerous. So we want everyone to know what it is, to prevent a few single-minded people from making decisions that could be catastrophic."

"Quentin, you have somehow managed to avoid National Security personnel with a device you say is very dangerous. And now you are behaving as fugitives on the run—with a weapon of unknown origin and destructive power. Do you understand our concern?"

Quentin's stomach sank. "When you put it that way, yes. But that's a distortion of what's really happening here. This thing is not a weapon. In fact, the reason we're running is to prevent it from being used to make weapons."

"I understand you brought this thing to the U.S. because you believed our people were best qualified to deal with it. It seems that was a subterfuge."

"Or we simply changed our minds. We aren't terrorists, if that's what you think. We have no intention of hurting anyone."

"I hope to God that's true, Quentin." There was a brief silence. "Tell me, what is your destination? What do you hope to accomplish by driving east?"

Quentin froze. "You know where we are?"

Mesner's voice was even, with no hint of condescension. "Of course we do. Quentin, I consider myself to be an honorable man. And I give you my word that this device will not be used in the way that you fear it will. In fact, Quentin, it seems that you are currently the expert on the device. Therefore, if you cooperate from this moment on, you will be included in the investigation of it. Your opinions seem sound and will be considered valuable."

Quentin put on the brakes and pulled the van onto the shoulder. "What I need is a promise that the first thing we do is make a live announcement on national television." He opened his door and stepped onto the road. The sky was orange to the east and deep blue everywhere else. It was actually quite beautiful—and dead silent. No vehicles were visible in either direction, and the sky was clear of helicopters and planes. "I want to make this announcement myself, before the device is examined by any experts."

Mesner sighed. "That's a rather difficult thing to promise, Quentin."

"I was afraid you'd say that," Quentin replied. "But that's the only way to ensure the safety of all the people of this world. I'm sorry." Quentin then stepped to the side of the road. He picked up a large rock from the rubble deposited there, dropped the phone on the ground, and smashed it in the desert sand.

CHAPTER TEN

SLEEPING WAS a lost cause for Quentin. He lay awake in bed, listening to the relentless twitter of katydids and crickets through the open window of their bedroom. He had nudged Lindsey awake, and they'd talked about the strange phone call, but her tone was rather dubious. She had no explanation for why the caller sounded so much like Quentin, or how the guy could know the details of their life he had described. She hadn't heard the phone ring, and so she'd suggested Quentin might have dreamt the conversation. Within minutes she'd fallen asleep again.

But sleep didn't come for Quentin. The caller had described in detail a key intimate moment of their relationship, when they'd been in a sleeping bag under an Ozark night sky and they had agreed to try having another child. His first thought was that Lindsey must have told someone about the event. But then the guy had described the fears Quentin had experienced at that moment—fears he had never revealed to Lindsey. This was simply not possible.

Quentin rolled to his side to feel Lindsey's breath in his face. He could think of only two explanations: he had dreamt the whole thing, or the guy was telling the truth—he really was a copy of Quentin. Ockham's simplicity principle, that the simplest solution tends to be the best, should've applied here. Logically, the call must have been a dream. But Quentin had now been awake for half an hour, and he was sure it hadn't been a dream.

Finally, he slid out of bed, grabbed his smartphone from the dresser, and walked to the kitchen. He looked at the most recent call and then tapped the number to dial it. Quentin heard ringing, but then it switched to voicemail. *"You have reached the voicemail of..."* Then a recorded voice stated, "Colonel Roger Richards." Quentin hung up.

He paced the kitchen floor. Who the hell was Colonel Roger Richards? He went to the bedroom they had converted to office space and woke up his computer. A web search for Colonel Roger Richards led him to the site for the U.S. Embassy in Jakarta. A Colonel Roger Richards was listed as the Defense and Army Attaché.

He sank into his desk chair and stared dazedly at the screen. The caller had said their Twin Otter had crashed in Papua, resulting in them finding something there, and they had brought it to the U.S. with the help of the military. A few days ago, about ten days after his group had returned home, Quentin had seen news reports of a skirmish between U.S. soldiers and Indonesians in Papua. A chilling tingle crept up the back of Quentin's neck. Something strange was happening.

A car door faintly slammed shut out on the street, followed by three more. Quentin's eyes flicked to the clock in the corner of his computer screen. Just before six a.m. The tingle on his neck spread quickly down his spine.

A knock on the door startled him out of his trance. And it woke Lindsey.

"Quentin? Where are you? Who is that?"

"I'm out here, Linds. I don't know, but you might want to get up."

The knock came again, this time louder.

Quentin was wearing only a pair of shorts, but he went to the front door and opened it. On the porch were two men in jackets and ties, in spite of the sultry July air. Behind them were two local policemen Quentin had seen around town before. In the street he saw two police cars, their lights flashing, and a dark sedan. Two more sedans were coming to a stop.

His first thought was that Addison had snuck out during the night and had gotten into trouble or had been hurt. Instinctively he swung around to look down the hallway to Addison's bedroom. But there Addison stood, his face bright with curiosity.

"Sir, are you Quentin Darnell?" It was one of the jacket-and-tie men.

"Yes. What's going on?"

The man held up an identification card that Quentin couldn't see. "I'm Gordon Carver. I'm a regional field agent for the Department of Homeland Security. May we come inside?"

Quentin motioned for them to enter, and they stood awkwardly in the foyer. The two local policemen eyed him pensively but did not speak.

Carver said, "Mr. Darnell, have you and your family been at your house all night?"

Quentin nodded. Lindsey and Addison were now at his side.

An inscrutable look passed between the men. "We are not aware of the details at this time, but it seems there was a fatal airline crash at the Los Angeles airport."

Quentin frowned. He couldn't think of anyone he knew who was currently traveling.

The man continued. "Apparently there is some confusion as to the identities of the passengers. For some reason it was believed that you folks were on that aircraft."

"Well, clearly we weren't," Lindsey said. "I take it there is more to the story?"

"Yes, there is." The men exchanged glances again. The policemen watched Carver as if they, too, were waiting for an explanation. Carver cleared his throat before going on. "But first, can you think of a reason why anyone would claim to have your identities?"

Quentin's thoughts immediately turned to the mysterious caller. The guy had said the police might show up. He had practically begged Quentin to say nothing about the phone call.

"We did fly back from Indonesia a few weeks ago," Quentin said. "Maybe they got our names from a passenger list or something?"

The man nodded at this, but the gesture was dismissive. He continued to stare at them, like a teacher out-waiting his students until they produced a satisfactory answer.

Quentin glanced at Lindsey, and she raised her brows at him. She was waiting for him to tell them about the caller. He shook his head slightly.

Perhaps the men read possible deception in this exchange, because their demeanor suddenly changed. "Our job at this point is to nail down the facts, so that we understand what we're dealing with. We'd like to see some identification for both of you. And we'll also need to search the premises. Then we can further discuss what we know about tonight's events. Will you cooperate with us on this, Mr. and Mrs. Darnell?"

Quentin sighed and waved his hand to the interior of the house. "Of course."

More police and federal men now stood on the front porch, and Carver motioned for them to enter. Lindsey fetched their driver's licenses and showed them to Carver. Then the men spread out to search the house and garage. For exactly what, Quentin had no idea.

A moment later two men came out of the bedroom office and asked Carver to come look at something. Quentin followed. One of the men pointed at Quentin's computer. On the screen was a web page describing the personnel of the U.S. Embassy in Jakarta, Indonesia. In the center of the screen was a short biography and photo of Colonel Roger Richards.

Bobby dropped a handful of crickets into the terrarium. Romeo walked out of the corner on all fours. His round tree frog eyes stared at the insects as they scattered, but he made no move to eat. Juliet was pressed flat against the glass at one end of the tank.

Bobby peered through the glass and frowned. "Those are the last ones, you guys. You'd better eat." The frogs hadn't had much appetite since Bobby had returned from the trip.

Bobby's mom called from the living room, "I have to get back to work. You want a ride to school or not?"

"I'm coming!" Bobby definitely wanted a ride. It had been a weird morning, with the police and FBI showing up. They'd said some people had come to the U.S. pretending to be Bobby and his teachers and classmates, and that the people were probably dangerous. And the FBI hadn't left. They had been parked outside all morning, just waiting.

And that wasn't all that had happened. Everyone on TV was talking about two things: A plane crash in California and something that was supposed to happen tomorrow right here in Newton. This last thing was most exciting of all. Supposedly, the guy who'd invented Kembalimo was making a big announcement, and for some reason he wanted to do it in Bobby's own town. Bobby loved Kembalimo. He'd been playing it for two years.

When he and his mom left the house a few minutes later, the FBI asked where they were going. Bobby's mom told them her lunchtime was over and she was going back to work, of course. And Bobby had summer school, if that was all right with them.

The guys politely explained that they would have to follow them.

As Bobby's mom drove, he could tell she was worried because she wasn't talking.

"Today we do our reports," he said. His class included two weeks of afternoon sessions after the field trip to study the data they had collected and make computer presentations with their photos. Today they would show their presentations in class.

"I'm sure you'll do fine," she said. Then she was quiet again.

"It's gonna be okay, mom. Nothing can happen."

More FBI cars were parked at the school. She pulled into the drop-off area and then sat quietly for a moment. "I knew the whole thing was a bad idea!"

"Mom, it wasn't—"

"It *was*. Your dad was the one who wanted you to go. Then you had to be evacuated from that awful place. And now we find out terrorists used your names to get into the United States?" She waved her hand at the cars that nearly blocked the drop-off area. "They must think the terrorists are coming to your school."

Bobby saw real fear in her eyes. "I know you didn't want me to go. You'd rather me just sit at home all summer. But this class has been the best thing in my whole life."

She stared straight ahead, but her frown relaxed a little.

The two men who'd followed them from the house stood outside her window until she rolled it down. "Ma'am, we intend to stay with your son until the situation we discussed is completely under control. You can be assured he'll be safe going about his usual business."

"This is probably the safest place in town today, Mom. Nothing will happen."

Finally she forced a smile. "Do good on your report. I'll take off early and pick you up."

Bobby got out. "You need the hours. I'll walk home."

"I'll be here, and you'll ride with me," she said. "I love you, kiddo." She drove away.

Bobby waved and then turned to the two men. "My mom said you guys think those people are coming here."

The taller man answered, "To be honest, we don't know what their intentions are. But we'd like to stick close to you for a while. Is that okay with you?"

Bobby shrugged and nodded. He had his own bodyguards, like a rock star or the president. The men followed him into the school. More government people were in the main office, but Bobby went straight to his science room. He wasn't the only one with bodyguards. Men were talking in the hallway, and more were in the room, either standing to the side like statues or walking around looking at the animal cages. Other than that, everything was normal.

"Here comes another Kembalimo nerd," Russ said. "Hey, Bobby, I hear the Kembalimo people are coming here to give you an award—the most time wasted on an online game."

"It's not a game," Addison said. From Addison's tone, Bobby guessed he had already gotten his share of teasing. And of course he always made it worse by getting mad.

But Bobby knew better. "It's okay; not everyone is smart enough to understand Kembalimo."

Roberto laughed. "You gonna take that from an eighth grader?"

Russ got up from his chair. Bobby knew Russ was just acting tough, but he figured he was in for a nuggie or wedgie. His bodyguards didn't seem interested in stopping it.

"Russ, sit down, or we'll tell Renee you have crabs." It was Ashley, and her threat worked. Russ groaned and sat back down.

Ashley didn't even look at Bobby. Girls like Ashley never looked at Bobby.

Bobby took a seat between Carlos and Addison, who were both busy with their smartphones and barely looked up. "Hey, guys," he said.

"You have bodyguards, too," Carlos said. "Ours showed up first thing this morning. Freaked my parents out."

"Yeah, freaked my mom too," Bobby said. He pulled out his smartphone and connected to the computer next to their table with a USB cable. He transferred his presentation to the computer.

"Happy last-day-of-school, everyone!" Miranda came in with an armload of white paper bags. She dropped one on the table in front of each of them. The bags were covered with hand-drawn animals and palm trees. She smiled at the FBI men scattered around the room. "I didn't make enough for you guys. Sorry."

Bobby opened his bag. Inside it were candies and cookies that looked homemade.

Ashley shook her head. "Barbie strikes again."

"Actually," Roberto said, his mouth already stuffed, "Miranda's awesome. Miranda, will you marry me?"

"She's way too good for you, man," Russ said, cookie crumbs spilling out of his mouth.

Mr. and Mrs. Darnell came in with two more FBI men, and everyone shut up.

Mr. Darnell spoke first. "This is Mr. Carver and Mr. Mifflin. They work for the Department of Homeland Security, although you probably already know that. I doubt we'll be able to focus very well today if we don't first talk about what's going on." Then he motioned for the man named Carver to take it from there.

The guy looked nervous. He cleared his throat and adjusted his suit jacket, giving them a glimpse of a gun in a black holster. "We're still sorting out details, but it appears that a group of people have breached our security measures and entered the United States under your identities. This might be linked to a fatal airline crash that occurred last night. It's possible these people actually caused the crash as some form of distraction, allowing them to get by our security."

Bobby sat up straight. The men at his house hadn't said this.

"And to make matters worse, these people may possess some type of weapon."

"What kind of weapon?" Ashley said.

"We don't know. But as you can imagine, we're taking this very seriously."

Ashley spoke again. "So shouldn't you be in Los Angeles where the terrorists are?"

The man glanced around the room. "We believe these people might be on their way here."

Bobby raised his hand, and the guy nodded for him to speak. "On TV they say something big is happening here tomorrow. Something about Kembalimo."

The guy frowned. "We didn't know about that until this morning. But yes, it seems that SouthPacificNet has selected this location for a public announcement."

More questions were asked, but Carver didn't know or didn't want to share much more than that. He and his partner moved to the classroom door and stood with their arms crossed. They obviously had no intention of budging until class was over.

Everyone whispered about this new information, but soon Mr. and Mrs. Darnell got the regular class session going by calling kids up to present their projects. By now there were at least ten FBI men in the room. They must have been bored, because they actually watched the presentations. They even clapped along with everyone else at the end of each one.

Addison ended up going last, and it was obvious he hadn't spent much time on his project. Mr. and Mrs. Darnell stared at the floor through most of it. Just as Addison finished, a man came in and spoke quietly to the others. Again Carver took front and center.

"We have new information. The suspects I told you about might well have been on their way to this very town. But I am pleased to report that they have been apprehended in Arizona."

In spite of the good news, Bobby saw that Mr. Darnell wasn't smiling.

As it had done every morning of the nearly ten thousand years of Mbaiso's existence, the sun rose in the east, throwing long shafts of light through the canopy. And as they had always done, the shafts of light moved steadily across the forest floor as if the sun were searching this place for something it had lost.

Mbaiso positioned himself in front of one of these searchlights and waited as the beam moved steadily across his body, briefly painting his fur a brighter rusty-brown and warming his weary muscles.

Mbaiso had been working days and nights to accomplish his last array of directives from the Creator. Tupela, who had been occupied with her own tasks, now joined him. The two tree kangaroos lazed about on the forest floor near the base of the largest tree in the area—the tree that supported the village's most important hut. The hut was joined to six suspended tunnels leading away from the tree to chambers where the villagers had gathered to be healed when necessary, to simply be near the Lamotelokhai, or to make requests through the tree kangaroos. Talking directly to the Lamotelokhai had long been a tribal taboo, the result of a villager fixated on personal rewards slaughtering nearly half the tribe. The same scenario had recently reoccurred with the boy, Addison. But it would not happen again—at least not in this place.

Now the central hut was empty. The surviving villagers had returned to their living huts, and the six tunnels with their ceremonial chambers hung silently above the tree kangaroos. There would be no reason for the villagers to use them again.

Mbaiso shifted positions to allow the sunbeam to paint his body again. The sensation was familiar, but everything else about this morning seemed different. A connection had been severed. No new instructions were coming in. There was no reason to gather information because there was no central database to transmit it to. The Creator was gone. And the villagers no longer needed help, because Mbaiso had carried out tasks that would help them live a self-sufficient existence.

Events had progressed, as they eventually had to. The tree kangaroos, like the ancient villagers, no longer had a role to play in what would come next, although they would likely feel the effects even in this secluded place.

Mbaiso examined the array of directives one more time. There was only one remaining to be carried out. He had examined it from every angle but could find no concealed meaning. The directive was clear: after completing the array of tasks, Mbaiso was to disaggregate Tupela's body and then his own, returning them to the soil.

His final task was to die.

Mbaiso contemplated the array of tasks that hovered there in his consciousness. He shook his head forcefully and then deleted the entire array. For the first time in his existence, Mbaiso had decided to disobey a directive from the Creator.

Tupela seemed to notice Mbaiso's agitation. She ambled over to him and used gestures to request details about the tasks they were to complete next. Mbaiso pushed himself up to a sitting position and signed to her: *Soon there will be much to do. For now you should rest.* She then wandered off and settled down at the base of the massive Lamotelokhai tree.

Mbaiso watched his beam of light move across the ground and then vanish as the structure of the forest canopy rendered the sun unable to search for whatever it had lost.

CHAPTER ELEVEN

Bobby had no idea it could take so long to drive across Arizona. The state was huge. And after spending weeks in the rainforest, the desert seemed so brown and dry, all sand and rocks and hills, speckled by wimpy little shrubs as far as he could see. They drove the back roads, so the desert was all there was to look at. It had been eight hours since Mr. Darnell had busted the cell phone, and they were still in Arizona. The only real excitement was when Mrs. Darnell had turned on the radio and the people were talking about Peter Wooley. Besides the plane crash, the top news of the day was that Mr. Wooley was making some big announcement at noon tomorrow in Newton, Missouri. They played a clip of Peter's voice, and Bobby recognized his accent. Peter explained that tomorrow's announcement was going to change the world, and everyone should watch it. Then the radio people made jokes about how it was a brilliant publicity stunt.

Mr. Darnell turned off the radio. "Peter said he would arrange something, and he meant it. I bet the media are already showing up in Newton."

Mrs. Darnell had been looking at maps constantly, and a big

one was spread out on her lap. "We're still something like twelve-hundred miles away," she said. "We'd have to drive straight through to be there by noon tomorrow."

They were passing through a town called Saint Johns, which was spread out, almost like it wasn't a town at all. But it had two gas stations, and they stopped at one. They filled up, and since the place had pizzas, Mr. Darnell bought two. They went to the restroom in shifts so their group wouldn't attract attention. But then a highway patrol car pulled in next to them. A chunky patrolman got out and walked into the store just as Mrs. Darnell and Ashley came out. He held the door open and nodded as they passed through. But instead of walking in, he turned and stared. Mirrored sunglasses hid his eyes, so Bobby couldn't tell if he was looking at the van or checking out their butts. Ashley opened the van's sliding door, and the patrolman then had a clear view inside the vehicle.

"Just don't look at him," Mr. Darnell mumbled as he backed the van out.

The patrolman was frozen in place, still holding the door open. Then they rounded the corner of the store, and he was out of sight. Holding his breath, Bobby turned and watched the gas station as they drove on. Two blocks away, then three.

"He's not following us," Bobby said, and he started breathing again.

The houses thinned out as they left the town behind. Ahead was a long stretch of highway through the desert, with nothing but gray mountains in the distance. The smell of hot pizza filled the van, and Bobby realized he was hungry. Before grabbing one of the boxes he took a last look at the town that was shrinking behind them.

And there was the highway patrol car, lights flashing. It was quickly gaining on them.

"He's coming!" Bobby cried.

Suddenly the van filled with frantic voices. Ashley and Carlos wanted them to gun it and outrun him. Mrs. Darnell was freaking out, since nobody had a driver's license. By then the patrol car was right on their tail, sirens blaring. Mr. Darnell pulled over and stopped.

A loudspeaker voice came from behind them. "Driver of the vehicle! Get out and stand where I can see you."

Bobby looked back. The patrolman had his door open and was crouched behind it, talking into a microphone. At least he wasn't pointing a gun at them.

"If you guys have any ideas, this is the time," Mr. Darnell said. He opened his door and stepped out of the van.

"Sir, hold your driver's license where I can see it and walk to the back of your vehicle."

Mr. Darnell walked toward the patrol car. "I'm sorry, but I've lost my license."

"Stop there, sir." The patrolman looked at something in his own hand, maybe a smartphone. Bobby guessed he was comparing Mr. Darnell to a picture. "What is your name, sir?"

"Quentin Darnell."

The patrolman put his megaphone in his car and talked without it, but Bobby could still hear him. "Mr. Darnell, place your hands on the back of your vehicle."

Mr. Darnell did this. His face was just on the other side of the rear window, and he silently mouthed something. He was asking them—asking *Bobby*—to do something.

The patrolman talked to someone on his radio. Finally he came forward and rapped on the van's rear window. "The rest of you exit the right side of the vehicle and stand where I can see you."

Mrs. Darnell got out and then opened the sliding door. Ashley and Carlos piled out.

Ashley poked her head back in. "Bobby, have Addison do something!"

Bobby turned to Addison. "We have to get to our home, but now we can't."

"You want me to help you, don't you?"

Bobby thought hard. The patrolman had already called it in, so others would be here soon. Right now there was only one man. Addison could do something to him, maybe make him go to sleep, or give him part of his body, like he did to Gregory. Maybe he could teleport them somewhere, but he could only do that to somewhere they had already been.

Bobby shook his head and slid toward the door. "I don't know what to do. Unless you can make this van fly."

Addison said, "You would like me to make this van fly?"

Bobby stopped. He had been kidding, but Addison was waiting for an answer.

"All passengers out of the vehicle, now!" The patrolman was on his loudspeaker again.

"We're coming!" Bobby said. He turned to Addison. "Sure, but we don't have any time."

Addison looked around him, and then out at the patrol car. "It will take some time."

"How long?"

"A unit of time is needed."

"Um," Bobby shook his hands desperately, "we use seconds and minutes. Here's what seconds are: Mississippi one, Mississippi two, Mississippi three. That's three seconds."

"Four-hundred seconds. If there are problems, maybe six-hundred."

Bobby blinked at him. "Really?"

Ashley stuck her head in the door again. "Are you trying to get us shot?"

Bobby stared into Addison's eyes. "Please do that—as fast as you can." He crawled out, and Addison followed. They all stood there squinting in the desert sun. The patrolman looked from them to his smartphone, and back to them.

Suddenly Addison walked between the vehicles to where the patrolman stood.

"Son, go back with the others."

Addison stopped just in front of the patrolman, his reflection showing in the man's glasses. "I am going to do something now," Addison said. "Do not be afraid. And please do not hurt my friends."

"No one's going to get hurt, son. Just move back to—"

The man stopped. Addison had put his hands on the patrolman's hood, and they seemed to melt into the car. The patrolman yanked off his sunglasses. His eyes were round. The metal around Addison's hands moved like white syrup, and his arms seemed to pour into it. Addison's head and shoulders started getting smaller as his parts moved into the patrol car.

The patrolman backed up. "What's happening?" Without taking his eyes off Addison, he leaned over and fumbled for something in his car, maybe his radio. But then he seemed to forget what he wanted and just stood there staring.

"It's okay," Mr. Darnell said. "We'll explain everything."

Addison's head and chest kept shrinking. Soon they were only half their normal size, and he looked like a deformed clay figure, except that he was alive and moving.

Oozing metal on the hood of the patrolman's car formed into small pieces that started moving around like mechanical gray crickets. The patrolman backed away and stood in the middle of the road. He wasn't paying attention to anything else. Bobby looked down the highway. A big truck was coming from Saint Johns but was still far away. The car's engine stopped running, and the desert became quiet except for the scuttling and scratching of the metal crickets as they spread out over the vehicle.

Mrs. Darnell said, "What's happening, Bobby?"

"I'm not sure. Addison said he would make the van fly."

They all turned and looked at him, except for the patrolman.

"Then maybe we can get home," Bobby said.

"What the hell are those," the patrolman said. He sounded like he might be sick. The truck was getting closer, and he let Mr. Darnell lead him by the elbow to the side of the road.

Scurrying crickets covered the patrol car, and the sound of their work was a constant buzz, like a radio that was only getting static. One of the tires popped with a loud hiss, and the car settled to one side. Seconds later, the other three popped. And then the car changed shape. The roof fell in, and the entire vehicle flattened out to the ground. Addison pulled back from the car and stood by Bobby at the side of the road. He looked like something from a nightmare. His legs were still normal, but the top part of his body was disfigured and shrunken. The patrolman, totally freaked, kept looking from his car to Addison, and back to his car.

The crickets were now on the move, thousands of them walking from the patrol car to the van. Bobby knelt between the vehicles to watch. Upon closer inspection he saw that they did not walk on legs. Instead they stretched and compressed their shape like fat inchworms.

"You should not touch them, Bobby." It was Addison, but his voice was like a cartoon animal. Bobby backed away from the little robots.

The semi truck finally reached them, and it screeched to a stop in the middle of the road. The driver leaned over his steering wheel to stare. The door popped open, and a bald man in a sleeveless denim shirt dropped to the pavement. "Everybody here okay?" he shouted.

The patrolman didn't answer, so Mr. Darnell told him they were fine.

The trucker pointed to the swarming, chittering mass. "What the hell are those?"

"It's a long story," was all Mr. Darnell said.

Soon the patrolman's car was completely transformed into crawling robot bugs. They swarmed onto the minivan. The scraping, squeaking sounds continued as the van's front end grew longer and a thick column formed from the floor to the ceiling between the two front seats. Some of the bugs flowed away from the van and formed a long pile on the ground. The pile became a solid object with a bucket-like cylinder at each end.

Addison stepped forward. His body looked almost normal now, just smaller than it should have been. "Your help is needed," he said. He grabbed the bucket at one end and lifted.

Mr. Darnell stepped up and grabbed the other bucket. He strained to lift his end. Bobby rushed forward to help. Together they lifted the huge object. Addison guided them to the front of the van, and they raised the thing high and placed it across the roof, just over the new column between the seats. The two buckets now hung on each side of the van.

A second, nearly identical object was already being formed. They lifted this one and placed it on the roof at the rear of the van. Then they backed away and watched. The remaining bugs swarmed the top of the van, reshaping it so the two sets of wings with their buckets became part of the whole machine. And then the bugs were gone and everything was silent. Except for the tires, the van was all white, and it gleamed in the sun.

Addison climbed into the driver's seat. He turned the key and started it up. The engine was now quieter, just a low pulsing sound, and Bobby could feel its soft rumbling in his bones. Addison touched some controls on the steering wheel and the four buckets swiveled, first one way and then the other. And then the buckets began to hiss. Bobby couldn't hear any kind of motor inside them, but air began to blow from the buckets so hard that the van came off the ground a little and then settled back down.

When Addison opened the driver's door and got out, his body

was back to normal. He looked at Bobby and smiled. "Five-hundred and eighty seconds," he said.

IT OCCURRED to Quentin that a minivan that had been converted into a jet in less than ten minutes might not be safe. When he suggested this, Ashley said they should trust Addison.

"And besides," she said, "if we die, no one will miss us anyway."

This pretty much shut everyone up, except for the highway patrolman. The poor guy looked like he'd just come out of a coma. He stepped over to Quentin and looked him in the eye. "I'm obviously involved in something way over my head here. I'm going to ask you this, and by God you'd best tell me the truth. What are you planning to do?"

Lindsey spoke first. "We don't intend to hurt anyone, if that's what you mean. As you've seen, we have something unusual with us. We were the ones who found it. We're avoiding the homeland security people because we know it *will* be used to hurt people. We have a plan to prevent that. You have a chance to keep the world safe if you help us."

The patrolman eyed the minivan jet. "What would happen if I tried to hold you people here for the feds?"

"We wouldn't blame you," Quentin said. "But we're pretty determined to go."

The man looked at his hands, which were shaking. He gripped his belt to keep them still and shuffled his feet in the roadside gravel. Finally he turned to the truck driver. "Sir, you're the only other witness here. I'm considering letting these people go. My gut's telling me it's the right thing to do. I'm gonna need you to work with me on this when the feds get here. Do you believe my judgment in this matter is sound, or are we going to have a problem?"

The truck driver nodded at the minivan. "Hell, I wanna see that goddamn thing fly. I think you should let 'em go."

The patrolman squeezed his eyes shut for a moment and then faced them again. "You don't have much time. You were right when you said the feds are looking for you. Hell, everyone's looking for you. If we were any closer to Gallup or Flagstaff, they'd be here by now. Have I made myself clear?"

Quentin nodded. "Very clear. And we're grateful. By this time tomorrow, you should know just how important this decision was."

The patrolman sighed. "I have no intention of being a liar, so when they get here, I'll explain just what you've told me—that you believe you're doing the right thing, and you convinced me like-wise. I'll take what's coming to me for doing it." He shook his head. "There'll be a special hell for you if you make me regret this." Then he glanced at the van. "I'll leave that part out. If they know you're in the air, they may shoot you down."

Addison stepped forward and held out a hand to each of the men. "This is a gift for you. You should eat it."

Warily, the men took the gray lumps offered to them. They made no move to eat them.

Quentin motioned everyone into the van. Addison took the driver's seat. Quentin eyed him warily and then slid into the seat behind Lindsey. Before pulling the door shut, he turned to the men. "Addison is right, you really should eat those. Oh, and I'm sorry about your car."

The patrolman just shook his head again.

Quentin shut the door. The four thrusters jumped to life, blowing air so hard that the van lifted at a startling rate. He watched the ground drop away, the two men below shielding their eyes from the blasting sand. The thrusters rotated, and the craft accelerated forward. Junipers and pinyons on the desert floor shot past in a blur. Quentin guessed they were flying several hundred miles per hour, but the rushing wind was surprisingly quiet.

"I'll tell you when to turn," Lindsey said to Addison. She already had the map in front of her and was navigating as if nothing had changed. "Just stay above highway 191 for now. Looks like we left just in time," she said, gazing at the ground.

Quentin peered at the road below. A string of vehicles raced south.

Although the van's exterior was changed, its interior looked the same as before, except for the thick column between the front seats and the addition of two joysticks on the steering wheel. The column, Quentin figured, contained some sort of drive shaft or mechanism that connected the four thrusters to the vehicle's engine. The two joysticks appeared very simple. Addison held one in each hand and seemed to control everything through them. Quentin gazed through the window at the foremost thruster on his side. It was obviously sucking air in the front and blowing it out the rear hard enough to lift and propel them. How could a six-cylinder minivan engine pull that off?

He said, "Addison, what did you do to the engine? It sounds different."

Addison kept his hands on the joysticks, but he turned to Quentin. "The engine needed to be different for the van to fly. So I made it different."

"Does it still run on gas?"

"Yes, but it was originally built to use more gas than is needed. Now it is different."

Another way the world is about to change. "How far can we get on the gas we have?"

Addison gazed down at the passing desert. "If things stay as they are now, forty-nine million, nine hundred fifty-four thousand, and eighty feet."

They were all silent for a moment. Then Bobby said, "How many miles is that? A mile is five thousand, two hundred and eighty feet."

Addison replied, "Nine thousand, four hundred and sixty-one miles."

Quentin said, "On one tank of gas?"

"We also have gas from the other vehicle."

The tiny robots must have carried gas from the patrol car to the van. Quentin stared at the thruster again. "Addison, this van uses a fairly conventional method of flight. In a dream you showed us the home of your creators. The people there flew some kind of sphere-shaped vehicle. Why didn't you just make the van into one of those?"

"Those vehicles were used only inside the towers you saw. The towers were made so the vehicles could fly inside them. Outside of the towers, the vehicles could not fly. So they could not fly here."

Lindsey was still looking at her map. She said, "We're a thousand miles from our home. How long will it take?"

Again Addison looked at the ground. "If things stay as they are now, it will take eighteen thousand, three hundred sixty-seven seconds."

Lindsey frowned. "Okay..."

Bobby helped out. "Sixty seconds is a minute. Sixty minutes is an hour. How many hours is that?"

"That is five hours, six minutes, and seven seconds."

Lindsey looked at the clock on the dash. "That puts us there at nine-thirty. Peter's news announcement isn't until noon tomorrow."

They all got quiet, probably imagining, like Quentin was, what it would be like to show up at their homes. How would their families react? How would their other selves react?

Bobby broke the silence. "Addison, did your nanobots get into these pizzas?"

"No."

Bobby kept one box and passed the other forward. "Don't want to waste them, then."

ADDISON HADN'T ALTERED the van's dashboard, so the simple digital compass was the only navigation instrument they had. But navigating was not difficult. Lindsey kept her eye on the map, and they flew north until she spotted I-40. The double ribbon of highway was easy to see from a great distance, and the next few hours passed in reasonable comfort. To avoid landing, Quentin convinced them to pee in the soda cups that had accumulated on the floor. This was not an easy sell for Lindsey and Ashley, but the van's back seat offered a modicum of privacy.

They followed I-40 through New Mexico and Texas, and into Oklahoma without incident. Occasionally they spotted small planes flying far below, and Quentin hoped none saw them. To avoid flying over Oklahoma City, they cut to the north to follow I-35 to Kansas City.

That's when their luck changed.

"Um, you guys, we have company," Carlos said.

Two military fighter jets were closing in on them from the east, their contrails streaming behind them into the distance. The jets passed overhead with a deafening roar. Quentin spun around and watched them split and circle around in opposite directions.

"They're not going to shoot us down are they?" Ashley said.

"Addison, can we go fast enough to outrun them?" Quentin asked doubtfully. The jets flew at terrifying speed.

Addison looked at the jet circling before them. "It would not be safe for you."

There was nothing they could do but watch the jets circle and fly by them again, one from ahead and one from behind. The relative velocity of the jet from behind was low enough that they clearly saw the pilot as he overtook them. He tapped the side of his helmet over his ear. Then he was past, and he cut off to circle back.

"He wants to talk," Lindsey said.

The jets made another pass from behind, and the pilots repeated the same gesture. Lindsey shrugged and shook her head to make them understand that they didn't have a radio. On the next pass, the pilot changed his approach. He held up a white clipboard. Written by hand was one word: *FOLLOW*. He flipped the board over. It said *TINKER AFB*.

Lindsey turned around to Quentin. "What do you want to do now?"

Ashley said, "You guys, I kind of have this fear of getting blown up in mid air."

They had little choice. If the Air Force thought they were terrorists—and they probably did—then they might actually fire on them. So now what? Quentin looked through the window again at the van's thrusters, which could turn in almost any direction. They couldn't outrun the fighter jets, but they could probably out-maneuver them.

"Everyone buckle in and hold on," Quentin said.

"What are you doing?" Lindsey said.

Quentin fumbled for his seatbelt, and suddenly the thin strap seemed ridiculously inadequate. "Maybe we can lose them if we fly closer to the ground."

"Okay, no," Ashley said. "That doesn't sound like a plan."

Carlos called from the back seat, "They're coming back!"

Quentin's mind raced. "Addison, wait until they pass by us and then try to descend without them seeing."

"Mr. Darnell?" It was Bobby. "I think it'll be better if you just let Addison figure something out. Just be sure to tell him that no one should get hurt."

Quentin hesitated. He gripped the arm of his seat.

The jets came up from behind on both sides. And there was the clipboard again. *FOLLOW*. The pilot flipped it over. *OR WE FIRE.*

Quentin considered Bobby's suggestion. "Addison, those jets

have weapons they can shoot at us. Can you get us away from them without getting us shot?"

"How do the weapons work?" Addison said.

"I don't know! Rockets, maybe. They shoot self-propelled rockets that have explosives in them. Or maybe they have guns that shoot metal bullets."

"Yes."

"Yes what?"

"I can get us away without getting us shot."

Before he could change his mind, Quentin said, "Then do it."

Without warning, the thrusters flipped around and blasted in the opposite direction. Quentin was thrown forward and the seatbelt dug into his flesh. The fighter jets shot ahead and rapidly shrank in the distance.

And then the van fell like a rock.

There was no screaming; they were all too petrified to scream. Quentin was lifted off the seat, and he felt his stomach in his throat.

"Do not be afraid," Addison said.

Quentin was pulled even harder toward the ceiling, and he realized they weren't in free fall. They were actually accelerating straight down. He wanted to scream at Addison that they would be killed, but he couldn't speak. The thrusters rotated again, and Quentin braced himself for a deceleration that would likely shatter the van's frame and crush their bones. But it didn't come. Addison skillfully slowed at a rate that was only barely uncomfortable. Then the pressure shifted again. Quentin was pressed into his seat as they shot forward. He looked out the side window. They were nearly on the ground. Trees flashed by in a blur of green, and then gave way to an open field, and then another flash of trees. The thrusters rotated once more, and again the seatbelt dug into Quentin's flesh as their velocity dropped to nothing in only a few seconds. A swirl of leaves and dust shrouded the van until the tires touched the ground, then the thrusters fell silent.

They were hidden in a patch of trees. The jets roared by overhead.

"I believe I have done what you asked," Addison said.

***

Bobby sat with Carlos on the ground outside the van. Dusk was coming, and the light under the trees that hid them was starting to dim. Bobby heard the pulsing of a helicopter in the distance. The Air Force was still searching.

Ashley said, "Let's just find a motel so we can get some real sleep."

Mrs. Darnell was still studying the map. "There should be several small towns just to the east. Maybe we can land near one and walk in."

Mr. Darnell sat in the van with his legs hanging out the door. "We can't do that. Flying in the dark is probably our only chance of making it to Newton. We have to keep going."

"I'm not sure I can navigate in the dark," Mrs. Darnell said.

Carlos said, "Can't they use radar? It probably doesn't matter if it's dark."

Dark or not, Bobby figured they were more likely to get caught the closer they got to home, since the FBI probably knew where they were headed. They needed a better way to get there. Bobby considered this for a moment, then rose to his feet and went around the van to where Addison still sat in the driver's seat. "Addison, can I talk to you?"

Addison stepped out and followed him away.

Before speaking, Bobby thought back to the disaster at the hospital. He would have to pick his words carefully. "Addison, I think the only way to get home is for you to teleport us there, or zap us, or whatever it is you do."

"I cannot do that because—"

"I know, because you haven't been there. So what I'm thinking is, you could leave us here and go there yourself first."

Addison's brows wrinkled. It was the first time Bobby had seen him do that. "Your home is three-hundred miles from this place. It would not be safe for you, even if I go there first."

"But could you do it?"

"Yes. But it would not be safe for you."

"Well, I know it's not safe for us to fly the rest of the way in the van."

"There is a chance you would be hurt."

"How much of a chance?"

"I cannot know."

"Okay, if you teleported us there a hundred different times, how many times would we get hurt?"

Again Addison wrinkled his brow. "Two times. Maybe three times."

"That's all?"

"As I said, it would not be safe for you."

THEY WERE in the air only a few minutes before spotting a town. Hovering low near the edge of it, Quentin strained his eyes to see details in the encroaching dark. Soon he saw two long structures with a parking lot between them. It looked like a motel. Only a few blocks away a small river lined with forest wound its way by the edge of the town. On the other side of the river was open farmland.

Addison landed in some trees on the far side of the river. They left the van hidden there and walked in the twilight along the border between the forest and a milo field. As they walked, Quentin asked Addison the same question for the fourth time.

"You really think there is at least a ninety-five percent chance it will work?" He had explained percents to Addison.

"I cannot know, but that is what I think. There is a chance you will be hurt."

"But less than a five percent chance."

"That is what I think."

The plan was crazy, but crazy had become a way of life. It now seemed unlikely that they could fly the three hundred miles to Newton undetected. But Addison said he could do it without them, because he could fly differently. Quentin guessed that meant faster, or lower—perhaps maneuvering in ways that would crush their bodies.

They came to a bridge Quentin had seen from the air. The bridge road would take them the few blocks to the motel. Only one vehicle, a pickup truck, passed them as they walked the road. Quentin glanced at the license plate to make sure it wasn't a government vehicle.

A blue and gold Economy Inn sign marked the motel. Only a few cars were there, but the office appeared to be open for business. The others waited behind one of the rows of rooms while Quentin and Lindsey went into the office. A red-haired woman in her sixties sat behind a counter watching a small television. When she saw them, she looked surprised.

"Didn't hear you drive up," she said. "Where's your car?"

"We had a flat tire," Lindsey said. "We left our car down the road a bit."

The woman nodded, picked up her phone, and started punching a number. "Friend of ours has a garage. He can probably fix it tonight."

"No!" They both said it at once. The woman held the phone.

"We can fix it ourselves," Quentin said. "We'll do it in the morning. Right now we're exhausted. We'd like a room."

Frowning, she replaced the phone and turned to a computer. "Just the two of you?"

They should have rehearsed this.

"We have our daughter with us," Lindsey said.

The woman looked out the front windows. "She didn't want to come in?"

Quentin raised his voice. "Can we please just have a room? We're very tired."

The frown faded and the woman's face became a concrete wall. "Certainly, sir." She started entering information on her computer. She asked for their license plate number. Quentin started to give her his own car's number then he changed his mind. Instead he gave her the number from the truck that had passed them minutes before. He told her they never carry a credit card and then paid for the room with twenties. They left the office before she could ask more questions.

The door to their room was in plain sight of the office. Quentin went around back and told Ashley to come now. The boys were to sneak in when the woman wasn't watching. The room was small, but at least there were two beds. A telephone and a small pod with a connector for wired Internet access sat on a table between the beds. Quentin eyed the phone and wondered if using it would bring the military down on them. Then he picked it up and dialed the number Peter had given him. A woman's voice came on.

"Economy Inn office. Do you wish to make a long-distance call?"

Quentin hesitated. The woman had caught him off guard yet again. "Yes, I do."

"That'll be an extra charge, sir. You can give me a credit card number or you can pay a cash deposit on the call."

Quentin gritted his teeth. He dug out another twenty-dollar bill and asked Lindsey to take it to the office. A few minutes later the woman came back on.

"I'll connect you now."

Quentin held his breath as the phone on the other end started ringing.

"Wooley here."

"Peter! This is Quentin. We talked earlier."

"Glad to hear your voice, Quentin! Are you safe?"

"For the moment. We've had some close calls. Peter, I can't talk long. I just wanted to check with you about the plans for tomorrow."

"I've managed to arrange a significant event. The secrecy of it has worked in our favor. The media channels are suitably intrigued. Should be a ripper party. Please tell me you will be there tomorrow, Quentin. If it ends up a bust, I may not be able to rally them again."

"If our current plan works, we'll be there tomorrow, at the address I gave you."

"Excellent. I can be there myself by noon, local time."

Quentin hadn't expected this. "I thought you were in Brisbane."

"I've worked most of my life for this, and I wouldn't miss it. I'm at LAX at the moment. Folks are rather cranky here. Why do I have the feeling you have something to do with that?"

"We'll have to explain later. I should go now. Noon tomorrow."

"Yes, indeed. But tell me Quentin, have you considered what you wish to say or do? Expectations will be high, you know. Mere words may not be sufficient."

Quentin knew what he meant. "Don't worry. When we're done, there will be no doubts." And then he realized he had left out an important detail. "Peter, if you happen to get there before us, there is something you should know. There is another person there by the name of Quentin. And there is a Lindsey and an Addison."

"I'm not sure I understand."

"Please just trust me. Those other people don't know the details, so try to humor them until we get there. I can't explain any more right now. We will see you then, okay?"

"Ace! Quentin, may I ask a quick favor? You have indicated

that it is in the form of a boy. Do you think I could speak to this boy for just a moment?"

Quentin hesitated. Then he held the phone out to Addison. "Peter wishes to speak to you."

Addison inspected the phone before holding it to his ear. "Peter," he said. There was a pause as Peter talked. "Yes, I can do that. At the time you were in the village, you were afraid you would die, because others would not know what you had learned. But there was someone you wanted most to know. You thought of her as Rose, but you knew her name to be Rosalyn. She was very important to you. Peter, did you return to Rose and tell her what you wanted to tell her?" There was a long pause. "I understand, Peter. I am sorry. Peter? Recently you have started having visions again when you sleep—visions of my creators." There was another pause. "Because it is time, Peter. Yes, Peter. Goodbye." Addison handed the phone back.

They stared at him. "What was that all about?" Quentin said.

"Peter asked me to prove to him that I am what you say I am. So I did."

Bobby peeked through the curtains. "It's pretty dark now. Addison should go."

Lindsey spread the maps out on one of the beds. From the room receipt, they knew they were in Pawhuska, Oklahoma. So she showed Addison where they were and how he could get to their hometown. Then she described how to navigate through Newton to their house.

Quentin's reluctance to let Addison go took him by surprise. After all, this was not his son. Why, then, did he have to fight the urge to hold the thing close to him?

Apparently Ashley had the same urge. She threw her arms around Addison. "You be careful," she said. "We'll be waiting for you." Addison did not embrace her back. Lindsey sat on the bed watching and made no move to get up.

Quentin and Addison slipped out the door and around the corner. Quentin had intended to walk Addison back to the waiting van, with hopes that he would come up with some adequate words. But Addison stopped just behind the motel.

He gazed at Quentin's face. "Do not be afraid, Dad." And then the boy was gone, replaced by darkness and a sharp pop of collapsing air.

IN NEWTON, Missouri, Quentin sat on the bed, nervously twirling his raccoon bone. This had been one of the strangest days of his life. He hadn't been able to shake the haunted feeling he'd gotten from the early morning caller claiming to be his identical copy. Then there was the mass of feds. And the false report that the suspects had been caught. And now the TV reporters. They were here for a different reason—Peter Wooley's mystery announcement.

Lindsey came into the bedroom with two glasses of wine. She handed one to Quentin and sat on her side of the bed. For a few minutes they sipped the wine and stared at the TV. The news stations were reporting the happenings in Newton, but they didn't know much, so the same sound bites were being repeated again and again.

Lindsey switched the TV off. "Addison's still watching this crap. Says he's not tired."

Quentin dropped the bone and put his hand on her thigh. "It's been a big day for—" A burst of wind outside suddenly cut him off. Then there were men yelling, the national security guys—so much for their promise to be inconspicuous.

The wind got louder. Quentin put his glass down. "What is that, a tornado?"

They went to the living room. Addison was already at the front door, looking out. Quentin pulled him back and peered into the front yard. "Jesus Christ," he muttered. He stepped out onto the porch, Lindsey and Addison at his side. An aircraft of some kind was landing in their yard. The craft had four jet engines mounted on top. It also had four tires, and its shape reminded Quentin of a car—more specifically, a minivan. The jet engines were actually very quiet. In fact, rushing air was all that could be heard. The thing came to rest on the grass, and the blasting air abruptly stopped.

A door opened and someone stepped out. The feds were out of their cars, guns drawn. Lindsey stepped back to the front door and switched on the porch light. The yard brightened, illuminating the person who was now approaching.

Quentin froze. It was Addison, or someone who looked exactly like him. At Quentin's side, Addison—the real Addison—whispered, "Dad, who's that?"

The person stopped at the steps just a few feet away. Quentin looked at his son and then at the stranger.

The boy spoke with Addison's voice. "You are Quentin Darnell and Lindsey Darnell." He pointed. "And you are Addison." The stranger then smiled. "I will be back, Dad. At noon tomorrow." He pointed to their feet. "The place where you are standing, you should keep it clear at that time. At noon tomorrow. The others will be with me."

There was a pop, and the boy was gone, a thin wisp of white vapor swirling in the air where he had stood.

CHAPTER TWELVE

The television cast an unnatural tint throughout the motel room, and the newscaster's voice droned on without emotion.

"Qantas officials are refusing to comment until the investigation is complete, but the Federal Aviation Administration and the FBI have made it clear that Qantas Flight 43 is at the very least a monumental case of mistaken identity, and quite possibly could be a brazen terrorist plot we have yet to see unfold. These facts we do know: Flight 43 was an unscheduled flight from Jayapura, Indonesia; a flight of unknown purpose, shrouded in secrecy. That airliner was an Airbus A380, one of the largest, most luxurious airliners made, with a passenger capacity of nearly five hundred. We are told that fewer than twenty passengers were on the flight. The cause is unknown, but Flight 43 crashed just before landing last night at 10:20 pm Pacific time. There were no survivors. But only minutes later, the very airliner that was thought to have crashed inexplicably landed safely—at nearby Long Beach Airport. Information on that plane's passengers, as well as the purpose of the flight, has not yet been released. It is still unclear if this was an act of terrorism. That of course is the question on the minds of many at this time. But perhaps the biggest mystery is, who was on the A380 that crashed?"

Bobby's neck tingled as he watched video of the crash scene. Fires burning. Scattered pieces of jet. Could some of those pieces be parts of his body? He asked if he could change the channel. Nobody answered, so he scanned through channels until he found a show talking about Peter Wooley and Newton, and all the FBI and reporters there. The reporters were there for Peter, but no one seemed to know why the FBI was there. Bobby wondered what his mom was thinking of all this. And then there was his other self. Thinking about that made him feel wretched, so he got up and paced around the tiny room. The clock on the night table said a quarter after ten. Addison had been gone for an hour. How long would it take him to fly to Newton? Could he even make it there without getting shot down? He had said he could survive a plane crash, but what about a missile?

Bobby stopped pacing. "Mr. Darnell? Can I talk to you about something important?"

He and Mrs. Darnell were sitting on one of the beds with their backs against the wall. Mr. Darnell grunted and got up. "Let's take a walk." He opened the door to look around and then waved for Bobby to follow. The night air felt dry, but it was filled with the familiar sounds of crickets and cicadas. And it smelled like home.

"I needed to get out of there anyway," Mr. Darnell said. They headed toward the bridge. There were no streetlights here, and the road was very dark. "Something on your mind, Bobby?"

"Yeah, everything."

"I know what you mean." The crickets got louder as they approached the river.

"When Addison gets back, I don't think we should take him to Newton," Bobby said.

Mr. Darnell kept walking.

Bobby went on. "He'll be caught, then the government people will tell him what to do."

"That *is* why we brought him to the United States."

"But it was a bad idea, and now we've messed things up. We keep messing things up. Addison's smarter than us. We should let him decide what to do."

"What do you mean?"

Bobby shrugged. "I mean let him make the decisions. Instead of giving him over to the government, we could hide him somewhere. We could tell him to only do things to help people. We could teach him what's right and what's wrong."

Mr. Darnell stopped walking. "We should probably head back." They turned and started back. "Bobby, I've never told you about my father, have I?"

"No, but I've heard things."

"Then maybe you know my dad was an anthropologist. A linguist, to be precise. He and my mom introduced me to Papua—actually it was West Papua. My dad was a good person, Bobby. The Papuans he worked with fascinated him. He believed he was helping them by exposing them to the rest of the world. But if there is one thing I know—one thing I feel deep inside me—it's that my father was wrong. He knew it too, but not until it was too late."

Mr. Darnell stopped again. "My parents didn't do anything bad, Bobby. They didn't force anything on the Papuans that was not wanted. But think about it. If you introduce metal knives—or maybe guns—to an isolated tribe, they are happy to use them. But then they become so good at hunting that they wipe out the game in their area. They have to switch to trading with other people, and using money. And then they can buy things like alcohol. Soon they are a changed people. The old ways of life are just a memory." Mr. Darnell kicked at something on the ground. "My dad couldn't live with that."

"And you think the creators of the Lamotelokhai are kind of like your dad, right?"

"Maybe. We probably won't know until it's too late."

"So, why don't you like my idea?"

Mr. Darnell started walking again. "Bobby, you're talking about giving up any control we might have and letting the Lamotelokhai make decisions that could affect everyone. What if its purpose is to change us into something we're not?"

"Maybe that's not such a bad idea."

They walked in silence until they were at the corner of the motel. Mr. Darnell stopped. "Bobby, you're a smart kid—probably smarter than I am. But we're talking about humanity's future. Don't you think we need to have control over that?"

Bobby looked him in the eye. "I guess so."

They checked around the corner and then snuck back into the room. Everyone was now awake, and there in the middle of the room stood Addison.

ADDISON HAD FLOWN three hundred miles to Newton in ninety minutes—in the dark. And instead of flying the van back, he had left it sitting in Mr. Darnell's front yard, surrounded by men with guns. Bobby was beginning to fear what might happen when they all showed up there.

They talked to Addison for a while, but soon Ashley and Carlos crashed and Bobby's eyes grew tired. He glanced at the clock on the night table, but then he noticed the little pod by the phone. Apparently the motel didn't even have Wi-Fi. Bobby looked from the pod to Addison. "Addison's a computer," he said. He pointed to the pod. "Maybe he can connect to the Internet."

Mrs. Darnell said, "Why would we want him to do that?"

Mr. Darnell slid his feet off the bed. "Maybe it would help.

Even if the news people get the word out, Addison will be taken away from us in a few hours. For all we know he could be hustled off to some military bunker and experimented on. If he knows more about humans and our history, maybe he'll recognize if he is being used recklessly."

He touched the port. "Addison, this is a connection to the Internet. It's how millions of computers share information. If you can connect to it, you could learn almost everything about us. Would you like to try that?"

Addison stepped over and put his finger on the cable port. His finger went inside, even though the hole was too small. For several seconds he didn't move. Finally, he looked up at them. "I can do this. But it will take some time to understand how the information can be learned."

Bobby thought about this. He knew information was sent in little packets, and Addison would have to figure out how to decompress those. Even then, the decompressed packets would result in typed information that was encrypted, such as HTML and Java code. Most likely, Addison had never seen typed words before. He probably couldn't even read. And then there were all the pictures and videos and animated Flash stuff.

Addison looked up again. "I understand now. You are right. This is a way to learn. I would like to learn more with the Internet."

Mrs. Darnell spoke up again. "The Internet has a lot of misinformation. This may be a bad idea."

"Yes, I see there is misinformation," Addison said. "I understand. I would like to learn more with the Internet."

Mrs. Darnel frowned, but Mr. Darnell just shrugged and said, "We're losing him soon." He rubbed his eyes. "Addison, will you be okay doing that while we sleep?"

"Yes," Addison said.

Ashley and Carlos were sprawled out in different directions on one of the beds, so Bobby grabbed a pillow and flopped onto the floor. His eyelids grew heavy as he watched the Lamotelokhai. Addison simply stood in place, his eyes seemingly focused on nothing.

STANDING ON HIS PORCH, Quentin glanced at his watch—ten-thirty a.m. It had been a long night. The place was now crawling with FBI and Homeland Security people. Guys with bombproof suits had inspected the extraordinary aircraft sitting in the front yard. After deciding it wasn't going to explode, they had brought a flatbed truck, winched the thing onto it, and took it away. Quentin never got a chance to go near it.

For several hours after the aircraft incident the feds had questioned Quentin, Lindsey, and Addison. Quentin had told them everything he knew, which wasn't much. There had been the strange phone call yesterday morning, and last night the aircraft had landed in his yard. He had no idea where it had come from or what it was. The one thing he was certain of was that the boy who'd emerged from the aircraft looked exactly like Addison. He had even called him Dad.

The boy had said he would be back at noon and the others would be with him. Who exactly were the others? Quentin was sure as hell going to be here at noon to find out. The feds had evacuated most of the surrounding homes, but Quentin had insisted that his family be allowed to stay near the front porch until the boy returned. And apparently they would be waiting there with several hundred armed men and women. Trucks and SUVs were parked haphazardly everywhere, including on the neighbors' lawns, forming a barrier around the house. Video cameras on tripods were stationed around the yard, many of them pointed at the porch. Addison's look-alike had said to keep the porch clear, and Quentin was determined to do so, even if it was the only place in the entire neighborhood clear of equipment and people.

Though there was a general air of excitement, Quentin was disturbed by all the guns. Many of the feds carried pistols in holsters. Some held larger automatic weapons as they paced back and forth between the vehicles. There were even truck-mounted, belt-fed machine guns.

"Mr. Darnell?" A federal agent approached from the street, followed by two armed men. The man stopped in front of Quentin and nodded. "My name is Darron Mesner, Federal Bureau of Investigation. May I ask you a few questions?"

"They've already asked everything," Quentin said.

Mesner's gaze was unwavering. "Humor me."

Quentin sighed and nodded.

Mesner looked at his watch. "Seventeen hours ago I spoke on the phone to a man who claimed to be you."

This got Quentin's attention. "So did I."

"You sound very much like the man I talked to. And then eight of our men claim they saw a boy identical to your son get out of an unidentified aircraft and speak to you." He waved to where the aircraft had landed in the yard. "So I'm trying to make some connections. Other than this man who claims your identity and the boy who looks like your son, have you made contact with anyone else in the last forty-eight hours?"

"You mean besides a hundred or so federal agents? No one out of the ordinary."

"Do you know Peter Wooley? Have you ever spoken to him?"

Quentin recognized the name. Wooley was the one making the big announcement in Newton that day. "I know who he is, but I don't know him personally."

Mesner studied him for a moment. "Wooley arrived here this morning. The guy has surrounded himself with an army of reporters. He's just down the road." Mesner nodded to the east.

"Says he has scheduled a live announcement at noon. Do you know where he wants to make the announcement?"

Quentin was completely alert now. "He wants to do it here?"

Mesner gave him a look indicating he was correct.

"Why?"

"I was hoping you'd tell me. The guy's got more media cameras focused on him than I've ever seen in one place, and I've seen a lot. He's live on the air and demanding to know why he can't show up for his appointment at your house."

Quentin could see that Mesner was scrambling for answers, almost pleading for him to shed some light on the situation. But Quentin was looking for his own answers. A boy who was Addison —but wasn't—had appeared in his front yard. And when Quentin had looked into the boy's eyes, he had begun to suspect this was not about terrorists or threats to national security. It was about some-thing else entirely.

"Here's what I can tell you, Mr. Mesner. I don't believe the people coming to our house have any intentions of hurting anyone. And I would like to invite Mr. Wooley and his reporters to our house to make his announcement. Do you have any kind of real evidence that Peter Wooley or our other expected guests are a threat?"

Mesner's steely eyes appraised him. "You sure sound like the man I talked to seventeen hours ago."

"Yeah, it's kind of uncanny to me too."

Mesner sighed. "We'll escort Wooley and a limited number of media teams through the cordon."

QUENTIN JERKED HIS HEAD UP. He thought he had heard voices. Bright sunlight made its way through slits in the motel room's curtains. He squinted at the clock on the night table. It was late—

after ten-thirty. He looked around. The others were sleeping, but Bobby and Addison were gone. He heard the voices again. This time they were recognizable. Bobby and Addison were talking in the bathroom.

Quentin laid his head back down and closed his eyes. In the next few hours the world would know what he knew. Lindsey shifted next to him. What would become of them? Where would they even live? They couldn't just show up in Newton and expect to share their house with their original selves. And then another thought hit him. He had lost Addison, and Addison's replica—the Lamotelkhai—would soon be taken from them. Today they would show up at their home, and there Addison would be, vibrant and alive and innocent. But that Addison was the son of another Quentin and Lindsey, and they would have no choice but to walk away from him—possibly forever. Remorse welled up in Quentin's consciousness.

He groaned and rubbed his temples. He needed to focus on other things, so he got up, woke the others, and then knocked on the bathroom door. "Bobby, we need the bathroom."

"Just a second!" There was whispering. The door opened and Bobby and Addison came out. Bobby said, "I wanted to talk to Addison, since they'll probably take him away today."

"What were you guys talking about?"

"Just talking," Bobby said. "Addison was on the Internet all night. I think he knows everything now."

Quentin appraised Addison. "Then maybe he can tell us what to expect when we get home."

"People are there," Addison said. "They are waiting."

Quentin was mildly surprised to get an answer. "How many people?"

"I cannot know how many. When I was there last night I saw eleven people, including you, Lindsey, and Addison. This morning I saw photographs of your house. The photographs showed ninety-four people. It is likely there were more the photographs did not show."

"That many? Did any of the people have cameras?"

"The photographs I saw were taken with cameras."

Quentin was too nervous to laugh at this. "No, I mean TV cameras. Were there television cameras there?"

"Yes."

Lindsey turned on the TV, and suddenly they were staring at the front of their house. In the foreground a reporter talked about the upcoming announcement. After listening for a moment, it was clear the reporter had no idea what the announcement was about.

Lindsey turned it off. "We'd better get ready. We don't want to disappoint them."

***

AN HOUR later they were cleaned up and ready to go. They still wore t-shirts and shorts from a truck stop, which were tacky and pungent, but at least they had showered.

Quentin had asked Addison to explain what would happen to their bodies as they were transported three hundred miles in a split second, but the answers were invariably frustrating. Would they be dismantled into atomic particles, transported at the speed of light, and reassembled? Addison more or less indicated this was not the case—so much for the Star Trek theory. Was the fabric of space somehow twisted so that they simply stepped from one location to another? Addison indicated this was closer to the truth. When asked for details, he started going on about entropy and quantum uncertainty, the inherent duality of space-time at its most basic level, alternate time lines, probability adjustment, stabilization— Quentin couldn't keep up.

Regardless of the exact mechanism, Addison had made one thing perfectly clear: they might get hurt. By hurt, Quentin assumed he meant mangled, boiled, or possibly exploded from the inside. As the minutes dragged by, he tried to avoid thinking of all the things that could go wrong. Finally, at six minutes before noon, they assembled in the center of the room.

"Addison, what can we do to make this safer?" Quentin said. "Should we hold hands?"

Before Addison could answer there was a loud knock at the door. They all froze.

"Yes?" Lindsey called out.

"Hello?" It was the lady from the front office.

Quentin stepped to the door and opened it just a crack. "Good morning."

"Hardly morning now, sir. Checkout was at eleven-thirty."

"We'll just leave the key here in the room, okay?"

"Supposed to check out at the front desk." The woman turned and walked away.

Quentin looked at Lindsey.

"Forget it," she said. "That woman only frustrates you."

"Are you suggesting I can't handle her?"

The kids laughed nervously at this. Lindsey said, "This is serious, Quentin."

He glanced at the clock—five 'til noon. He was so nervous that those minutes would be excruciating if he didn't find a distraction. "It won't take but a minute." He slipped out the door and headed to the office. The woman was already behind the counter watching TV. She looked up at him and glared. He smiled anyway. "I'd like to check out."

She still glared at him. "I was right."

"Excuse me?"

"You're one of them."

Quentin's smile faded. "What do you mean?"

"You're one of them people on the TV. The ones they're looking for. That's why I called Chief Sommers." She nodded over

Quentin's shoulder. He turned around in time to see a police car pulling to a stop directly in front of the office door.

Quentin turned back to her. "Shit, lady!"

"Don't you try nothing mister."

He spun around again. Chief Sommers was out of his car and approaching the door.

Quentin darted behind the counter.

"You stay away from me!" the lady shouted.

The policeman was in the front door. "Hey, stop where you are!"

Quentin looked down the narrow hallway behind the counter. There was a back door. He ran and threw it open. He turned and saw Sommers racing toward him. He seemed intent on tackling Quentin, which would be easy since he outweighed Quentin by at least fifty pounds. He was a barreling hulk.

Quentin ran out the back door and headed straight for the river. Sommers followed at full speed. There were enough trees near the river that Quentin hoped he could lose Sommers there and get back to the room with enough of a lead for Addison to transport them. So he ran with everything he had. The police chief was surprisingly fast, but his extra bulk slowed him down. Quentin approached the river and then circled to the left. Sommers yelled, but Quentin couldn't make out his words.

After a wide loop, Quentin was back at the motel well ahead of Sommers. He rounded the corner just as another police car careened into the parking lot. And hanging out the office door was the motel manager, waving to the car. She saw Quentin. Rather than waiting for the police car to stop, she actually sprinted toward Quentin, screaming.

Quentin threw open the door. "We have to go now!" Without a word they all jumped up and stood in the center of the room.

"Addison, please be careful," Lindsey said.

Addison was as calm as ever. "Try to move as little as possible."

Quentin shot a glance at the clock. It was exactly noon.

Suddenly the woman was in the doorway. For a moment, she seemed shocked that there were six people in the room. But then she turned and started shouting, "They're in here! All of them!"

Quentin clenched his eyes shut. "Now, Addison!"

QUENTIN DROPPED TO THE FLOOR. The drop was at least six inches, and he stumbled briefly. He opened his eyes. Before him was something he had thought he might never see again—his own front door. He looked down at his body. It was not inside out. He looked at the others, and they seemed fine too, but they were staring out at the front yard. Quentin turned, and suddenly he felt weak in the knees. The yard was filled with people. Dozens of military trucks and government cars blocked the street and filled the neighbors' yards. Cameras were aimed at them, mounted on tripods, held on cameramen's shoulders, even held high above with extension booms. And every single person was looking directly at them.

Three people emerged from the crowd. After a moment of confusion, Quentin suddenly knew who they were. The three stepped onto the porch, and each of them stood before their respective mirror image. No one spoke. Quentin's eyes moved from the father to the wife to the son, Addison—not the Lamotelokhai but the real Addison. Not a boy who had endured injury, psychological mayhem, and being abandoned by his own parents. Instead, this was his son, and for a moment Quentin almost forgot every horrific thing that had happened.

As they stood gazing at their counterparts, the crowd remained silent. Addison wasn't the only one who was different. There was something about all three of them. It wasn't just from the injuries. The Lamotelokhai had healed those. It was subtler than that, something that had changed in them gradually, so that Quentin had grown accustomed to it without noticing. They had seen death and miracles, and they held knowledge that the world was about to turn upside down. They were now strangers to this house.

Two men approached them. One of them appeared to be in his thirties. Below his white button-down shirt he wore blue jeans and leather sandals. He sported a closely trimmed beard with a smattering of grey, revealing that he might be somewhat older than his smooth skin suggested. His hair was pulled tight into a ponytail. Before he even spoke, Quentin knew this was Peter Wooley.

"You folks are punctual, I'll give you that. And your entrance was wicked impressive. You must teach me how you did that." The man smiled broadly, showing perfect white teeth. "I'm Peter Wooley. I've been waiting for you for some time. But then you know that, eh?"

The man next to Peter cleared his throat. He was clearly a federal agent of some sort. Who else would wear a suit jacket and tie in July? "My name is Darron Mesner." He looked from one Quentin to the other, and his gaze settled on the one who had just arrived. "I believe we spoke on the phone yesterday morning."

Quentin nodded, still out of breath. "Sorry. I just finished outrunning a police chief in Pawhuska, Oklahoma."

Both men stared at him.

Peter Wooley chuckled. He then waved to someone in the crowd of people to come to his side. An elderly woman who looked to be in her eighties approached them. Like Peter, she wore a white shirt, jeans, and sandals.

"I'd like you to meet Rose," Peter said. "My wife, and my partner in crime." He flashed a smile to Mesner. "Pardon the expression."

Mesner's eyes grew wide as he appraised the woman who was old enough to be Peter's grandmother.

Rose smiled at Mesner and extended a mottled hand to Quentin, then to Lindsey. "I'm quite used to such reactions. Peter and I are an anomalous couple. But you understand, don't you? I see it in your eyes."

Lindsey said, "We understand. It's a pleasure to meet you, Rose."

Rose's eyes sparkled. "I wasn't sure I'd live to see this day."

Mesner cleared his throat again. "We have a media fiasco here. We've agreed to allow Mr. Wooley to make whatever announcement he intends to make. But I'm shutting this show down right now unless you convince me your intentions are one hundred percent peaceful. You've carried something halfway across the country that witnesses say could be a weapon. This will not be taken lightly."

Lindsey spoke up. "Didn't you talk to Colonel Richards? He knows what we have and how important it is. It was his idea to organize this media event."

"Some of us don't agree with Richards."

"Well, as you can see, we've brought nothing threatening with us," Quentin said. "We only wish to share some important news."

Mesner looked at the Lamotelokhai. "I understand this boy is not what he appears to be."

Quentin put his arm around Addison's shoulder. "That's the news we've come all this way to share."

"Why do you look just like us?" It was the real Addison.

Quentin stepped toward him and was surprised when his other self pulled Addison back. "We don't mean to scare you. Something happened when you were flying from Wamena to Sentani. There was a strange event that affected the passing of time, and then there were two airplanes, and two of each of us. You probably didn't notice when it happened."

The real Addison wrinkled his forehead. "I did see something. But I never told anyone, because I wasn't sure."

Bobby said, "I saw you, Addison. I was looking out the window and I saw you there, looking back. Do you remember?"

Addison remained tucked under his father's arm. He nodded.

Quentin wanted to tell Addison the truth. "Your Twin Otter was fine, and you made it home safe. But ours crashed. It took us all this time to get here."

The real Addison looked from one of them to the next. "Where are the rest? Where's Miranda, Roberto, and Russ?"

Quentin took a deep breath. "We had problems. Some didn't make it back."

"You mean they died?" It was the other Lindsey.

"Yes. And there's something else." With some difficulty, Quentin looked directly at her. "Addison didn't make it back, either."

All three of them, this other family, turned to look at the Lamotelokhai. The other Quentin said, "I don't understand."

Quentin shifted uncomfortably. "Well, that's why we're here. And that's why the reporters are here, and the FBI. There's more to the story."

Peter cleared his throat. "Speaking of that, we're live on the air at the moment. Are you folks ready to tell the people what they should hear?"

Quentin looked around. The number of guns outnumbered the cameras pointed at them. He glanced at Lindsey and she nodded. "We'll do our best," he said.

Mesner added, "Be aware that any threatening action you take will be dealt with swiftly."

Peter turned to face the crowd. He waved the reporters closer. Several microphones on long booms were positioned over his head. He paused for a moment, waiting for the crowd to become quiet, displaying impressive self-composure. Not until the area was totally silent except for the summer breeze did he speak.

"My name is Peter Wooley, and I have promised you an announcement that will change the world. A sizeable promise indeed, and I do not fault you for your skepticism. But the moment of truth has arrived, and it is time for you to decide. Were my words merely hype? Or were they an understatement of the truth?"

Again he paused, as if savoring the tension. "When I was a younger man—for the record it was more than forty years ago—I stumbled upon something I did not understand. But from that moment on, this phenomenon became the only truly significant purpose for my life. At that time I could not share it with others. Perhaps that was as it should have been. Perhaps the world was not ready. But today, whether we are ready or not, the time has come."

Quentin had thought it impossible the crowd in his yard could become quieter, but it did.

After another controlled pause, Peter continued. "I must confess that my role in this event is relatively minor. These good people are the ones truly responsible for bringing this phenomenon to us all." Peter motioned for them to come forward.

Lindsey hung back and smiled at Quentin as he stepped forward. The boom mics shifted so that they were over his head. The television cameras were turned on him, and everyone waited. His mind reeled. He'd thought about this moment during the night, had decided upon a plan. But he had underestimated how difficult it would be. Perhaps he had never truly believed they would make it to this point.

He turned to the others. Addison—the Lamotelokhai—smiled at him, the smile he had learned to use when people were afraid. Quentin knew what he had to say first.

"I have lost my son." His voice cracked, but he quickly brought it under control. The people in the yard remained silent. "My son Addison was hurt when our plane crashed in Indonesia. He would have died. He should have died. But we found something there. It is something that can do wonderful and impossible things."

Quentin looked at Addison the boy. His son watched him, innocent, not understanding. He turned back to the crowd. "When people have access to such a thing as that, decisions are made based on emotions. We don't consider the consequences. I have come to realize this is the difference between power earned versus power given. Power we have earned is used with caution, with an understanding of consequences. Power that is given to us, on the other hand, is misunderstood. And so we toy with it.

"This phenomenon Peter mentioned is a gift. It is unimaginable power that has been given to us." Quentin paused to look at Darron Mesner. The agent raised his brows, as if he were waiting patiently for Quentin to make a point of some kind. Quentin turned back to the cameras. "I'm afraid we're in trouble, my wife and I. We brought this gift with us to the United States, and then we ran away with it, to avoid having it taken away. After this announcement we will probably be arrested. So we want everyone to know the truth. Here are the reasons for our actions: We used this gift without considering the consequences. We used it to save the life of our son. But he was beyond saving. We didn't realize the magnitude of this mistake until it had cost the lives of dozens of innocent people. We then tried to use this gift to ensure our own safety, only to witness the consequences as more innocent people were killed. And after enduring that, we have come home, only to find that we have no home anymore."

Quentin paused and tried to look at each of the cameras. "When you have seen proof of what we have to say, I think you will agree that we must allow the whole world to determine how best to use this gift." He motioned toward a group of federal agents standing nearby. "With all due respect, we did not believe we should simply hand over such a thing to those who might think first and foremost of ways to use it to make our country more powerful than others."

The crowd seemed transfixed by his words, but Quentin had nothing more to say. He looked at the others, and his eyes met Bobby's. If he were to ask Bobby, he was pretty sure the answer would be, *let Addison take it from here*. Aware that yet again he was putting their lives into the hands of an unknown entity, Quentin leaned closer to the Lamotelokhai and said quietly, "Addison, you mustn't hurt anyone or do anything that will make these people shoot us. But you need to tell them what you are. And they won't believe you if you just tell them. You will have to show them something to help them believe."

"I understand." Addison stepped forward. He gazed at the crowd and then spoke firmly, "Peter Wooley and Quentin Darnell told you about a gift. But they did not tell you I am the gift." A ripple of murmurs drifted across the yard, but Addison cut them off. "I am not a living thing like you are. You can think of me as a computer if you want to." He then paused as if aware they would need time to process this. "Those who created me wished to share some of what they had accomplished. That is why I am here." He paused again. "I have waited here for more than six hundred million years, but until recently there have been no living things here who could talk with me."

The drifting whispers turned to indignant laughter and ridicule.

Addison ignored this. "I would like to show you one of my creators. This might help you to understand." He smiled. "Do not be afraid."

Addison held his arms at his sides and looked at his feet. After perhaps ten seconds of uncomfortable silence the crowd's laughter returned. Suddenly Addison collapsed on the porch and became a shapeless mass. The other Darnell family backed away, horrified. One of the reporters said, "God almighty!"

The mass began to take shape. It resembled a large turtle, or an armadillo, curled up on the floor. Then it unfurled itself and stood up. Cries of alarm rose from the crowd. Quentin feared that a nervous gunman might open fire, but he couldn't take his eyes off the creature before him. It stood about four feet high on two hind legs, but the main torso tilted forward at a forty-five degree angle.

Protruding from the chest was another leg, longer and much thinner than the other two, providing the support that allowed it to lean forward. There were two arms, looking almost human, except that the hands had four fingers in opposing sets of two. The torso appeared to be covered with hard brown leather. Most disturbing were its heads. They were side-by-side, each of them looking like a sock puppet with two eyes and no mouth. A large mouth was positioned just below where the two head-stalks attached. Quentin realized the top of the body was the same anatomical arrangement as the fish-like creature Addison had shown them days earlier.

Suddenly the spindly chest appendage moved. Before, when it supported the body, it had appeared to have only one joint about midway between the body and floor. But when it lifted off the floor it became obvious that it was multi-jointed. The appendage snaked out and reached down to the first step below the porch. The multiple joints locked into place and the limb was rigid again, allowing the creature to lean forward. Its hind legs lifted off the floor and swung forward, straddling the center leg and passing over the two remaining steps. The creature landed lightly on the sidewalk. The motion was graceful, yet it was so shockingly alien that the crowd gasped, and those nearest the porch backed away. An authoritative voice commanded, "Hold your fire. Do not fire!"

Quentin had seen the impossible in recent weeks, but this disturbing yet beautiful creature was so foreign in its structure and movements that he could only stare in disbelief. The creature shifted from side to side, possibly waiting for the crowd to calm down. Its two head-stalks acted independently, each pair of eyes inspecting different areas of the crowd at the same time. The boom mics were quickly wrangled into position over the creature's head, in case it was capable of speaking.

And then it did speak. Its mouth was much larger than a human's, but the lips were extremely dexterous. "Do not be afraid," it said. The voice was no longer Addison's. "I have changed to the form of one of my creators. This individual was one of those who designed me, and many others like me. She lived more than six hundred million years ago. It is almost certain that her kind no longer exists. They were aware of their finite existence, and I was created so that others may know of them and remember them."

As the thing spoke, waves of color expanded and contracted on each head-stalk, reminding Quentin of the iridophore cells allowing chameleons to rapidly change color. The color changes seemed to be an integral part of the thing's verbal communication, and they included a broad palette of bright and subtle hues.

The creature paced a few steps one way and then back, using its center limb like a crutch. As it turned, the head stalks swiveled to allow the eyes to remain fixed on what they were looking at. The movements were mesmerizing, and Quentin wondered how much of this the television audience could see, and how many of them actually believed it was real.

The thing stopped and faced the cameras again. "I came to this place long before your kind existed. My purpose was to wait for beings capable of understanding my creators' accomplishments. During the time I waited, I encountered many different living things. All of them eventually disappeared, to be replaced by more. But none of those living things were able to talk to me and under-stand my purpose—until recently. Approximately thirty-seven thousand years ago, I encountered beings of your kind. They were unlike all the previous living things I had known. These people had learned to move across water from one part of the planet to another with boats they had made. They were the first living things I had encountered here who could talk to me.

"Approximately one hundred and fifty years ago, another of your kind came to me. Because of experiences in his life, he asked for my help with tasks that previous people had not, such as culti-vating food.

"A short time later, approximately forty-two years ago, another of your kind came to me. His name is Peter Wooley, and he is here with us now." Both head stalks turned to Peter, and both of the graceful forearms pointed at him. "Peter's experiences allowed him to talk to me in new ways. But Peter was forced to leave that place, and I did not encounter him again until today.

"Twelve days ago I met the people who stand before you." The creature motioned to Quentin and the others. "Bobby Truex is one of them. Bobby's experiences in his life were influenced by the efforts of Peter, even though they had not met until now. And so Bobby was able to talk to me in new ways. Because of that, I am now here in this place, talking to you.

"I have told you these things so that you will understand that Bobby is the primary communicator for your kind at this time. And Bobby has told me of fears that he has. Bobby fears that the accomplishments of my creators might endanger all of you. He is correct. I have not come here to instruct you on how to use the accomplishments of my creators. You may use them to destroy some or all of your kind. If you do that, I will wait here, as I have done since I arrived. Others may eventually replace your kind. Perhaps those who replace you will be better suited to use the accomplishments of my creators."

The thing pointed at Bobby again. "Bobby does not want the accomplishments to be used in ways that hurt and kill. Bobby is the primary communicator at this time, and I follow his requests. But soon, others of you will be primary communicators." The creature then stared at the cameras, as if waiting for this to sink in.

Finally, it said, "I will change my form back to what is more familiar to you." Its heads lowered, and the tiny arms dropped. The creature collapsed again. As the crowd and the cameras watched, clothing and human skin became apparent in the folds of the mass. A few minutes later it straightened up, and Addison stood before them. He said, "It is time for what is to come next." Addison then stood motionless, waiting.

Darron Mesner waved at some men to approach Addison, but the men were hesitant. They approached with guns drawn.

"Please put your guns away," Lindsey said. "They only make your intentions obvious, and they can't hurt him anyway."

The men ignored her, and Addison allowed them to escort him toward the street.

Mesner eyed Lindsey, and then Quentin. "You all need to come with us, so we can determine exactly what's going on here."

Bobby said, "They'll be careful with him, right? It's easy to make a mistake."

"They'll be careful," Mesner said. "You people should have trusted us from the start. Would have saved us all a lot of trouble."

"Bobby is trying to tell you something we've learned the hard way," Quentin said.

Mesner frowned and stepped closer to Quentin. "There are some, Mr. Darnell, who will likely consider your actions to be treason. But that's not for me to decide. I withhold judgment until all evidence is examined. I only wish you had done the same, rather than taking off across the country like self-righteous lunatics. Perhaps you should hold more trust in your country's leaders."

Quentin's face flushed with anger. "Our trust is in humanity, not in a few individuals."

Mesner stepped even closer. "Your ignorance is shocking and dangerous. Do you really think it would be our leaders making the decisions you fear? It will be the people, for God's sake! If this thing holds the power that you imply, it will be the general population crying out for its use as a weapon. Perhaps not at first—at first they'll demand that it be used to feed the hungry, or cure disease. Perhaps the general level of comfort will rise. But not everyone can have everything they want. There isn't enough space or resources on the planet to allow that. The more people have, the more they consider anything preventing an optimum level of comfort to be a threat. People don't like to feel threatened, Darnell. When they do, they become something different from what your naïve idealism would like them to be. They'll demand that this *gift* of yours be used to eliminate any perceived threat, perhaps even if it means using it as a weapon of mass destruction. Do you see where I'm going with this?"

Disturbingly, Quentin did see. He had to forcibly remind himself that he held more faith in humanity than Mesner obviously did. He started to say something, but Mesner backed off and waved for more men to come.

"We've set up a temporary facility for examining you all." Mesner hooked his thumb toward the street. "The other one will be taken to a more robust facility."

"His name is Addison," Quentin said.

Mesner nodded. "Addison, then." Without another glance at them he headed toward Addison, who was being led to the back of an armored truck.

"Son of a bitch!" Quentin muttered.

Lindsey was now at Quentin's side. "We've done what we came to do. We let the world know. They wouldn't dare make decisions now without consensus."

Quentin realized he was clenching his fists and tried to relax.

One of the agents gestured toward the street. "We need you folks to come with us."

"Mr. Darnell?" It was Bobby. "I did it anyway."

Quentin looked at him. "You did what?"

"What you told me not to do. I thought you might change your mind, so I talked to Addison this morning while everyone was asleep. I got him ready."

"Ready for what?"

The agent closed in. "I have to insist you people stop talking now and come with us." The other men moved in on them, too.

Bobby ignored them. "I taught him what he needs to know. You know, about what's right and wrong. He's ready. I just need to tell him." The agent gripped Bobby's shoulder and started leading him away. "Do you want me to tell him?" Bobby called to Quentin.

The man roughly clamped a hand over Bobby's mouth and put his other arm around his chest. "We're not playing games, son!"

Before Quentin could respond, Ashley cried out, "Addison! We need help!"

Everyone froze. Addison emerged from a group of agents at the rear of the armored truck. Several of the men moved to stop him, but Mesner warned them back.

"This guy's hurting Bobby," Ashley said.

The agent's eyes shifted, but he didn't release Bobby. The other men kept their guns trained on Addison as he approached.

"Bobby, would you like my help?" Addison said.

The man's hand prevented Bobby from speaking, but he nodded.

Addison stepped directly in front of them. "You should let go of Bobby now."

Quentin rushed forward. "Everyone stop!" he yelled. "Addison, don't do anything."

The agent still held his hand over Bobby's mouth, and Quentin looked the man squarely in the eye. "Sir, do you have any children of your own?"

"Yes," the man said, barely a whisper.

Quentin nodded to the television cameras. "Then your family is probably watching. I don't pretend to know exactly what Addison is, but he is not what he appears to be. He doesn't understand how tragic it would be for your family to watch you die before their eyes. I'm begging you, please let the boy go."

Addison's eyes turned golden yellow as he reached for the man's arm. "Do not be afraid," he said.

The guy released Bobby and stepped back before Addison's hand touched him.

Bobby wiped his mouth. He spoke to Quentin. "He's ready. Should I tell him?"

Quentin nodded. "Do it."

A slight grin materialized on Bobby's face. "Addison, phone home."

There was a pop, a tendril of water vapor, and then silence. Addison was gone.

CHAPTER THIRTEEN

THE CHAOS at Quentin's house eventually gave way to a more methodical investigation. The camera crews wouldn't leave, and Mesner was reluctant to have them forcibly removed on live television. But they were obviously growing weary of waiting for Addison to return and getting only clipped answers to their questions.

Addison would not return. Quentin had told the feds this again and again. Bobby had instructed the Lamotelokhai to disappear, and it was too late to get it back. Agent Mesner had ranted, had threatened them and even pleaded with them. "How could a fourteen-year-old boy have the right to do this?" he'd asked. "How could a boy make a decision for the entire country?" Quentin had reminded Mesner that the Lamotelokhai was for the entire world, which didn't help to placate him.

Quentin was sure he and Lindsey would be taken into custody. Perhaps they would even be locked away. But for now they were held at the house, in case Addison returned. Quentin sat with Lindsey on the front porch steps, surrounded by National Security personnel, while the kids were still being questioned individually inside. The front door opened and Mesner stepped out, followed by the other versions of Quentin and Lindsey. Mesner told his men to vacate the porch and move to the street. He then withdrew into the house, leaving the two identical couples somewhat alone. The other Quentin and Lindsey sat on the steps next to them.

"So Mesner wants *you* guys to question us now?" Quentin said.

The other Darnells eyed them warily, obviously uncomfortable. "Why not?" the other Quentin said. "We all need answers."

"There's one thing I'd like to know," the other Lindsey said. "How did Addison die?"

Quentin took a deep breath. "Actually, we don't know exactly."

"What does that mean?" the other Quentin said.

"There were some things that happened." Quentin sighed. "We had to leave him there, in the forest."

The other Quentin looked incredulous. "What? What could possibly happen that would make you—"

The other Lindsey put her hand on her husband's knee. "It can wait, Quentin. You're talking to yourself, remember? They're us. We can assume we would've made the same decision." This was followed by contemplative silence.

The other Quentin said, "This thing you found—this Lamotelokhai—it's not really gone, is it? You know where it is?"

"I have no idea," Quentin said. "Bobby convinced me we'd all be better off if we let it hide somewhere and decide on its own what to do next."

Another incredulous look. "Bobby convinced you."

Quentin simply gazed back at his copy.

"Even though this thing could change the future of our species."

"Don't assume I made the decision lightly. You have no idea what we've seen."

The other Quentin looked around the yard, trying to gather his thoughts. His left knee began bouncing, and his hand impulsively patted his pocket for the raccoon bone, but apparently it wasn't there. Quentin realized he hadn't seen his copy of the bone since crashing in the rainforest, and suddenly he missed its presence.

Finally the other Quentin said, "This goes against every instinct I have. It seems we are now at the mercy of some unknown force. My parents—your parents—imposed the same kind of influence on Amius and Gupy and their people. That's the first thing that comes to my mind when I think of what you've done, so how could you not have thought of that? Do you think Dad would've agreed to this?"

Quentin suppressed his contempt. "We had no choice." But doubts were again beginning to arise within him.

The other Quentin eyed him. "So what's next? Are we ever going to see this Lamotelokhai again?"

"If we told you where it is, would you tell Mesner? That *is* why he wanted you to talk to us, right?"

The couple exchanged glances, and then the other Lindsey said, "Somehow you both reached the conclusion that it should disappear. We don't know why. But how ironic would it be to not trust the two of you?

AGENT MESNER WAS FURIOUS, but Bobby stuck to his story—he had no idea where the Lamotelokhai was, and he had told it to stay hidden forever. Half of this was actually true. Bobby had been separated from the others and was being questioned by Mesner and two other feds. At least he was in the Darnells' kitchen and could get a soda whenever he wanted. He was on his third.

Except for the Lamotelokhai's location, Bobby had told the truth. Just like with Colonel Richards, Mesner had wanted to know everything, starting from the beginning. Finally it seemed he was out of questions, and he sat across the table from Bobby shaking his head.

"Now I have a question for you," Bobby said. "What would you do with it? If you had it—and it can do anything you want—what would you ask it to do?"

"I guess we'll never know, will we?" Mesner said.

"No, really. I answered *your* questions. What would you do with it?"

"I would turn it over to the authorities, which is what you—"

"No, I mean you. If you had it, what would *you* do with it?"

Mesner sighed. "Okay, Bobby. If it could do anything?" He thought for a moment. "I would ask it to make a rocket that could take regular folks like me into space. I've always wanted to go into space, probably since I was your age."

Bobby took a drink of his soda. "That's a pretty good wish. For me it's dinosaurs. I wanted the Lamotelokhai to make real live dinosaurs."

Mesner was actually smiling now. "And it did, right? At the hospital in Papua."

Bobby looked at the can in his hands. "Yeah. That didn't go so well."

"You're trying to make a point, aren't you Bobby?"

"No. I just wanted to talk about it. You know, like normal talk."

Mesner nodded slowly. "Like normal talk."

An agent leaned in the doorway. "Sir, I got a couple people here. Considering the circumstances, we allowed them entry."

Mesner nodded. The agent stepped aside and Bobby's mom appeared in the kitchen doorway. Bobby was behind her—the other Bobby. Their eyes got wide when they saw Bobby at the table.

"It's true!" his mom said. She approached slowly. The other Bobby stayed behind her.

Mesner glanced from one Bobby to the other, and then he

waved the other two agents out of their chairs so the other Bobby and his mom could sit. There was an awkward silence.

"I don't understand what's happening," Bobby's mom said.

No one responded to this. Finally Agent Mesner got up and said he would let them talk. He and the other agents left the kitchen.

"Where's Dad?" Bobby said.

She hesitated, almost like she didn't grasp the question. "Travis is on his way. He called when he saw you on TV."

The other Bobby finally spoke. "Are you really me?"

"A copy of you. Or you're a copy of me. I don't know."

"Do you know what I'm thinking?"

Bobby smiled. "No. How could I?"

"Are there any more copies of you?" his mom said.

"There was another one. He died in a plane crash at the airport."

His mom gazed at him silently. Her eyes turned wet. Bobby reached across the table and touched her hand. Instead of pulling away, she gripped his hand tight.

The other Bobby said, "Where's he going to live?"

His mom blinked. Obviously she hadn't thought of this. "Live?" she said.

Bobby fumbled for words in the silence that followed. "I guess I don't have a home anymore." He half-laughed. "They'll probably put me in jail or something, anyway."

His mom gripped his hand tighter. "You'll live in your home, with us."

Suddenly Miranda's voice was in the living room. Bobby jumped up and left the kitchen, followed by his mom and his twin. There was Miranda, alive and well. And the other Ashley was with her. The two Ashleys were face-to-face, probably feeling the same awkwardness Bobby had just experienced.

Ashley saw him come out of the kitchen and seemed relieved to have a distraction. She waved Bobby over. "It's Miranda, Bobby. She's alive! And the other Carlos is outside—with Roberto. I haven't seen Russ yet, but they're all alive!" She laughed nervously. "And this is the other me, of course."

Bobby said hello to the girls. They both looked dazed and didn't respond. Four adults stood behind them—probably their parents. Bobby wondered which were Lori and Brent.

Bobby didn't really know what he had expected, but this wasn't it. There was fear in the parents' eyes. Miranda and the other Ashley looked as if they might turn and run at any second.

Ashley must have sensed this, too. She was trying to stay positive. "I have so much to tell you guys. You would not believe the last two weeks! I don't think we'd even be here if not for Bobby." She moved closer and actually put her arm around Bobby's shoulder.

The other Ashley's eyes grew even wider when she saw this, and she exchanged a look with Miranda. She obviously didn't approve.

Standing there in the new Ashley's embrace, Bobby simply smiled.

CHAPTER FOURTEEN

Marjorie Temple fumbled for the keys to Room 4. It had been a doozy of a day already, and now that the mercury was pushing a hundred, she wanted to finish housekeeping and settle into the cool office before the worst of it. Only three rooms were filled last night, but she had saved Room 4 for last. To be honest, she would've been happy to bolt the door and never set foot in 4 again. But travelers passing through would have no clue what'd happened there, so she might as well make good use of it.

She took a deep breath and opened the door, half expecting somebody to be there. But the room looked normal enough. The police tape had been removed when the FBI got word that the real criminals were found in Missouri. Chief Sommers had said he never actually got a good look at the man he'd chased out back. And then they had all looked at Marjorie like she was a crackpot. But she knew darn well what she'd seen with her own eyes. The whole gang had been there, the same six from the TV, plain as the nose on her face. And then they weren't there. Gone, like spooks. The FBI, they just said don't worry about it, like it happened to everyone—everyone who was plum crazy, most likely.

Marjorie muttered to herself as she cleaned the bathroom. The bathrooms were always first—best to get them out of the way. The towels were a sight. This wasn't the mess from three folks—more like a gang of six criminals on the run. She swapped out the towels and wiped the tub and floor, stopping now and then to look into the main room to make sure she was alone.

Still muttering, she pulled the sheets from the beds. She glanced at the clock on the night table. And then she looked across the far bed and frowned. There was a new night table between the beds. The old one was in the far corner. If Luther had bought another one, he would have told her. Or more likely, he would've dropped it off up front, expecting her to put it in the room. She examined the table. It was just like the other one, only brand-spanking new. Not a scratch or water ring on it. But the table was off center. Luther had bothered to put the Internet plug and clock on the table, but didn't have a care to situate it right. She dropped her armload of sheets on the bed and gripped the night table with both hands. It wouldn't move. She tried harder. The table budged, but it was heavier than heaven. She opened the drawer. It was empty. She stared at the confounded thing.

"Good enough right where you're at," she muttered.

Marjorie moved the old table next to the other side of the bed. She stood back and appraised her work. Good enough. She finished changing the sheets and locked the door, more than happy to leave Room 4. Soon she was back at her desk, sipping a cream soda and watching the idiots on TV try to figure out what was going on in Newton, Missouri.

In Room 4, the new night table stood in silence, holding up a glowing alarm clock and an Ethernet connection pod that was now strangely fused to the table itself. Suddenly the table shifted three inches to the left, so that it was precisely halfway between the two beds.

And then it settled back in and continued its work.

CHAPTER FIFTEEN

Five Months Later

The canoe cut a clean line through the green water of the Sittee River. Bobby kept his eyes focused on the thick canopy to his right, watching for a flash of orange or green. They had already spotted thirteen iguanas, and one more would be a new record. In fact, this morning's paddle had been an all-around success. They had seen a family of coatimundi moving along the edge of the river, rooting around with their long snouts for bugs and lizards. And just as they had turned back, some two miles up the river, the melon-sized snout of a manatee had surfaced next to the canoe. It stared at them for a few seconds and then went under—the closest Bobby had been to one of the gentle brutes.

In spite of Bobby's efforts, they spotted no more iguanas on the last stretch of river. The weeks-old record would still stand, at least until tomorrow. From the canoe's stern, Quentin guided them to the put-in. The boat scraped gravel as it ran aground, startling

Bobby out of the daze the last hour of quiet had left him in. After they climbed out, Quentin pulled the canoe onto the grass, flipped it over, and lifted it to his shoulders. The black Kevlar was light, and there was no need for Bobby to help.

"I'll see you inside," Quentin said. "Don't be too long." Looking like a boat with legs, he headed to the shed.

The canoe was a gift from Peter, and so was the shed where they locked it up. In fact, everything was a gift from Peter, including the house. It usually took a long time to build a house in Belize, so instead Peter had bought the Sittee River Lodge, which used to be rented out for rainforest vacations. The locals who had worked for the Lodge were now paid to care for the place and to make sure nobody knew who really lived there. To Bobby the place was paradise, and now that it was winter the days weren't too hot.

Bobby counted anole lizards along the path to the house. If it were up to him, he'd stay outside all day. But Quentin and Lindsey were home-schooling him, and they made him do lessons every afternoon. Bobby didn't mind so much. Most of the lessons were online, and Peter had bought him a screaming fast 30-inch all-in-one.

After a couple months of trying to live at home, Bobby had decided to move in with the Darnells—they now made him call them Quentin and Lindsey. Living with his mom and his other self was just weird. Nobody seemed to know what to say. And going to the same school had been the worst part. Even though there were also two Carloses and two Ashleys, Bobby had felt tormented more than the others. He had then tried living with his dad. It was a different school there, but things were still awkward, especially when the other Bobby came for the weekends. And so it didn't take much arguing for Bobby to convince his mom and dad to let him come live with Quentin and Lindsey.

As Bobby made his way along the corral, a shadow appeared over the top of the fence.

"Hey, science boy, there's something for you at the house."

Bobby looked up, shielding his eyes from the sun. Ashley gazed down at him from the saddle of her horse, Marley. "Another box from Peter?" he asked.

"Nope. This one you'll want to open right away. In fact, I want to be there when you do." She cantered away, heading for the stable. "You're riding with me this evening," she called back. "No excuses!"

Bobby pretended to be afraid of the horses, because he liked when Ashley teased him. But he wouldn't miss riding with her for anything.

Ashley had stayed in Newton longer than Bobby. But like Bobby she'd said that school was the hardest part. Her friends and teachers didn't know how to act around her. They called her the Ashley twin. Miranda had seemed okay with being a friend to twin Ashleys, but after she heard about how the other Miranda had died, she started giving excuses for avoiding both of them. And so Ashley had eventually decided to come live with the Darnells. This made her kind of like a sister, and that was weird. But it didn't matter. Bobby was going to kiss Ashley again, and not just once. He recalled every word of their conversation on the plane that night. She had said if he were older she would probably kiss him again. All he had to do now was keep the local Garifuna boys away from her. And then there was the expat family living a mile down the river, halfway to the coast. They had a son who might be a problem.

Carlos was the only one still living back home, and it appeared he would stay there. He was so happy to get his brother Roberto back that he didn't mind being an extra twin to the other Carlos. His parents were the kind of people who could handle it. They had always made everyone feel welcome at their house, including Bobby.

Bobby was happy for Carlos, but he was also a little envious, particularly when he missed his old life. Bobby had lost his mom and dad and almost all his friends. He was trying to make a new home in a country he had never seen before. It was better now that Ashley was here, but sometimes it was still hard.

Bobby entered the lodge, flipped off his muddy sandals, and went straight to the table in the screened-in living room where they always put the mail. Their home's location was a secret, so Peter had set up a public mailing address for them in Brisbane. He had people there who sorted through their mail and only forwarded pieces that were really important. There were lots of gifts, including checks for different amounts of money. But those were always donated to charities. Peter gave them everything they needed, anyway. Peter had said a few weeks ago there had been a check for a million dollars. It was from the family of a man who'd had AIDS.

Addison was staying hidden, but people knew where the break-throughs were coming from. The whole world had seen the videos from Newton. So when a cure for AIDS had suddenly appeared on the Internet, the drug companies were ready to try it within a few weeks. Big surprise—it worked. And then a cure for diabetes had mysteriously appeared. It worked, too. Now people were saying there might be a new drug that simply makes people healthy, no matter what their ailments. Bobby didn't know if others could see it coming, but it was obvious to him that this might cause another problem: too many people on one little planet. How would Addison solve that one?

There had been other breakthroughs, too: new ways to slow down global warming, new kinds of food, new computer chips, and especially new breakthroughs in nanotechnology. Recently, micro-scopic machines had been introduced that could clean up smog over a city.

At the beginning of all this, Quentin and Lindsey had been afraid that cultural diffusion of the Lamotelokhai's knowledge would totally change the human species. But Bobby's plan to hide

Addison had changed that. The alien knowledge and technology was now just trickling into human culture without turning the entire world upside down. Instead of diffusion, Bobby liked to think of it as careful, measured infusion of ideas.

Three boxes and some letters were on the table. The first box looked like it might be a part they needed for the car. All of those had to be sent from the U.S. or China. The second box was from Peter. Probably some new gadget he wanted them to have. That could wait. Bobby picked up the third box. It was heavy. But the strange thing was that it hadn't gone through the sorting office in Brisbane. Instead, it had come directly from Pawhuska, Oklahoma.

"Hey, you guys, what is this?" he shouted.

Lindsey entered from the study and examined the package. "Perhaps we shouldn't open it. It may not be safe."

Quentin came in. He still had streaks of water on his shirt from hoisting the wet canoe. "Don't open what?"

"It's from Oklahoma," Lindsey said. "Sent directly here."

Quentin squinted at the box. "Must be a mistake."

But it wasn't a mistake. The box was addressed to Bobby Truex. "It's from Addison," Bobby said. "It has to be."

Ashley came in, breathing hard. "You better not have opened it without me, Bobby."

Bobby hefted the box. "I think it's from Addison."

There wasn't much debate. Everyone wanted to know what was in it. Quentin cut into the box and pulled out a note and a large lump of brown stuff wrapped in plastic.

Quentin handed Bobby the note. "It's for you."

The note had only a few lines:

> Bobby, please use the web browser on your
> computer to go to the following address:
> http://lamotelokhai.weebly.com

Bobby went straight to his room and sat at his desk. The others gathered behind him. He woke up his computer and typed the address.

Ashley said, "The computer from an advanced alien civilization has a Weebly site?"

Bobby shrugged. "Not a bad way to blend in."

The page loaded, but it appeared to be a blank white background with nothing on it.

Suddenly some black text appeared. "*Hello Bobby.*"

A text box and submit button appeared near the bottom of the screen. Bobby typed, "*Who is this?*" But he knew exactly who it was.

Instead of answering, the Lamotelokhai responded with, "*Am I correctly doing what you asked me to do, Bobby?*"

Bobby thought about this. "Yes. But you don't have to solve all our problems at once. You could slow down if you want."

Amazingly, the next thing that appeared on the screen was an emoticon: :-)

"He did *not* just text-smile at us," Ashley said.

The smile disappeared, followed by: "*There are many problems that people do not yet know about. There is much to do. But I can slow down if you wish it.*"

Bobby looked at the others. Quentin just shook his head and shrugged. Lindsey said, "We're not qualified to decide how fast the human race progresses."

Bobby typed, "You decide, Addison."

"*I understand. It is interesting that you call me Addison. I do not have Addison's form at this time.*"

"It's a habit."

"*Bobby, do you have the package I sent to you?*"

"Yes. What is it?"

"*I am learning about things that influence the emotions of people. I believe the contents might be something that will make you happy. You should remove the packaging and place your hand upon it. It must be your hand, Bobby. Other hands will not work. After some time has passed, please contact me again and tell me if I am correct.*"

Lindsey said, "The Lamotelokhai is using you for an experiment?"

"*Goodbye Bobby. Use this address when you want to contact me again.*" A few seconds later, the white screen was replaced by the home page of the city of Pawhuska, Oklahoma—Gateway to the Tallgrass Prairie.

Bobby returned to the table and eyed the stuff wrapped in plastic. Better open it now before anyone could try to talk him out of it. He grabbed some scissors and cut open the plastic. It was exactly what it looked like through the wrapper: a lump of clay about the size of a bowling ball. He put his hand on it.

As the seconds passed, the only sounds heard were the birds outside. The lump started to change. Bobby pulled his hand away. Creases formed as it took shape, and then fur grew on the surface. A few minutes later, the thing uncurled and sat up on two hind legs and one thick tail. Golden eyes peered at Bobby over a black and tan snout.

Bobby blinked, scarcely believing his own eyes. The creature blinked back.

"Mbaiso!"

CHAPTER SIXTEEN

Three Months Later

With clawed fingers, Mbaiso lightly caressed the termite tunnel that ran from the ground up to a massive nest high above, providing the industrious insects a sheltered corridor on the tree's surface. Mbaiso felt the vibrations of termites making their way up and down the tree. Much could be learned from such elegant and practical designs. The tree kangaroo turned his snout upward to gaze at the hanging tunnels there. The tunnels formed a network of corridors with rooms serving as nodes, each node connecting six tunnels. These newly constructed tunnels and rooms were half of a day's travel to the south of those used by the ancient villagers, and they were smaller.

Mbaiso withdrew his paw from the termite tunnel, leaving it undamaged. He then climbed to the nearest hanging tunnel and entered an opening in its floor. Other tree kangaroos bustled in both directions, carrying raw and processed materials like busy termites. Mbaiso made his way through the tunnel, which was just wide enough to allow two tree kangaroos to pass each other, until it opened into a six-armed hut. He ambled to the center of the hut, stepping around several amorphous masses of flesh that lay quivering on the floor. He leaned forward until he was nose to nose with Tupela. He inhaled her scent, received her cognitive signals, and visually assessed her condition. The data indicated she was within healthy parameters, but she was somewhat weakened. Accelerating production would not be wise. Mbaiso counted seven fleshy masses on the floor around her, new tree kangaroos in various stages of completion. Each of them had originated from a hefty chunk of flesh extracted from Tupela's body, merged with a smaller portion from Mbaiso, then frequently supplemented with raw materials brought from the forest floor and the river.

Events were progressing satisfactorily.

Mbaiso exited the network of tunnels. Today he would travel north to visit the larger hanging village of the humans. But he would not stay long. The villagers there no longer needed help, and much of his time was required for providing leadership to his growing colony. In the absence of instructions from his Creator, Mbaiso had resolved to devise his own plans for preparation. Being idle did not suit Mbaiso, particularly with his understanding of what was soon to come.

Mbaiso descended to the ground. As a habit developed over many years, he inspected the forest floor and understory brush, looking for any disturbance to the leaf litter or any debris that might reveal that the area was occupied. Satisfied, he moved to a beam of sunlight, sat back on his haunches, and closed his eyes.

Suddenly a shadow fell over him, and Mbaiso instinctively hopped to the side to avoid danger. But the approaching figure was no threat. In fact, it would not have been possible to construct the hanging tunnels and chambers without its help. The figure stood waiting. Mbaiso had agreed to take the human with him to the larger hanging village today. It was not possible to know what the result might be, but it was time.

Silently, the two began making their way to the north.

CHAPTER SEVENTEEN

Five Days Later

QUENTIN ENJOYED PETER'S VISITS. Not only had Peter made their new life in Belize possible, he had also become a close friend to them all. He insisted on cooking for them when he came and somehow always managed to have a box of fresh ingredients show up at the house the very morning of his arrival. This was no small task, considering the nearest moderately stocked grocery was in Dangriga, twenty miles away by potholed roads. Peter had declared that after his ordeal in New Guinea, he had given up adventure for cooking. It was a healthier pastime. Today he was preparing something called Coronation Chicken, with apricot jam and mango chutney, and he seemed to be doing a nice job of it in spite of their rather spartan kitchen.

This visit had a particularly significant purpose: to discuss moving the Lamotelokhai. Until today, they had never told Peter the Lamotelokhai's actual location, and to his credit he hadn't asked. But he had convinced them it would have to be moved. Somehow it had avoided detection, in spite of efforts by the world's best networking experts. But eventually it would be found. Besides, there was only so much it could do with limited bandwidth. What it needed was a secure facility with a fiber optics backbone, cutting edge firewall and server technologies, and diesel generators in case of power outages. And that's exactly what Peter had built just outside of Oklahoma City. The facility would operate under the guise of a Kembalimo server farm for North America. Kembalimo's popularity had swelled since the media event last summer, and a new facility was needed to accommodate the growth anyway. Hidden deep within the facility was a server room with unprecedented security measures and bandwidth infrastructure, the new home for the Lamotelokhai. All they had to do was transport it there.

To say that Quentin and his new family were involved in this transfer was an overstatement. Peter and his most trusted employees had done everything. All Quentin had to do was reveal the specific location of the Lamotelokhai, which he had already done this afternoon. Bobby would contact it and tell it about the move. The Lamotelokhai would change itself into the form of a human being, walk out of Room 4 of the Economy Inn, ride in a company van to the new facility, and walk past the unsuspecting employees into its new home. By necessity there were three employees at the facility who knew the truth. The remaining three hundred had no idea the place would serve such a world-altering purpose.

Ashley had just come in from working the horses. She sniffed the air. "This place hasn't smelled this good since the last time you were here, Peter."

Lindsey made a face. "Thanks, Ash."

"Not that I'm complaining. What girl wouldn't love to eat rice and beans a hundred different ways?"

Peter chuckled. "Besides the cooking, are your folks here giving you a fair go?"

This reference to Quentin and Lindsey as her folks seemed to throw Ashley a bit. She exchanged glances with Bobby. "Yeah, actually they are."

Dinner was ready. Shortly they were seated and digging in.

Ashley spoke around a mouthful of food. "Peter, next time you come you should bring Rose. We miss seeing her."

Peter frowned, a rare expression for him. "Rose is not feeling so well." He shifted in his seat, obviously finding the topic difficult. "Rose and I both are eighty-three, did you know that?"

"I'm sorry she's not well," Ashley said.

Peter shook his head. "No worries, Ash. It's a funny thing—I have no need of medicines, but there are no medicines that can help her."

The rest of them were silent while Peter looked at his plate.

Finally, he said, "I hope you folks don't mind this, but when I meet the Lamotelokhai face-to-face, I have a favor to ask of it."

Lindsey reached across the table and put her hand on Peter's. "Yes, you should do that, Peter."

A brown shape suddenly sprang from the floor and crashed onto the table, spilling a pitcher of water.

Lindsey lit into the tree kangaroo, "Get your sorry carcass off the table!"

Bobby jumped up and scooped Mbaiso into his arms. "I forgot to put him out!" He went to the screen door and dumped the creature into the yard. Quentin heard him say, "I'll bring you a salad when we're done."

"Why does that thing need to eat?" Ashley said. "It's not even real."

Bobby sat back down. "That's how it gets energy. Just like you, only different."

She snorted. "Okay, now I understand."

Bobby went on, as he tended to do. "The real Mbaiso used to eat, too. This one's just a copy, but I guess it works the same way."

Ashley used her fork to push some food around on her plate. "Well, that's something we have in common. We're all just copies."

Mbaiso had been in trouble several times recently, so Quentin changed the subject for Bobby's sake. "So Peter, you feel like everything's ready for the transfer?"

"My team is standing by. I just need your final blessing."

"I want to go with you to pick it up," Bobby said.

Peter looked at Quentin and Lindsey. "I have no objection to that. It might facilitate communication, Bobby being the thing's mate."

Quentin could think of a dozen reasons why this was a bad idea; primarily, the hassles that might ensue if people recognized him. Bobby was not a fugitive—the FBI had finally given up their questioning—but their privacy here depended on the deception Peter had created regarding their whereabouts. The whole world believed them to be living in a secure residence within Peter's SouthPacificNet corporate campus. If Bobby were spotted in North America, he'd be hounded by reporters, or worse. But upon reflection, the other reasons had to do with Quentin's fear of letting Bobby out of his sight.

Finally he said, "If you can make sure he won't be recognized, I suppose he could go."

Ashley dropped her fork. "I'm going too! Do you know how long we've been stuck here, Peter?"

"She's right," Lindsey said. "Maybe they'll better appreciate what they have here if they go on a trip."

Quentin threw up his hands.

Peter grinned. "That settles it. You two are assigned to a secret mission. But I'm leaving here in one hour. If you can't be packed and ready, you're not fit for such a mission."

This is how it came to be that Quentin and Lindsey found

themselves alone in the house for the first time in months. The occasion was not squandered. Later that night they lay together in the screened living room, catching their breath. They held each other without speaking, listening to the insects and frogs that had lived on the banks of the Sittee River since long before humans had set foot in this part of the world.

Just as it always happened in the last quiet moments of the day, Quentin's thoughts turned to the forest of Papua, and the life-altering trials that had occurred there. But he would not speak these thoughts. Everything that could be said had been said far too many times. Lindsey had found a way to move forward, at least on the outside. Sometimes Quentin was awakened in the night by her stifled sobs. But she would never talk about it, and in the mornings she would be a role model of composure and vivacity for all of them.

Finally, Lindsey's breathing let Quentin know she had found sleep, and he hoped it would be free of dreams. Peter had promised that the Lamotelokhai would occasionally teach them more about its creators through visions as they slept, but so far this had not happened. When they did come, those dreams would be welcome. For now, all others were silently feared.

Quentin allowed Lindsey's rhythm to draw him away from awareness. As he descended, he pushed away the image that would forever visit him at this fading moment: a dark figure moving like a ghost through endless trees.

"Quentin, it's the sat phone."

Lindsey shook him awake. This time Quentin heard the chirping device Peter had given them. It was an unfamiliar sound, because Peter was the only one who had the number. Actually, that wasn't quite true. There was one other.

"Why would Peter call so soon?" Lindsey asked. "Something has to be wrong."

Quentin pushed himself off the mattress they had placed on the floor and stumbled to the phone. "Hello. Peter?"

"Greetings, Quentin. It is a pleasure to hear your voice, but rather unsettling that you are not before me as we speak."

Quentin knew the voice, the accent. "Samuel? Is that you?"

"It is indeed, thanks to the help of our good friend, Obert."

Quentin wondered if he were dreaming. He had asked Peter to arrange delivery of one of his newly developed satellite phones to Obert in the village of Navera, where they had radioed for a rescue plane. It was a long shot, but if Samuel somehow made his way back to Navera, he would have the opportunity to contact them. Besides Peter, Obert was the only other person on the planet who could call this phone.

Quentin punched the speaker button and set the phone down so Lindsey could hear. He said, "Samuel, it's great to hear that you're well! When the Indonesians took you away, we feared the worst."

Samuel chuckled. "Yes, of course. There was that. I informed those people that I would guide them to the place where we found the plant—the one they believed to hold the powers of healing."

"But Addison created that."

"Quite right. And upon entering the wilderness I gave it to them. And then it was a simple matter of waiting for my opportunity to escape. I fear, Quentin, that they failed to estimate my ability to outrun them."

Quentin smiled. "Well, you are surprisingly fit for a man your age."

Lindsey spoke up. "Hello, Samuel. I'm glad you're okay."

"Lindsey, is that you? My goodness, this machine is truly a wonder!"

"Well, you can thank Peter for that," Quentin said. "Tell us, Samuel, what have you been doing all these months?"

There was a pause, as if Samuel wasn't sure he should answer. "I have returned to the village where you found me. The indigenes who remain there have been kind to me, and I like to believe that I can provide them with various services. Perhaps a day will come when I will be ready to venture to the outside world. But my brief exposure those months ago convinced me that it is not yet my time. Perhaps it will never be."

"We understand, Samuel," Lindsey said. "We've also decided a simpler life is the best choice. But you are in Navera. It must have taken you days to travel there. Did you do that just to tell us you are alive and well?"

This time there was a longer pause. "Actually, I have come here for a specific reason. There is something I must tell you."

They waited.

"Your son Addison has returned to the village of my indigene hosts."

Quentin suddenly felt faint. "What did you say?"

"He wishes to know where his mother and father are. It seems the mbolop have provided him with the assistance he has needed to survive."

Quentin could not manage to formulate a response. Lindsey seemed to be struggling as well.

After a moment of silence, Samuel spoke again.

"Quentin and Lindsey, you will scarcely believe what your son has been doing these past months."

1948
Dutch New Guinea

Samuel Inwood trudged up a densely-forested hill, slipping in mud from a recent rain and bearing a heavy pack made from woven sago leaves that had been softened by chewing. He stopped at the hill's summit, hefted the pack to the ground, and sat beside it. His bare arms and legs were scratched and bleeding, but they would heal soon enough. He inspected his spider silk vest and fingered a ragged hole. That would have to be mended.

The sound of claws scuttling on tree bark made Samuel glance up quickly. A tree kangaroo, locally known as an *mbolop*, was clambering up a tree a few yards away. The creature had followed him from the village. Samuel frowned. He would have preferred to do this without being observed, even by the mbolop.

The surrounding trees upon the hill's crown were relatively sparse. Many years ago Samuel had been on a hill similar to this one. It had been his first hunting excursion with the Papuan savages who had long ago captured him and killed his companions —savages he now considered to be friends.

Today, though, Samuel had not come here to hunt.

"I estimate the village to be nearly three miles distant," he said, not necessarily to the mbolop nor to anyone in particular. During eighty years living with the tribe, he had developed a habit of speaking aloud when he was alone.

He opened the pack. Inside were twelve pouches, each of them made from the skin of a bandicoot, and each of them containing a lump of clay slightly smaller than his fist. He pulled forth one of the pouches. He held it upside down until the lump of clay fell out onto the ground before him. He then pulled forth a second pouch and dropped a nearly identical lump of clay next to the first. This was followed by a third lump, and then a fourth. Eight lumps still remained in the pack, contained within their own skin pouches.

Samuel had discreetly collected the lumps over a period of three months, carefully storing them in his hut. Each was contained within a pouch so the lumps would not touch, as his purpose would be ill-served were they to be mixed together before this particular day. He had pinched off the lumps, one at a time, from a much larger source, a mass of clay over two feet in diameter. The Papuan villagers called the clay *Lamotelokhai*, which meant *the end of the world*. Eighty years before, Samuel had briefly believed the clay might have been a portal to God. Since then, however, he had seen that it was something even more astounding.

Samuel studied the four lumps before him. A pinch from any one of them could be used to perform seemingly impossible tasks. If he wished to cause an object to dissolve into soil, he would need only to apply the clay to the object. If he or a companion were injured, applying the clay would heal the wounds—even if the wounds would otherwise have been fatal. If he wished to cook a meal or fire-harden a spear tip, he could apply the clay to the wood before burning it, resulting in a smokeless fire that would not reveal his location.

Unique tasks requiring more specific instructions, however, could only be performed by the larger source of the clay, the Lamotelokhai. Or so Samuel had previously believed. Recently, however, an idea had been circling about in his mind. What if it were possible to combine bits of the clay into a mass smaller than the Lamotelokhai but large enough to carry out complex tasks? If this were possible, the benefits would be numerous beyond imagining.

The question was this: how large would the mass need to be?

He looked again at the sparse hilltop trees. "Am I alone?" he shouted, and then again in the language of the villagers. "*Nu bai-khokhüm?*" There was no response, although he sensed the mbolop watching him from above. Returning his attention to the lumps of clay, he shifted his position on the ground and straightened his back, attempting to drive away his misgivings.

"Let no man deceive himself," he muttered. "Let him become a fool, that he may become wise." He then pushed the four lumps together and molded them into one.

He plucked a river stone from the pack and placed it next to the clay. Then, he placed his hands on the clay and closed his eyes to create a clear vision of his request. He stirred up a well-rehearsed series of thoughts, running them through his mind in a specific order: a vision of the river stone becoming smaller and taking on a golden color; a silent explanation that the rock had turned to gold, the heaviest of metals; a vision of a gold nugget tipping a scale, outweighing a stone on the opposite end.

Samuel opened his eyes, pinched off some of the clay, and smeared it upon the stone. He then sat back and waited.

Nothing happened.

He pulled four more skin pouches from the pack, removed

lumps of clay from them, and pressed the lumps into the larger mass. He placed his hands on the clay, repeated the series of thoughts, and smeared another pinch of clay on the stone.

Again, nothing.

"God blind me! Have I embarked upon another fruitless path of inquiry?"

He pulled the last four skin pouches from the pack, extracted the clay lumps from each of them, and pressed them into the mass, resulting in a lump that was now as large as his head. If this didn't work, he would have to conclude the experiment was a failure, as it was impractical to gather more. He placed his hands on the clay and repeated the sequence of thoughts. After anointing the stone, he sat back and watched, softly singing an old song from his childhood to calm himself.

"A-hunting we will go, a-hunting we will go, we'll catch a giraffe and make him laugh, and then we'll let him go."

The stone shifted. Or did it? Perhaps it was just his imagination.

"A-hunting we will go, we'll catch a bear and cut his hair, and then..."

The stone shifted again. This time it continued changing. It was becoming smaller. Its edges seemed to soften, and its surface turned to shimmering golden yellow. Samuel held his fingers above it to be sure it wasn't hot, and then he picked it up. The bottom of it had conformed to the twigs and soil, as if it had melted and cooled, although no debris was stuck to its surface. Its weight indicated that indeed it was gold. He looked more closely. It was imperfect, with speckles of minerals showing on its surface. This was peculiar. He had made this same request of the Lamotelokhai many times, always resulting in perfect, pure gold specimens. Nonetheless, the results were encouraging.

He proceeded to the second experiment he had prepared. He

placed his hands upon the lump of clay, closed his eyes, and conjured another sequence of thoughts. In his mind's vision, the gold specimen transformed its shape. First it elongated and formed a head, thorax, and abdomen. Then two broad wings sprouted from each side of the thorax, gradually spreading wider until the entire object was an intricate gold sculpture of a butterfly. He opened his eyes and smeared a pinch of clay onto the impure gold.

He waited, softly humming the old song.

The gold began to change. It narrowed in two places, forming the three insect body regions. Then, however, the sculpting process went astray. Instead of delicate wings blossoming from each side, tendrils of speckled gold spewed forth into shapeless extensions. The insect body curled up and writhed, as if it were a malformed creature in great pain. Samuel watched, mesmerized, as the object's shape continued shifting. For a moment the gold resembled a giraffe, and then a bear, and then it even resembled the face of his beloved Lindsey, whom he had left behind in London and who had no doubt grown old and passed away years before. When he saw this, he glanced away, unwilling to be tormented by the sight. When he returned his gaze to the gold, the transformations had stopped, leaving an amorphous mass that bore no resemblance to a butterfly. He touched it with his finger, half expecting it to change again, but it was cold and solid.

"Most... extraordinary," he said. He turned to the lump of clay. "You seem to understand my requests but are hardly capable of granting them. Of what use are you? I shall have to endeavor to discover what you can and cannot do."

He got up and began searching the area for a beetle or other large insect, which he would need for his next experiment. After sifting through leaf litter on the forest floor for some minutes, a slight movement in a low bush caught his attention. He approached the bush and soon was eye-to-eye with a slender arboreal lizard perhaps two feet in total length. Its yellow-spotted black body sharply contrasted with a brilliant blue tail.

Samuel sighed and shook his head. This was yet another new species of the genus *Monitor*. He would have a most impressive collection of specimens, had his life not taken such a calamitous turn of fate.

He slowly inched his way closer and then thrust his hand out in a blur and snatched the lizard. He inspected the struggling creature, holding it out so that its lashing tail could not whip his face.

"If you are indeed new to science," he said to the lizard, "then I have the honor of naming you." He used his free hand to subdue the tail. "*Monitor cerulean* seems to fit you well, as your tail is as blue as the evening sky. Let us see what we can do to make the name even more fitting, shall we?" He then carried the lizard back to the lump of clay and sat upon the ground.

He placed his free hand on the clay, closed his eyes, and formed a mental vision of the lizard. Then, he imagined the blue pigment of the creature's tail spreading forward, transforming the scaly skin on the rest of the body from black and yellow to the same brilliant cerulean hue. He opened his eyes and smeared a pinch of clay onto the lizard's back. By this time the creature had stopped struggling, so he released it, keeping his hand ready above it in case it tried to run. The lizard tilted its head but remained where it was.

Samuel waited.

Soon his mental vision began materializing. Beginning at the base of the lizard's tail, bead-like black scales faded to gray and then became blue. This alteration progressed until its entire body and head were blue with yellow spots.

As the yellow spots began changing to blue, the lizard abruptly wrenched its head to the side. Its mouth snapped open and emitted a menacing hiss. Samuel pulled his hand back, thinking the lizard was about to lunge at him. Instead of attacking, however, the creature spasmed and tumbled onto its side, its legs kicking desperately, as if gripped by seizure. Suddenly its body split in two, spewing forth blood and entrails.

Samuel rose to his feet. "What in God's—" He stopped short. The two halves of the lizard were now moving—transforming. Torn skin rolled up into itself and fell away from each portion of the carcass. The elongated rolls of skin then began crawling away, moving on their own like macabre grubs. Exposed organs detached themselves from the lizard's body. Some of them began oozing away, while others sprouted rudimentary legs and began crawling.

Horrified, Samuel realized he was stumbling backwards.

The lizard's tail broke free from the body and thrashed about. Its haphazard movements became more coordinated and deliberate, until finally it slithered away like a snake. The head portion of the body was still floundering about, going through its own revolting transformation. As it rolled on the ground, its jaws snapped shut on some dry leaves and small plants, which then began changing, eventually assimilating into the creature's head. The unholy beast then began snapping up every living and once-living object within its reach, as if it had discovered a new life-sustaining food source. Each thing it clamped upon became part of its abhorrent and growing mass.

Samuel could hardly look away from this disturbing sight, but suddenly his attention was drawn again to the snake-like tail, which had slithered and spiraled its way up a sapling tree and was now at the height of his chest. The thing was tightening around the sapling like a snake constricting its prey. Carefully keeping his distance from the creature's voracious head, Samuel stepped closer to the sapling to observe. But then he stepped back again when the trunk softened where the tail was gripping it, the entire tree folding and collapsing toward him. The autonomous tail then somehow melded into the folded joint of the sapling's trunk and was gone.

And then the entire tree began to move.

"God save me," Samuel uttered.

The tree continued changing its shape as it slowly writhed about. Samuel backed away, but he tripped and fell over something. Sprawled on his back, his feet and knees rested atop a hulking mass that only moments before had been the head of a small lizard. The thing was now the size of Samuel's body, although its form was unrecognizable. No longer resembling the lizard it once was, it had grown body parts of many different creatures, all of them squirming and fighting as if they desired to escape from the horrifying conglomeration to which they were bound.

As Samuel tried to comprehend what he was seeing, a creature's head materialized from the mass and clamped its jaws onto his bare calf. The head was the size of a small dog's, but it appeared to be reptilian, with round yellow eyes and vertical pupils. Samuel kicked it with his free foot, tearing its teeth loose from his flesh. He rolled out of its reach and then sat up, pressing his hand against his bleeding leg.

The multifarious masses continued to squirm and grow before his eyes, including several smaller blobs that had originated from the lizard's entrails and hind legs. With every passing moment they grew larger as they engulfed leaf litter, soil, and living plants. The reptilian head that had bitten Samuel gaped and screeched as it fought to free itself from the jumbled body parts of a dozen or more different creatures, all of them squirming in the same frantic manner.

Several sharp cracks drew Samuel's attention upward. He rolled to the side just in time to avoid being killed by the trunk of a large falling tree. Smaller limbs on the now horizontal tree folded where they joined the main trunk and then broke off. The limbs began bending and cracking on their own accord, taking on new shapes. One of them emitted a dry, twittering shriek, unlike any sound Samuel had heard before.

He stared at the scene before him, too shocked to run or to try to stop the accelerating process. Suddenly he was aware of a curious sensation in his bitten leg. He looked down. The wound was changing. His skin was peeling back, exposing red muscle and pale fat. The underlying tissues were moving about, transmuting into something else. For a brief moment a three-toed claw emerged from the wound and grasped at the air before sinking back into his calf muscle. Another bulge formed, and a pair of eyelids parted. A rust-colored eye stared back at him.

Samuel tried to cry out in despair and crawl away from the transforming flesh, but he could not escape his own body. He curled up on his side and pummeled his leg with his fist, desperately hoping to stop the monstrous transformation by beating it to a pulp.

In his panicked frenzy, his flailing arm struck something beside him. It was the mbolop, the tree kangaroo. Samuel's inadvertent blow sent it tumbling, but it quickly righted itself and sat up on its haunches. The creature scratched at its belly. It then ripped open its own skin, plunged one paw deep into its abdomen, and extracted a bloody lump of flesh, which it held out as an offering.

Samuel stared at the mbolop, then looked down at his leg. The wriggling, transfiguring wound was steadily growing larger. It had expanded down to his foot. One of his toes was now six inches long and was thrashing about, looking much like a lizard's tail. His entire body would soon be transmogrified.

He snatched the lump from the mbolop's paw and shoved it into his mouth.

———

In his desire for haste, Samuel ran directly through a patch of *yalün*, or stinging nettles. The unnatural transformation of his leg had stopped, but the wound was still wide open, and the nettles pricked and lacerated his raw flesh, injecting their astringent sap.

The pain nearly caused him to collapse, but dread and remorse pushed him onward.

He continued fighting his way through dense jungle for nearly two hours. At last, exhausted and bleeding, he arrived at the village. He made his way straight to where the Lamotelokhai was concealed. Soon he stood at the base of an enormous, buttressed tree. Wasting no time, he extracted a thin rope with evenly spaced loops—a rope ladder—that had been tucked away in the crevices of the tree's bark. He began climbing toward the hut, which was over a hundred feet above the ground. His leg was now nearly healed, and soon he ascended directly through a hole in the hut's floor and stepped away from the ladder.

To his surprise, three Papuan natives were there in the hut. One of them stepped away from the others and blocked Samuel's path. He was about Samuel's height, but he had dark skin and wore no clothing other than a sheath made from a gourd, fitted tightly over his sexual organs. A band of white paint, made from palm oil and the crushed shells of river clams, extended from one ear to the other like a mask. Green lorikeet feathers protruded in random directions from his frizzly hair. His name was Sinanie, and Samuel had lived with him and his fellow tribesmen since 1868.

Sinanie appraised the scratches and filth covering most of Samuel's body, a deep frown forming on his face. He said, "Samuel, *ge sumo abül lép-telo* (you have the smell of a man who is afraid)."

Samuel was still trying to catch his breath. "Sinanie, *nu khof-e-kha lamoda-Lamotelokhai tekhén-mo* (I must touch the Lamotelokhai)."

Sinanie furrowed his brow. He did not step aside.

There was no time to explain. Samuel walked around Sinanie and kneeled down before a low table. Upon the table was the Lamotelokhai, a shapeless lump of clay approximately the size and mass of a man's body. This was where Samuel had gotten the smaller lumps of clay he had secretly combined on the remote hill.

And the Lamotelokhai was the reason Samuel had remained in this forest for eighty years. Without waiting to see if the natives intended to stop him, he placed his hands on the clay. He formed words in his mind without speaking them, although his lips moved slightly to facilitate the process.

"I must confess, I have again done something foolish and am in desperate need of your assistance."

PAPUAN LANGUAGE GUIDE

First, I must say that I have the deepest respect for the unique cultures of the Papuan peoples. Obviously I have taken liberties in developing the characteristics of Sinanie's tribe, but I intended no disrespect by doing so. I have also taken liberties in developing the crocodile cannibal tribe, the tree kangaroo hunters, and Obert's village, although nearly all of their characteristics are based upon actual Papuan cultures.

Compared to Book 1 (Diffusion), Book 2 (Infusion) contains relatively few native language phrases used by Sinanie's tribe. The phrases used in Book 2 are provided below.

I adapted this language from the amazing work of Gerrit J. van Enk and Lourens de Vries in their studies of the language and culture of the Korowai, a Papuan community of treehouse dwellers of southern Irian Jaya (now called Papua). Astoundingly, the Korowai had never come into contact with outsiders until the early 1980s.

Papuan Dialogue from Book 2 (Infusion):

1. *mbayap* (Penis gourd. Typically called a *horim* in Wamena)
2. *Nu ne khelép-té. Wolakholol be-lembu-té-n-da.* (It is clear to me. The world will not get out of order.)
3. *Mbakha-lekhé-nggolo? Nokhu be-khelép-telo-n-din-da!* (Why? We cannot know!)

4. *Nggé, gu mbakha-to-fosü le-bo?* (Friend, Where have you come from?)

RESEARCH SOURCES

I am thankful for the hard work of those who have painstakingly researched the cultures, wildlife, and ecosystems of Papua. The following are recommended books (and one video).

Flannery, Tim. *Mammals of New Guinea*. Chatswood, New South Wales: Reed Books Australia, 1995. Print.

Flannery, Tim. *Throwim Way Leg: Tree Kangaroos, Possums, and Penis Gourds – On the Track of Unknown Mammals in Wildest New Guinea*. New York: Atlantic Monthly Press, 1998. Print.

Marriott, Edward. *The Lost Tribe – A Harrowing Passage into New Guinea's Heart of Darkness*. New York: Henry Holt and Company, 1996. Print.

Merrifield, William, Gregerson, Marilyn, and Ajamiseba, Daniel, Ed. *Gods, Heroes, Kinsmen: Ethnographic Studies from Irian Jaya, Indonesia*. Jayapura, Irian Jaya: Cenderawasih University, 1983. Print.

Muller, Kal. *New Guinea: Journey Into the Stone Age*. Lincolnwood, Illinois: Passport Books, 1997. Print.

Souter, Gavin. *New Guinea: The Last Unknown*. New York: Taplinger Publishing, 1966. Print.

Van Enk, Gerrit J. and de Vries, Lourens. *The Korowai of Irian Jaya – Their Language in its Cultural Context*. New York: Oxford University Press, 1997. Print.

Sky Above Mud Below. Dir. and Perf. Pierre-Dominique Gaisseau (organizer and leader) and Gerard Delloye (assistant leader). Lorimar Home Video, 1962. VHS.
    This is an amazing video filmed as it happened in 1959, when a group of explorers set out on a seven-month attempt to cross the jungles of Papua (then called Dutch New Guinea). Winner of the 1961 Academy Award for Best Documentary Feature.

ACKNOWLEDGMENTS

I am not capable of creating a book such as this on my own. I have the following people, among others, to thank for their assistance.

When it comes to editing, my son Micheal Smith is extremely talented, and his tireless and meticulous suggestions are invaluable. If you find a sentence or detail in the book that doesn't seem right, it is likely because I failed to implement one of his suggestions.

My wife Trish is always the first to read my work, and therefore she has the burden of seeing my stories in their roughest form. Thankfully, she kindly points out where things are a mess. Her suggestions are what get the editing process started. She also helps with various promotional efforts. And finally, she not only tolerates my obsession with writing, she actually encourages it.

I also owe thanks to my former colleague, Monique Agueros. She provided expert editing suggestions in spite of being an amazingly busy person. Thanks, Monique!

Finally, I am thankful to all the independent freelance designers out there who provide quality work for independent authors such as myself. Jake Caleb Clark (www.jcalebdesign.com) created the awesome cover for *INFUSION*.

ABOUT THE AUTHOR

Stan Smith has lived most of his life in the Midwest United States and currently resides with his wife Trish in a home nestled within an Ozark forest near Warsaw, Missouri. He writes adventure novels and short stories that have a generous sprinkling of science fiction. His novels and stories are about regular people who find themselves caught up in highly unusual situations. They are designed to stimulate your sense of wonder, get your heart pounding, and keep you reading late into the night, with minimal risk of exposure to spelling and punctuation errors. His books are for anyone who loves adventure, discovery, and mind-bending surprises.

Stan's Author Website
http://www.stancsmith.com

Feel free to email Stan at: stan@stancsmith.com
He loves hearing from readers and will answer every email.

ALSO BY STAN C. SMITH

The **DIFFUSION** series

Diffusion

Infusion

Profusion

Savage

Blue Arrow

Diffusion Box Set

The **BRIDGERS** series

Bridgers 1: The Lure of Infinity

Bridgers 2: The Cost of Survival

Bridgers 3: The Voice of Reason

Bridgers 4: The Mind of Many

Bridgers 5: The Trial of Extinction

Bridgers 6: The Bond of Absolution

INFINITY: A Bridger's Origin

Bridgers 1-3 Box Set

Bridgers 4-6 Box Set

The **ACROSS HORIZONS** series

1. Obsolete Theorem

2. Foregone Conflict

3. Hostile Emergence

4. Binary Existence

Genesis Sequence

Stand-alone Stories

Parthenium's Year